CITY OF SMALL KINGDOMS

JONATHAN CULLEN

LIQUID MIND PUBLISHING

www.jonathancullen.com

Liquid Mind Publishing

liquidmindpublishing.com

ALSO BY JONATHAN CULLEN

Shadows of Our Time

The Storm Beyond the Tides

Sunsets Never Wait

Bermuda Blue

Port of Boston Series

Whiskey Point

City of Small Kingdoms

The Polish Triangle

Sign up for Jonathan's newsletter for updates on deals and new releases!

https://liquidmind.media/j-cullen-newsletter-sign-up-2-jody/

"There are no miracles for those that have no faith in them."

French Proverb

CHAPTER 1

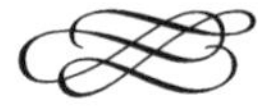

OCTOBER 1945

WE BEAT UP A PRIEST, but we really had no choice. We didn't just beat him up—we kicked his skull, gouged his eyes, and ripped out his hair. By the time we were finished, he was lying on the ground in a pool of blood, groaning and half-dead.

It was the last thing Sweeney, Russo, and I expected when we went out that night. But it wasn't just any night—it was the first Halloween after the war. We had finally walloped the Japs, and after four years of rationing and blackouts, people wanted to live again. It was a wild and unpredictable time, filled with a restless energy that bordered on lunacy. Music blared from every front parlor; couples danced openly in the streets. The bars were busy every night of the week, and it was impossible to get a taxi.

By nine o'clock, most of the younger kids had gone home. Trick-or-treating was over, and it was time for mischief. Gangs of rowdy teens roamed the neighborhood looking for trouble. They broke bottles, smashed windows, and got into fights. Their hoots and cries echoed throughout the streets and, at times, turned Roxbury into a real-life horror show.

But Sweeney, Russo, and I stayed in the shadows and out of their way. Tired of walking and with our candy bags overflowing, we stopped at a corner and stood behind a giant oak tree.

"Hands up!" Russo said, pointing a cardboard laser gun.

With his clothes painted silver, I wasn't sure if he was a Martian or The Tin Man. I pushed the gun away, and he made an electric hum that sounded more like a foghorn.

I pulled out my plastic sword and put it under his chin.

"Where's me tribute, matey?" I said.

Dressed as a pirate, I made a pirate's sneer and pushed it harder.

"Stop," he whined. "That hurts."

I released the weapon with a hearty laugh and shoved it back in my belt. Then I turned to Chester, who was sitting on the curb, and said, "Who are you supposed to be again?"

"Thomas Aquine-*ass*," Russo blurted. "Aquine-*ass*, Aquine-*ass*!"

With his brown cowl and large hood, Sweeney looked like Friar Tuck without the tonsure. A thick wooden cross hung from his neck.

"Who the hell is Thomas Aquinas?" I said.

"He's the greatest Saint who ever lived."

I started to laugh but stopped when I saw that he was embarrassed.

"My ma made me wear it," he mumbled, looking down.

Chester "Chesty" Sweeney was that lovable but hapless friend everyone had. Short, fat, and clumsy, he stuttered when he spoke and stumbled when he walked. He was shy to a fault, and the mere sight of a girl would send him into convulsions of self-conscious angst. He was so chunky that he appeared to have breasts, and the kids in school taunted him with the nickname Chesty.

Like most of us, Sweeney was poor. He lived in a cold-water flat outside of Dudley Square with his mother, a religious fanatic who called herself an "Old Catholic" and believed demons were out to get her. His father died when he was eight after the trawler that he worked on was lost at sea in the Hurricane of '38. As the only children in school who didn't have siblings, Russo, Sweeney, and I hung out together as much for protection as for friendship.

"Thomas Aquinas?" I said. "I guess it can't hurt to have God on our side."

"Or this."

When we looked, Russo pulled out a pint of rum. Even in the darkness, I could see the brown liquid swishing side to side, and it gave me a nervous thrill. He twisted off the cap and handed it to me first.

"Go on, have your grog, matey."

"Cheers," I said, smelling inside.

I took a swig and instantly my throat burned, my eyes got teary. Nevertheless, I held the liquor down and had some more.

"Your turn, your holiness," I said, giving it to Sweeney.

His fingers trembled as he took it, and he gazed at the bottle like it was poison.

"C'mon fat boy!" Russo said.

When he tried to force Sweeney to drink, I shoved him away.

"No! He don't have to do anything he don't want to."

"Take it easy, Jody," Russo said, flaring his arms. "I ain't makin' him do nothin'."

It was then that we heard the low murmur of Sweeney's voice.

"I want to. I want to drink it," he said.

While Russo and I watched, he took a deep breath and raised the bottle. He closed his eyes with the solemnness of prayer and brought it to his lips. Then he began to guzzle.

Suddenly, we heard a noise. Sweeney let go of the bottle and it smashed.

"Aw, look what you—"

"Shhh!" I said.

I peered around the tree and saw a gang of older kids coming towards us. They were loud and drunk, swaggering down the middle of the road like a posse out for blood.

Russo looked over my shoulder.

"Who is it?" he whispered.

When they crossed under a streetlamp, I recognized the leader and gasped.

"Vigliotti!"

Anthony Vigliotti was a local thug who left school at fifteen and lived off the streets as a petty thief and swindler. Tall and thin, he had lanky arms that went almost to his knees. As an Italian with bright blonde hair, some people suspected he was adopted but no one ever dared to ask.

"Whadda we do?" Russo said nervously.

They were a half block away and moving with the slow yet all-consuming fury of a tornado. I watched as one of the boys tore a mirror off an automobile and threw it in an alley. Then another howled and pulled off a fence post. When some lingering trick-or-treaters fell into their path, they were pushed, jostled, and shoved to the ground. Even under the calming influence of the alcohol, I was frightened beyond words.

"We gotta go," I said.

The gang was now at the opposite corner of the intersection and moving fast. Together, we crept back from the tree and went in the other direction. We had only gone a few steps when Chesty stopped.

"My candy."

"Quick, quick," I said.

He scurried over, got the bag, and started walking back to us.

"Oh, what do we have here?" a voice said, and I cringed.

They spotted us.

"Run!" I shouted.

We spun around and sprinted for our lives. Russo tossed his cardboard gun; Chesty dropped his bag, and the candy went everywhere. For some reason, I kept my plastic sword even though it was useless.

By the time we reached the next crossroads, Sweeney was lagging behind. With his fat legs, he was as slow as a bison in a stampede, and I worried they would get him.

"C'mon, man," I said, turning back to encourage him.

The gang was closing in—I could hear their voices behind us. We cut right and went down a small street. A long and rambling stone wall, eight feet high and hidden behind weeds, ran down one side, and by some miracle, I spotted a gate.

"This way," I said.

We ran over, but it was locked. Standing in the overgrowth, the three of us looked at each other and silently agreed that our only escape was over the wall.

"Chesty first," I said, and Russo nodded.

We took Sweeney under the shoulders and hoisted him up. He teetered for a moment then fell forward into the blackness, landing with a thud.

Vigliotti and his gang were only seconds away. Russo grabbed one of the iron slats, lifted himself up, and was quickly over. Alone and exposed, I was more afraid than ever, and my heart pounded. When someone threw a rock, it missed me by inches and bounced off the gate with a gong. I looked up and started to climb, expecting at any moment to be pulled down and beaten.

Just as I reached the top, blue lights flashed across the night. I glanced back, and a police car was speeding down the street. Instantly, the gang scattered, leaping through bushes, tumbling over trashcans, darting down driveways.

I thought the nightmare was over, but it had only just begun.

WHEN I OPENED MY EYES, I was lying on my back and staring at the stars. In those first few seconds, I didn't know where I was, but I was comfortable and not afraid. Out of the corner of my eye, I saw the sliver of a moon hovering over the tree line. Then somebody shook my shoulder.

"Jody? You okay?"

I turned my neck, and the back of my head was sore. In the pitch dark, I saw Russo's silver costume and then his face. He was standing over me, and I hadn't even noticed.

"What happened?" I asked.

"You slipped and fell. I think you hit your noggin."

I sat up on the damp grass and looked around dizzily, rubbing my crown and wondering where I was. When I saw the moss-covered wall beside me, I remembered what had happened.

"Where's Chesty?" I said.

"Don't know. He kept running."

I stood up and dusted off my clothes.

"Let's go find him."

We went up a short stretch of lawn and came to a courtyard with gravel walkways, hedgerows, and flower beds. All the vegetation was dead, but there was a cold lushness I couldn't explain.

"What is this place?" Russo wondered.

"Don't know."

We walked with a slow fascination, past benches, birdbaths, and statuettes of religious figures we knew but could not name. At the center of the courtyard was a large white sculpture of Jesus, seated on a rock and ministering to three boys. Two were on his lap, but the third was standing and facing away from the others.

Something fluttered above, maybe a bat, and we both jumped. I looked up and saw a bell tower rising above the buildings. With its open belfry and huge glass windows, I recognized it immediately. A chill went through me that was a blend of fear and awe.

"Kilda," I mumbled, staring hypnotically.

It was a structure I had only ever seen from a distance, and now it was right in front of me.

"Kill what?"

The old Christian abbey was only four miles from downtown Boston, but it might as well have been in the Himalayas. Built when the area was farmland, it was strangely out-of-place in the urban slums that surrounded it.

"It's an abbey," I said.

No one I met had ever been inside the property, and it was so isolated that even birds seemed to avoid it. As far back as I could remember, its name was never printed or published; it wasn't carved into an archway or marked somewhere by a plaque. Yet everyone knew it as St Kilda.

"Gives me the creeps," Russo said, stopping to look around.

"Let's keep moving."

Suddenly, we heard someone. We dove behind a hedge and got down on our stomachs. Peering through the branches, we saw a figure in the shadows of the portico. Whoever it was stepped out of the darkness and began to go across the grass. As he got closer, we realized it was not one person but two.

"He's got Sweeney!" Russo said in a quiet panic. "Who is he, Jody? Who is he?!"

I elbowed him and told him to shut up.

"A priest. Maybe a monk."

The man held Sweeney close, but I couldn't tell if it was a headlock or an arm restraint.

"Come out, boys."

When he called to us, Russo and I froze.

"Come out now," he repeated, this time louder. "I know you are there. Don't make me come get you, righto?"

Growing up in Roxbury, we had heard lots of foreign accents, but this one was unfamiliar. Russo looked at me for an explanation, and I just shrugged my shoulders.

When the man reached the middle of the courtyard, he stopped at the statue of Jesus with the children. Sweeney didn't seem to struggle; it looked like he couldn't move. We all respected, even feared the clergy, but for him, there must have been a deeper terror because his mother was so devout.

"Come out now boys," the priest continued, "or your friend is in mighty trouble. You don't want that, righto?"

In the moonlight, his silhouette cast an enormous shadow. He had on a long, black overcoat that should have reached his ankles but ended at his knees. Beneath it was a brown tunic which, ironically, was the same as Sweeney's costume.

"I count to ten then I take your friend away. Okay?"

With Sweeney firmly in his grip, he began to move in a circle, scanning the hedgerows and bushes, searching.

"Von, two—"

He spoke with a drawn-out emphasis that was probably meant to coax us but only made us more scared.

"He's crazy, Jody," Russo said, and he was right.

There was something sinister in the man's voice, and when he finally turned in our direction, I understood why. His eyes were wide, and his tongue was slack. He slurred and seethed like a rabid dog. He might have been drunk, but I had no doubt that he was insane too.

"He's got something, Jody!"

"Dree, vor," the priest said.

Squinting in the darkness, I looked closer and realized he was holding something to Sweeney's neck. My heart raced, and I began to feel sick.

"Whadda we do, Jody? Whadda we do?!"

"Vive, seeeex..."

When Sweeney whimpered, Russo began to panic, his legs shaking. I leaned in close, whispered in his ear.

"Go distract him," I said.

"Distract him?"

"I'll get him from behind."

"Get him?" Russo said, his hushed voice cracking. "We can't—"

I grabbed him by the back of the neck.

"He's gonna fuckin' kill him!"

"Seven, Eeet..."

The hideous enumeration continued.

Without another word, Russo got up and stepped out into the open, and the priest saw him immediately.

"Ah, come now," he said with a devious smile.

Russo went towards him, the man urging him with each wary step.

"Good boy. Closer now. Don't be afraid."

As he did, I darted behind the hedgerows and circled the courtyard, reaching down and loosening a white brick from the walkway. I stepped out onto the gravel and crept up behind the man when, suddenly, he lunged forward and grabbed Russo.

"Jody!"

Now he had them both.

What spell of courage or foolishness came over me, I didn't know. But I walked up and raised the brick as high as I could. Hesitating for a half-second, I thought about what I was doing and knew I had no choice. Then I swung the brick and smashed the back of his skull.

Instantly, everything went quiet. The man wobbled but didn't fall over. He let go of Sweeney and Russo and slowly turned around, looking at me with the dumb glare of an idiot who has been taunted. Even from ten feet away, I could smell alcohol on his breath, see the madness in his eyes. When a trickle of blood came down his ear, he wiped it and looked at his hand.

Then he snarled and charged straight at me.

"Get him!" I shouted, and all hell broke loose.

Russo jumped on his back and got him in a chokehold. I kneed him in the balls, and he was briefly stunned. When we finally wrestled him to the ground, Russo gouged his eyes while I battered him with kicks and punches. But the priest continued to resist.

"Stop!"

I looked back and Sweeney was standing in the distance, his tunic torn at the seams, tears streaming down his face. Even in all the chaos, I somehow noticed that his wooden cross was no longer around his neck.

"Help us!" I shrieked, but he wouldn't move.

The man grabbed me by the throat, and I bit his hand. Russo took one step back, wound up, and booted him in the jaw. The priest's head dropped to the ground, and he lay panting and snorting like a slain beast.

I ran over to Sweeney and said, "C'mon! We gotta go!"

"You killed him. You killed a priest."

"That's no holy man," Russo said, spitting blood. "Let's go fat boy. We just saved your life."

We ran towards the wall and were halfway there when the priest yelled out, "Boy, don't leave me here..."

Sweeney stopped so we stopped too.

"...You're a good boy, righto?"

He had the weak, quivering voice of someone in agony, but I had no pity.

"I gotta help him," Sweeney said. "I gotta—"

I stormed over and brought my face to within inches of his.

"You gotta do nothing. That guy is bats…bananas…nuts!"

But he wouldn't look at me. He just stood there shaking his head back and forth like a stubborn child.

"To hell with him," Russo said, hissing in disgust. "Let him go."

"Boy," the man cried. "My leg…it's broken. Help me."

Sweeney looked towards the courtyard, his cheeks flush and lips trembling.

"Jody," he said, "I have to—"

Without an explanation or even a goodbye, he turned and started across the grass. Russo and I watched as his plump figure lumbered towards the cloister and vanished in the shadows.

Tired, cold, and sore from the fight, we headed back to the gate. Once Russo was safely over, I climbed up and stood balancing at the top. I cupped my hands in front of my mouth and called out, "Chesty?"

Scanning the darkness, I looked for movement but saw none.

"C'mon, Jody," Russo said.

I tried one last time.

"Chesty?"

All I heard was the echo of my own voice.

CHAPTER 2

January 1968

I HADN'T BEEN warm in two months. The winter chill seemed to dig into my bones and settle there like a deep and permanent ache. It hurt when I sneezed, and each time I coughed, I could taste bile. Half the department was out sick, and we were so short-staffed that Chief McNamara had to borrow officers from nearby Somerville. Even Captain Jackson, who hadn't missed a day since Truman was president, had been out for almost a week.

I looked up from my desk in a drowsy stupor. Through the foggy window, I could see only the outlines of buildings, the headlights of cars along Cambridge Street. I scribbled something on the document I was working on and put it in the drawer. I got my coat, turned off the lights, and locked the office door. Another workday was done.

The hallways of headquarters were desolate at night. The only sound was the muffled footsteps of the evening staff two floors above. I turned into a stairwell, went down three flights, and burst into the frigid night. It was the last week of January—the bowels of winter—and with the parking lot covered in black ice, I stepped carefully.

I had just got to my car when a voice called out, and I almost slipped.

"Mister!"

I turned around and saw someone coming out of the shadows. I put my hand on my .38 out of instinct, not because I felt threatened. When my eyes adjusted, I realized it was an Asian boy, perhaps fifteen years old, dressed only in a work shirt and white smock.

"Are you a police officer?" he said.

"Why? What's wrong?"

"We found something. Can you come?"

When I nodded yes, he turned around, and I followed him. We went down an alleyway that ran between the buildings, the underbelly of the city and a hidden world that most residents would never see. The pavement was rutted—there was litter and sludge everywhere. Rats scuttled in the darkness, and somewhere a tabby cat hissed.

We turned right, then left, then right again, and soon I was lost in the urban maze. Finally, we came to a dead-end, and in the distance, I saw a floodlight above a narrow door. A small wooden sign mounted above the lintel read: Lantern House Restaurant – Employees Only. A group of Asian workers was gathered by a dumpster, smoking obsessively, speaking in their native tongue.

"Please, just over here," the boy said, waving.

As I approached, the crowd parted, and a couple of men even bowed. They were all dressed the same, with rubber boots, soiled aprons, and white undershirts. Hours laboring in the hot kitchen must have made them resistant to the cold, I thought, because anyone else would have had hypothermia.

"What's this all about?" I said impatiently.

The boy looked at the men and then to me.

"They found something...inside."

I eyed them skeptically and walked over to the dumpster. Gripping the metal rim, I pulled myself up and looked in, but all I could see were dark piles of garbage.

"No," the boy said. "Under the hood, near the back."

I reached for my lighter, and it took three tries to start. I held out the flame and saw plastic bags, empty boxes, and canisters. Woven throughout was the organic muck of restaurant waste—fish heads, onion skins, pork rinds, rotten mushrooms. Even with a stuffy nose, the odor was enough to make me gag. A solitary seagull, as bold as he was hungry, landed in the heap and began to pick at a chicken bone.

I looked down at the boy.

"I don't see anything," I said.

He glanced over at the men, who were huddled together and watching.

"They were sure they saw it."

I shook my head.

"I don't see anything. Can they show me?"

"They won't."

I frowned and said, "Whaddya mean *they won't?*"

"It's a bad omen, Sir."

Suddenly, the bird flew away with a morsel in its mouth, and the workers all gasped.

My hand was getting numb from holding the cold metal. Just as I was ready to give up, a chunk of ice fell from a building ledge and went into the dumpster. Like a reflex, my eyes followed to where it landed, and I noticed something shiny in the corner. I held the lighter out again and, wedged between a plastic bag and an empty tin of canola oil, was a burgundy shoe—a woman's shoe.

I looked closer and shuddered when I saw the smooth skin of a human leg.

CHAPTER 3

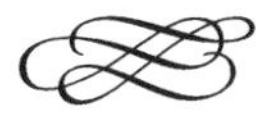

I TIPTOED INTO THE BEDROOM, AND SHE WAS ON HER SIDE, A DOWN comforter wrapped around her body. Her eyes were closed but that didn't mean she was sleeping. I took off my suit and hung it next to her nurse uniforms, which she had ironed and folded neatly. When I heard the bed creak, I turned around and whispered, "Ruth?"

"You're late."

"Something came up."

There was a dreamy pause.

"Funny thing about life. Something always comes up."

As I peeled the damp undershirt off my body, I realized I was sweating all over. I had witnessed hundreds of murders, but they never got any easier, and each one presented a new trauma.

"I made meatloaf," she said with a yawn. "You can reheat it."

"No appetite, but thanks."

"Since when?"

"There was a body in a dumpster near headquarters."

The moment her eyes popped open and she sat up, I regretted mentioning it.

"My gosh. How?" she asked.

"A porter found me in the parking lot. Took me to it."

"A murder?"

"I'd say so."

The light from the hallway broke across her face, and I could tell she had been crying.

"How was the appointment?" I said.

When she didn't answer, I thought she might not have heard me. But as I went to ask again, she blurted, "More drugs."

"More drugs?"

"More drugs."

I reached out to turn off the hallway lamp, and the whole apartment went dark. I climbed into bed and put my chest against her back, my arms around her stomach. Her purple negligee was absurdly unsuited for the weather, but she was never one to sacrifice femininity for comfort, and she was the only woman I ever met who wore perfume to bed. As I lay snugly against her warm skin, I was for a moment aroused, until I gave in to exhaustion and was out cold.

RUTH WAS STILL ASLEEP when I got up the next morning. I crept out to the kitchen and opened the cabinet above the stove. I reached for the empty Maxwell House tin that I kept hidden behind a row of soup cans. Inside was a small black box with the gold necklace I had purchased a week before for our first wedding anniversary. The actual date wasn't for two more days, but with the unpredictable schedules of a nurse and a cop, I had to improvise.

I sat at the table sipping tea, crunching on a raisin English muffin. The first rays of dawn came through the windows and filled the kitchen with light. When I looked out, I saw that it had snowed. On the side lawn, a cardinal was bathing in the flakes, a solitary left-behind from the hordes of birds that had long since fled.

Before I left, I put the box on the counter along with a small note I had asked a secretary at work to type for me. My penmanship had always been bad, and I knew that nothing would ruin a gift like a sentimental card whose sentiments were unreadable.

As I drove to work, I imagined the moment Ruth would awake to find it, knowing that the snowstorm would only add to her joy. She may have been from Southern California, but she had taken to New England like a Puritan. She loved the cold and hated the heat, which put her at odds with that large portion of the local populace that resented winter. She didn't always fit in, but she always knew where she stood, and although we grew up on different coasts, our hearts were on the same city block.

I loved her endlessly.

CHAPTER 4

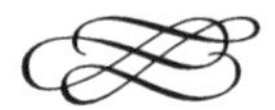

WITH ITS SCHIZOPHRENIC SHAPE, BOSTON DIDN'T HAVE A GEOGRAPHIC center. But if there was one, police headquarters would have been it. Built during the Civil War, it was a six-story mammoth of granite and yellow brick, with rows of double-hung windows. It looked more like a warehouse than an office building and lacked the ornamentation of the historic structures around it. Because it was originally a gunpowder store, everyone called it The Armory, including the press, and anyone who referred to "headquarters" was considered an out-of-towner.

Inside, the corridors were bustling with detectives, patrolmen, crime specialists, secretaries, and other officials. The ancient radiators gave off a steamy and must-ridden heat that was no less uncomfortable than the bitter cold outside. As I approached my office, Harrigan came around the corner with his briefcase in one hand, a fedora in the other.

"Morning Lieutenant," he said.

"You're bright and cheery."

"My years in the sun."

As I put the key in, he asked, "How was the drive?"

"Streets were a nightmare. Took back roads, mostly."

I opened the door, and we both walked in.

Detective Trevor Harrigan and I had worked together four years and never once had I regretted the partnership. Tall, black, cleanly shaven, and always dressed in a single-breasted suit, he was a Victorian image of the distinguished law officer. He spent the first half of his childhood on Saint Kitts in the West Indies and the second half in Roxbury. From the former, he inherited a mild-mannered island propriety, from the latter a street-savvy cool. We attended the same high school, although we were four grades apart, and the mutual experience of our hardscrabble youth made us as tight as brothers despite the racial divide.

I took off my coat and threw it over a chair. I invited him to sit, but he declined, and I knew why. The office was a mess. I had been there for two years, and it looked like I just moved in. There were stacks of boxes against the walls—furniture was everywhere. Framed citations and other wall décor sat in piles in the corner, still wrapped in moving paper. Luckily for me, Harrigan accepted my sloppiness like he accepted my smoking—with silent scorn.

"So," I said, climbing over things to get to my desk, "any news on Cinderella?"

"How do you mean?"

"Anyone reported missing?"

"Lots of people missing, Lieutenant."

As I reached in my top drawer for a cigarette, the radiator behind me made a loud bang, and I jumped.

"Chrissakes," I said. "They need to fix that damn thing."

I held up my lighter but refrained from using it when I saw Harrigan's expression.

"Where's Jackson?" I asked.

"The captain is home sick, unfortunately."

"Still sick? That makes—"

"Two days this week, one last, three the week before."

"We may have to send flowers."

Unsure whether I was serious or joking, Harrigan didn't answer.

Someone knocked at the door, and a pretty young secretary

peeked in. With a pleated navy skirt, collared blouse, and white beaded necklace, she reminded me of Audrey Hepburn, and just the sight of her made me more awake.

"What can we do for you?" I asked.

"Good morning. There's a man here to see you."

"A man?"

"A man and a boy. Oriental man and boy. They're in the lobby."

I gave Harrigan a curious look and got up. As we walked down the hallway, the secretary was twenty feet ahead, and she strutted like she knew we were watching.

We came out to the reception area, and the boy who had led me to the body the night before was there on a bench. Beside him, an elderly Asian man sat gazing at the floor, a set of crutches by his side. As we approached, the boy looked up, but the old man did not.

"You get some rest last night?" I remarked.

Clutching a wool cap, he nodded nervously but didn't speak. He was thin and pale, with the tired eyes of someone who had been up for days. But it wasn't an uncommon look, and in January everyone seemed to walk around in an anemic funk that made you think the world was dying.

"What've you got for us?" I said directly.

The boy looked up at me, then glanced around the lobby. Phones rang, typewriters clanked, and people moved around like fretful ants. I could tell that all the activity made him uncomfortable.

"My uncle, Sir. He saw something last night."

His voice was unsteady, his eyes darted.

"Wasn't he interviewed?" I asked.

"No, he doesn't work there—he doesn't work anywhere." He glanced down at his uncle's crooked legs. "He comes by the restaurant to see friends. He was there last night—" He stopped abruptly and said, "Can we speak somewhere else?"

I looked over at Harrigan, who stood with his arms crossed, listening.

"What's your name, son?" I asked.

"Theodore—Teddy."

I started to grin but stopped when I realized he was serious.

"Your Chinese name. What's your real name?"

"We're Korean," he said. "That *is* my real name."

I looked at the floor, partly embarrassed and partly surprised.

"My apologies. What's your uncle's name?"

"Jong-soo."

When the old man heard his name, he twitched once and turned to his nephew. His tiny eyes flickered, and he chewed his gums with the few teeth he had left.

"Let's all take a walk, Teddy," I said.

He got up to help his uncle, and when I tried to assist, the old man shooed me away and grumbled something. In one thrust, he pushed himself off the bench and was standing.

We proceeded down the hallway, people moving out of the way when they saw the crutches. I leaned into Teddy and said, "Polio?"

"No," he replied, shaking his head. "It happened in the war. He was beaten. Broke five vertebrae."

I looked at the man in pity and noticed that the crutches were covered in Korean writing, tiny symbols carved into the wood like ornamental swirls.

"And the decorations?"

As we talked about him, the old man hobbled along but I wasn't convinced he was unaware.

"It's like a diary," Teddy whispered. "Things that have happened in his life."

"A cultural thing?"

"No. His own idea."

We came to the elevator bank across from the copy room and waited. I had never used the elevators so the journey was as new to me as it was to them. When the doors opened, I held it for the old man and then pressed the button for the basement. Having served in the war, I understood the Korean tradition of order and cleanliness and wouldn't have insulted him by taking him to my office.

Downstairs we pushed through the swinging doors and into the cafeteria. It was a large room with a low ceiling, fluorescent overhead lights, and two dozen tables lined in perfect rows like a military mess hall. At the far side, the kitchen staff was filling the buffet with pans of hot food, preparing for the lunch rush. In the corner, some patrolmen were drinking black coffee and trying to shake off the fatigue from the overnight shift.

I led Teddy and his uncle to a table by the wall and invited them to sit.

"Can I get you something?" I asked.

The boy politely declined, and his uncle just looked off with a hypnotic stare.

I turned to Harrigan and said, "Get me a coffee, will ya?"

"I'm your partner, Lieutenant, not your errand boy."

"My treat, get something for yourself."

As Harrigan waited, I reached into my coat, but my wallet wasn't there.

"Damn it," I said. "Must've left it at home."

"A man could go broke being treated by you," he said as he walked off.

The vague change of expressions on the boy and the old man could have together added up to a smile. They may not have heard exactly what Harrigan said, but sarcasm was a universal language.

"Tell me," I said to Teddy. "What did he see last night?"

"An ambulance."

"An ambulance?"

When he turned to his uncle and spoke, I experienced a bitter-sweet nostalgia at the sounds of peasant Korean. During the war, I had overheard the whispered conversations of villagers who the military hired to deliver supplies and munitions to division rear. After 18 months in the Korean mountains, I grew so familiar with the language that, even if I didn't know what they were saying, I somehow knew what they meant.

The old man squinted, the wrinkles in his face contracting, and he looked like a mummy. He peered up to me, perhaps for the first time, and suddenly began to talk. He made strange hand gestures, moved his eyes, shook his head, and wobbled. Once finished, his shoulders slumped, and he stared blankly at the tabletop. The outburst was as comical as it was bizarre, and I sat with a stunned grin.

"He insists it was an ambulance," Teddy said.

Harrigan returned and put a cup of coffee down in front of me.

"There was an ambulance," I said, recalling the scene, "and a coroner's van...and two cruisers..."

The boy translated as I spoke, and his uncle listened. When I was done, the man again broke out into a hysterical spell of words and motions. I looked aside to Harrigan, who stood frozen with a donut in his mouth, as amused as I was by the performance.

"He says, Sir," Teddy continued, "that he got off the bus at 7:00. He walked down the alley to the back of the Lantern House. He stopped to urinate in a small space between the buildings. As he walked back, an ambulance drove up the alleyway back to the street."

"Did he get a plate number?" Harrigan asked, wiping his mouth with a napkin.

"No. It was too dark."

"Any markings? A company name on the side?"

The boy asked the man, who gave a terse reply and pounded his fist once on the table.

"No, Sir. It happened very quickly," Teddy said.

I turned to Harrigan, and our eyes locked in a brief and wordless deliberation. We were both skeptical, that was obvious, but as eccentric as the old man was there was no reason for him to lie. Immigrants were never easy witnesses, and too often they were reluctant to come forward about a crime. Living at the fringes of their adopted country, they were vulnerable so I appreciated the risk Teddy and his uncle were taking.

"Well," I said with a sigh. "Thanks for coming to see us."

"You're welcome, Sir."

We escorted them back to the reception area, where they slipped quietly out the front doors and back into the world. As Harrigan and I headed back to my office, a young woman in a blouse and tight skirt came barreling out of a doorway, and we almost collided. A curt smile was her only apology, and she continued down the corridor, her heels clicking in the distance.

We returned to the office, and I shut the door. There we sat in the quiet of the room, pondering the interview, savoring the silence. It wasn't a long meditation, however, because the faulty radiator began to knock again, and talking seemed the only defense against its annoying clamor.

"What's your take?" I said.

"I think the old man is being truthful."

"Wanna look into it?"

"Not particularly," Harrigan said, and he paused a moment before adding, "But I will."

"Make some calls. See if any ambulances got heisted last night. Have someone check with the shop owners. I'm going home to get my wallet. I'll stop at the coroner on the way back."

He nodded and reached down for his briefcase. As he went to leave, I said, "Another thing," and he spun around like he was expecting it.

"If the...um...captain calls in, let me know? Get me on the two-way?"

"You'll be the first to know. I promise."

CHAPTER 5

DRIVING AFTER A STORM WAS TREACHEROUS IN BOSTON. THE NARROW streets were narrower, and the constant spinning of tires created a layer of hardened ice that was like trying to maneuver on a hockey rink. In the South End, a newspaper truck almost glided into me; In Jamaica Plain, I watched an elderly driver spin out. At Forest Hills, my tires slid on the trolley tracks and almost sent me headlong into a bus. By the time I got home, I had experienced more traffic events than most commuters would in a year.

Such were the sacrifices of living in the city. A week after returning from our honeymoon, Ruth and I moved into a third-floor apartment on a shady street in Roslindale. Situated at the top of a small hill, it had a spectacular view of downtown. It wasn't the Taj Mahal, but it was clean and neat, and my only complaint was that there were no screens for summer. The owner was a retired cop who lived just two blocks away so we never had to worry if there was a clogged drain or if the boiler wasn't working.

I parked out front and left the Valiant running. As I walked up the front steps, I saw tiny footprints in the snow and knew that Ruth had gone to work. Inside, the necklace and note were gone, and it made me smile. I found my wallet and headed out.

To avoid traffic, I took a different way back, but I only got as far as Forest Hills Station before everything came to a standstill. It was complete gridlock. I considered using my sirens but knew that people wouldn't move if they had no place to move to. In a flash of impatience, I cut the wheel and turned down a side street. In the calculus of driving aggravation, an hour on backroads was better than thirty minutes of stop and go.

I disappeared into the residential maze, down streets and small lanes lined with triple-deckers. Constant plowing had created snow drifts on both sides, covering stairways, burying trashcans and even a few cars.

At some point, I crossed the invisible boundary into Roxbury. As bleak and rundown as it was, I loved the neighborhood because I had grown up there. It wasn't so much nostalgia—I was never away from it long enough to feel estranged—but more the warm familiarity wrought by years of memories, experiences, first loves, and heartbreaks.

I knew the area as intimately as a woman, but something about either the snow or the morning glare made me confused. At the next crossroads, I stopped to look for a landmark but saw only more and more triple-deckers. Square, plain, and colorless, they stretched for miles unending like the boxcars of a freight train. I had to admit to myself that I was lost.

I punched the gas in frustration, and my tires spun. I turned down a street, then another, driving blindly and hoping to see something I recognized. Finally, I came over a small hill and noticed a crowd in the distance. Dozens of people filled the sidewalks, spilled onto the street.

I drove slowly to the bottom and saw a wide entranceway. With its wrought-iron gate and brick colonnades, it could have been a mansion if it wasn't in the slums of Roxbury. I peered into the property as I passed and saw a snow-covered hill with a cluster of stone buildings at the top. The vast space was like finding a pasture in a jungle, and I knew it could be none other than St Kilda.

A driveway wound up the right side of the hill and led to the main building. Yet people avoided the road and instead went straight up the slope, stopping at the base of the bell tower. I hadn't been to the abbey in over twenty years, but I was sure that, on the night we encountered the priest, Russo, Sweeney, and I had entered from the back. Those memories should have been enough to turn me away, but I was bound by both curiosity and duty to find out what was happening.

I rolled down the window and called to the first person I saw.

"Pardon," I said. "What's going on here?"

An old man in a trench coat came over and leaned in with a warm smile.

"A miracle," he said in broken English. "The most beautiful miracle."

"Miracle?"

"In the window. The Madonna. See for yourself."

He tipped his hat and continued towards the entrance.

I got out and stepped over a snowbank to the sidewalk. Despite all the people, it was remarkably calm, and the only sounds were restrained voices and soft whispers. It was an incredible diversity of humanity—old and young, rich and poor, healthy and sick. Behind me, some men were talking in Spanish, and up ahead an old woman in a shawl was praying in Polish. Some people were alone, and others had brought their children. I saw a woman carrying a baby, its tiny body swaddled in a patterned blanket. Everyone walked towards the gate with a solemn steadiness, undeterred by the ice and the cold.

I blended into the crowd and went through the front gates. When I walked onto the lawn, my shoes sank in the snow and my socks got wet. But I continued up the hill and soon reached the bell tower, where a couple of hundred people were gathered. It was even larger than it looked from the road, and with its thick walls and crenelated belfry, reminded me of a castle. On the front were three arched windows, twenty feet tall and built of leaded panes.

At the foot of the obelisk was a makeshift shrine of candles, votive plaques, and other Christian offerings. Old women, hunched and frail, knelt down and chanted on the pavement. Somewhere somebody was reciting the Our Father in Italian.

I walked over to a woman and asked, "Where is it?"

She leaned towards me, pointing.

"There."

I tilted my head back and looked up, squinting in the sun. At first, I saw nothing, only three windows covered in ice. But the longer I stared, the more a shape began to form. Then suddenly I could see it: the unmistakable image of the Madonna and Child etched into the frost. The likeness was eerie, and I just shook my head in astonishment.

I turned around and looked out across the property. In the distance, the entire city unfolded under a blue, wintery sky. People were continuing to come up the hill, trudging over the frozen ground in overcoats, scarves, and gloves while down below on the road the traffic was increasing. Everything was orderly so far, but I wasn't convinced it would stay that way.

I walked away from the tower and followed the side of the building, coming to a paved turnaround where the long, winding driveway ended. I assumed it was the main entrance because it had a large double door with a knocker. I swung it twice, and some startled birds burst out of the eaves and scattered. Moments later, the latch creaked and the door opened.

"May I help you?" a voice said.

I looked into the darkness and two eyes peered back. The door opened a little more, and I saw a man in a brown cloak. He had a pitchfork beard and tiny eyes, and he stood with his hands clasped.

"I'm a detective," I said, pointing behind. "You've got some uninvited visitors?"

The monk stretched his head out and looked.

"Are they uninvited?" he said.

"There's an image...in the tower window. They think it's the Madonna."

"Well, is it?"

I blinked at the strange response.

"I'm not here to philosophize. You need to either lock the gate or get a police detail. It's not safe."

He paused for a moment then said, "Very well, Officer. Please come in."

I stepped over the threshold and into a long, dark hallway that smelled musty and old. The walls were unfinished, as was the floor, and it was like entering a cave. When I hesitated, the monk turned back and waved for me to follow.

"I'm Brother Emmanuel," he said.

I wasn't familiar with the etiquette for shaking hands with a member of the clergy, so I just nodded.

"Joseph Brae," I replied.

We turned into a small office with a desk and phone and not much else.

"Please," he said. "Make any necessary arrangements."

I dialed The Armory and explained the situation to the dispatcher. When I hung up, I thought the monk had left but he was standing right behind me.

"Did you know about the image?" I said.

"We do. Brother Lionel informed us last evening."

I looked around the sparse room.

"What is this place?"

"We're a Benedictine abbey. Forty-six monks, some part-time laypeople and, of course, our abbot."

"And where is he?"

"Not here at the moment, I'm afraid. Can I give you a short tour? Is there time?"

Before I could say yes or no, he walked out, and I found myself following him out of curiosity. We continued down the hallway and came to an atrium, where the walls were covered with portraits of men in cassocks and vestments, solemnly posed and reflective. Suspended ten feet in the air was a wooden figure of Christ, his limbs mounted to the cross, his body writhing. Although hand-painted and finely sculpted, it was heavily damaged, with a missing nose and charred limbs.

"You like the relic?" Brother Emmanuel asked. "It's from St. Hedwig's Cathedral—Berlin."

"Must have cost a fortune to transport."

He closed his eyes and smiled.

"Brother Vogt, our abbot, brought it with him when he came to this country. The Cathedral was destroyed by American bombers. This was saved from the fire."

I glimpsed up respectfully at the statue but couldn't refrain from sarcasm.

"Divine intervention?" I said.

"And the help of the faithful. Four men were terribly burned, I am told. One died."

"How about the abbot?"

"He was, of course, spared."

We went through an arched doorway and down another corridor that had doors at regular intervals. Along the walls were antique sconces, black and corroded, and their bulbs emitted a dull, yellow glow. The only windows were tiny apertures built into the stone, decorated with burgundy shades.

"This is one of our dormitories," the monk said, pointing. "There's another on the other side of the cloister."

"The cloister?"

"The garden, some might call it. Or courtyard. An open space for contemplation. For nature."

As we walked, my mind drifted back to that cold Halloween night. It was so long ago that it seemed nothing more than a bad dream from childhood. Maybe it was the alcohol, I thought, or the fact that I had fallen on my head, but I couldn't remember much about what happened. I had only scattered images and hazy impressions: the wet grass, the sinister voice of the priest, the kicks and punches, the terror.

"Detective?"

But the incident was real enough to still startle me because when I looked ahead, I realized that I had stopped.

"Sorry," I said, quickly catching up.

When we reached the end of the hall, Brother Emmanuel opened a heavy door and daylight flooded in, temporarily blinding me. I followed him through, and when my eyes adjusted, I realized we were at the cloister. It was smaller than I recalled, no larger than a city playground and bordered on three sides by buildings. In the distance, I saw the grassy slope that went down to the old stone wall—the wall we climbed that fateful night.

"This is where we come to reflect," he said, raising his eyebrows. "In warmer times, of course."

I looked around and, at the center, I saw the statue of Jesus and the children. A chill went through me that I attributed to the cold, but which I knew was probably from something more disturbing. I turned away and changed the subject.

"Where're the others?"

"In the presbytery for midday prayer. We pray six times a day."

I started to ask another question but was distracted by the sound of sirens.

"That's my call," I said.

He opened the door and held it for me. We walked down the corridor, through the atrium, and back to the front entrance.

"What will happen now?" the monk asked.

"We'll get traffic moving, get people off the street. After that, it's up to the brass." As I stepped out, I added, "Thanks for the tour."

He smiled humbly, took a bow.

"I'm happy to share our house," he said.

Again, it seemed proper to shake, but his hands were clasped. So I nodded with an awkward smile then put up my collar to leave.

"Oh, Officer?"

I stopped and turned around.

"How did you come to find us?"

I made a confused wince.

"Driving by...I was just driving by."

"Do you always pass this way?" he asked.

I thought for a moment.

"No. never."

CHAPTER 6

THE MORTUARY WAS IN THE BASEMENT OF BOSTON CITY HOSPITAL, AND the only entrance was by the loading dock at the back of the building. I went through a narrow door, down a staircase, and followed a dimly lit corridor that was more like an underground tunnel. The ceiling was so low I had to duck to avoid pipes. The stench of coal and mold was everywhere.

Finally, I came to a single gray door with no sign or marker. Because of where the office was located, someone had long ago dubbed it The Crypt, and the nickname stuck.

I knocked twice and waited. Seconds later, the door swung open, and the doctor appeared in a white surgical gown. His glasses were hanging at the tip of his nose, and in one hand he held a fat cigar. I squinted in the clinical light, and our eyes met.

"Can I come in?" I asked.

He took a puff, looked straight at me, and blew the smoke in my face.

"May," he said.

"Pardon?"

"*May* I come in."

"Okay, *may* I come in?"

With an annoyed look, he turned around and waved for me to enter.

Short, squat, and nearly blind, Doctor Ansell wasn't easy to get along with, but he was always amusing. With his slanted face and prominent nose, he looked like a miniature version of Alfred Hitchcock. He was raised by immigrant parents during the Depression and grew up on the streets of Roxbury. The only reason he liked me was because we were both veterans, and the only reason he liked Harrigan was because he was black. As a child of the Jewish ghetto, he naturally sided with the underdog.

"Didn't know you could smoke down here," I said.

He shrugged his shoulders.

"Who knows, kid. I don't make the rules. I only break 'em. Besides, who the hell's gonna rat on me? Everyone here's dead."

The Crypt had only three rooms—the front office, the lab, and the morgue, which was at the back. The whole place was nothing more than a former storage area whose plywood walls had been plastered over and painted white. The floors were all cracked, and the drop-ceiling had stains from age and water leaks. It was cold and dank, always.

As I followed him over to his desk, I heard a clank and turned to see a timid and bespectacled man in his twenties. Coming out of the lab, he had bumped a metal table and knocked some things over.

"Dammit, Mannett! Be careful."

I chuckled and said, "It rhymes."

Ansell rolled his eyes with a smirk.

"Hardly. It's really *Manet,* like mayonnaise."

"Like the artist."

"Can you believe it? A regular stinkin' aristocrat. So I call him mayonnaise. White and tasteless, just like he is."

The assistant maintained a reluctant composure, enduring the insults because he had no choice. As we stood watching, he clumsily put the equipment back in order and returned to the lab room.

"So," the doctor said, flicking an ash into an empty can of Moxie. "What can I do for you?"

"Looking for an update on the murder last night."

He raised his eyes—gave me a sideways glance.

"Get in line. Won't be done 'til the end of the week—if you're lucky."

"A witness came in The Armory today. An old man. And a boy. The old man said he saw an ambulance back down the alleyway a few hours before the body was found."

Ansell tilted his head, vaguely intrigued, and took another drag. When he exhaled, the thick cigar smoke was enough to make even me —a smoker—wince. Without a word, he started to move again, and I was having trouble keeping up.

"They get a plate number?" he asked.

"Nothing. And no company name..."

He pushed a gurney into the corner, picked up some boxes the post office had delivered and put them on a shelf.

"...that's what the old man said anyway..."

Next, he got some surgical gloves from the drawer and stretched them over his large hands.

"...he didn't speak a lick of English, was a bit loony."

The doctor stopped.

"Just cuz someone don't speak English don't make him loony, kid."

"He was loony anyway," I joked, and he walked away.

"You'll need more info than that. Hundreds of ambulances in this city. Maybe it was a salt truck, a delivery van. Without decals, who can say?"

Putting the cigar back in his mouth, he continued to speak, but I couldn't understand what he was saying.

"Huh?" I said, finally.

He took it out and licked his lips.

"I said *the irony is killing me.*"

"Irony?"

"She should've been getting picked up by an ambulance, not dumped off by one."

When I frowned, he turned around and looked me dead in the eye.

"The broad was pregnant. She had just delivered. There's a child out there, Lieutenant, somewhere—"

CHAPTER 7

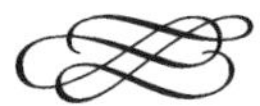

Captain Jackson didn't return to work until the end of the week, a record absence for any senior official but a sacrilege for him. In my fifteen years on the force—including six years working under him—he had never missed a day. He was not only dedicated to the job but he was also committed to the mission of law enforcement, a rare idealism in a department where civil-service mediocrity prevailed. He had been out so much that even the office clerks started to notice, and people were stopping me in the hallways to ask where or how he was.

When I got to The Armory on Friday and saw his letterbox empty, I knew the captain was finally back. I walked towards his office with a heavy dread, as concerned about him as I was about our caseload. If I could have avoided going in, I would have. But in our work timing was everything, and any delay could mean the difference between arrest and escape, conviction and acquittal, life and death. We didn't have the luxury of waiting.

I knocked once and opened the door.

"Ah, Detective."

I immediately sensed a change in his voice. He was naturally hoarse—strange for someone who never smoked—but this was something more. I leaned against the doorway and looked in but not at him.

"Morning, Capt.," I said.

He coughed before speaking.

"Well, are you going to enter or hold up the building?"

I grinned and walked reluctantly across the floor. I took one of the two chairs opposite his desk and sat with my legs crossed. The captain was working—he was always working. With a pencil in hand, he was face-deep in a report dossier, and my presence did nothing to distract his concentration. I sat still and waited for him to finish.

Like most his age, Captain Ernest Jackson was an Eisenhower man, a fact that was emphasized by the framed portrait of the general and former president on the wall. But he hardly fit the mold of the straight-edged disciplinarian.

He had a great mound of white hair, unkempt and often unclean, which seemed to consume his whole head. He wore glasses so thick they magnified his eyes and hence his character. He was almost never in uniform, rarely carried a sidearm, and seemed to delight in his own eccentricity. Born and raised in Cornish, Maine, he was one of the few Yankees in a police force dominated by white ethnics from the city's insular boroughs. Because he was an outsider, his enemies saw him as a threat, and his friends saw him as a savior.

The captain had many quirks, but his most prominent was that he hummed while he worked. It was always amusing and sometimes annoying, but Harrigan and I accepted him like dutiful sons because in many ways we were. He was in the front row at my wedding; he was the first in line at Harrigan's father's wake. We exchanged gifts at Christmas and went fishing each summer. He had other detectives, but as the core of the homicide unit, the three of us operated like a close-knit family. For me and Harrigan, the only thing that rivaled our respect for Jackson was our love for him.

Finally, he closed the file and put it aside.

"So," he said, looking up. "You're late."

I knew from his tone that it was more an observation than an accusation.

"Ruth had an appointment. I drove her."

He tapped his fingers together, his eyes averted, thinking.

"Some things are more important than the job. *Some things*. That happens to be one of them." He covered his mouth and coughed and then continued. "Harrigan filled me in on the young lady you found Monday night. What a sin. What a shame."

"I was leaving work," I said. "A kitchen worker hailed me in the back lot. An Oriental."

He hacked again, and his entire body shook. I took a clean napkin out of my pocket and handed it to him, but he declined.

"Who has the audacity to leave a body a hundred yards from headquarters?" When he looked at me, his eyes were gaunt, tired. "Tell me what we know, Lieutenant."

"To begin with," I said, "she was pregnant."

His mouth dropped—he leaned forward and squinted.

"Pardon?"

"She had just given birth, probably a few hours before she was killed. I was at The Crypt on Tuesday. Ansell informed me—"

Someone knocked on the door, and when I turned around, Harrigan stuck his head in.

"Please, Detective," Jackson said, beckoning to him. "Come in..."

He took the chair beside me, and I could smell fresh cologne.

"...We were just discussing the homicide from Monday."

Harrigan sat still, his back arched and shoulders wide.

"There was no apparent sign of trauma," I continued. "We should have the full autopsy early next week."

Harrigan said, "We might have a witness."

I glanced at him and said, "I was getting to that." I faced the captain and explained, "The boy who took me to the woman came in with his uncle. An old Korean—a real nutcase. Said he saw an ambulance in the alley a couple hours before the body was discovered."

"So, was he mistaken?" Jackson said.

"I...I mean...I think—"

"The gentleman was quite senile," Harrigan said. "But why would he invent such a thing?"

"Seemed unreliable to me," I added.

"An unreliable witness," the captain said, coughing yet again, "is… still…a…witness." He quickly reached for a paper cup on the desk and drank, his eyes strained and lips quivering. Once his throat was soothed, he continued, "A pregnant woman…and an ambulance?"

"A link?" I wondered.

Jackson grimaced.

"A tenuous link, but better than nothing. Perhaps it was a failed delivery, the paramedic panicked?"

"Or maybe she was left for dead," Harrigan said, "Someone heard her cries and called an ambulance. Then they couldn't find her."

"Maybe a botched abortion."

"Maybe all these things," the captain said. "We have to start somewhere—"

The phone rang and broke the momentum of our brainstorming. Jackson picked it up and said hello. As the caller spoke, his face tightened, and his eyes moved anxiously. For a moment, I thought there had been another murder. But he put his hand over the receiver and mouthed the words, "I have to take this."

Harrigan and I immediately got up and left. As we reached the corridor, the secretary who almost knocked us down earlier in the week walked by and smiled. With her hair in a bun, pink lipstick, and dark suit, she was like a new woman. The only way I could tell it was her was by the large gap between her teeth, a flaw that was mysteriously sexy on her but wouldn't have looked so good on someone else.

When I craned my neck, Harrigan gave me a scolding look.

"Don't step where you shouldn't walk," he said.

"I'm married, not dead."

We lingered for a moment in the hallway, unsure where to go or what to do. The meeting had ended so abruptly we didn't have a plan.

"Let's head to the cafeteria," I suggested.

"As you wish."

"I'm buying."

"I'll believe it when I see it."

We turned at the first stairwell and went down two flights. I nodded to some colleagues, then we pushed through the swinging doors. I glanced back to Harrigan and lowered my voice.

"Does the captain seem alright to you?" I asked.

"Alright, yes. Well, no."

We got two Styrofoam cups and filled them up from a large, metallic urn that had probably been out all morning. I waited near the register while Harrigan proceeded to pick out a banana, fruit cup, glazed donut, and muffin. When he came over, I looked at the tray and said, "What's this?"

"Aren't you buying, Lieutenant?"

The lady behind the counter grinned.

"A coffee," I said.

"I'm sorry, but you didn't specify."

I rolled my eyes and handed her a five. She gave me change, and we walked over to a table.

"I like when you have your wallet," he said.

"I don't wanna have to drive home again. Took me an hour to get back last time."

I took a sip; the coffee was hot but stale.

"Didn't you get lost?"

"Lost?" I said, reaching for a copy of the Herald Tribune someone had left behind. "No. More like sidetracked. There was a little incident at—"

I stopped when my eyes caught a small headline at the bottom of the page. For some reason, a chill went up my back.

ROXBURY MIRACLE DRAWS
HUNDREDS OF THE FAITHFUL

CHAPTER 8

THE STREETS WERE COLD, DARK, AND BUSY AS I DROVE TO PICK UP RUTH. Along Tremont Street, the bars and restaurants were already filling up, and everywhere I looked pretty women in long coats and short skirts sashayed over the frozen cobblestones.

When I pulled into City Hospital, the gates were flanked by mountains of hard-packed snow, the accumulation of storms that had been pounding the city since mid-December. The charm of that first fall was long gone, and what remained was dirty and perilous.

As I came up to the entrance, people were rushing in and out of the main doors. Many more lingered beneath the portico, smoking, standing on crutches, and waiting for rides. Cars pulled up, taxis left, and the place had the non-stop buzz of the departures gate at Logan Airport.

I stopped at the curb, and Ruth was standing beside a column, hands in her pockets, earmuffs around her head. A security guard started to come over to tell me to move but quickly changed his mind once he recognized the car. When I tapped the horn, Ruth looked and stepped over the slush to get to the door.

"Whoa," she said as she got in. "It's chilly."

"How come you didn't wait in the lobby?"

She took off the earmuffs, ran her hands through her hair.

"I've been cooped up all day, needed some fresh air."

"Nothing fresh out here," I said, but she didn't reply.

I turned the radio on low, and we drove through the South End, past block after block of rundown brick townhouses. What were once stately homes for the city's executive class had deteriorated into efficiency apartments, rooming houses, and the occasional brothel. The jazz clubs around Columbus Avenue were already beginning to heat up, and I watched a group of beatnik students pile into Wally's Café. With black turtlenecks and tight jeans, they were over a decade behind in fashion, but I preferred their chic modernism to the hippies.

Ruth hadn't said anything since we left, and her silence made me worry. As we continued home, a tacit tension was building that neither the radio nor my offhanded comments could break. It wasn't natural for her to be so glum, but in the past few months, I had seen a side of her that made my dark moods look like bliss. I was sure I knew the reason, but I wasn't sure I could face it.

"Did the test results—"

"Yes and no," she said.

"Are you—?"

Before I could finish, her head was slumped, and she was sobbing.

"No, I'm not okay," she said. "I'm angry. I'm tired. And I'm ashamed."

As we approached a red light, I slowed to a stop and turned to her.

"I accept the first two, but there's no reason to be ashamed."

"Maybe I'm not supposed to have children," she said, sniffling.

"Even if that were true, we don't know. Have some faith."

I reached over and rubbed her shoulder, but she was cold and unresponsive.

"Every day I see young women," she said, "girls really...unwed and uninterested, give birth, not caring a rat's ass about motherhood. I'm not saying they don't love their kids, but it's so easy, so effortless." She pushed tears from her eyes and gazed out the window. "One came in last Monday, gave birth, and an hour later was gone. Skipped out of the ward with the child like an impatient little hussy..."

She spoke so fast, with such mumbling bitterness, that I almost missed it. I blew through the light and pulled to the side of the road.

"What the hell are you doing?" she said.

I slammed the Valiant in park and turned off the radio.

"You said Monday night?"

"It was Monday night. Yes. Why?"

"The woman, what do you remember about her?"

With her back against the door, she looked at me with a confused pout, her mascara smudged.

"I was there when they brought her in. She looked like any young woman. Dark hair, pretty."

"Please, try to think. Did she have red shoes?"

Her expression changed and she sat up.

"Actually, she did. More like burgundy, but yes. Red. Why?"

I gripped the wheel and stared through the glass.

"Could be nothing," I said. "The woman we found in the dumpster was pregnant. Just delivered. Hours before, according to the coroner."

By now, her tears were almost dry. I didn't want to upset her again, but I had to keep pressing for information.

"How many patients leave right after giving birth?" I asked.

"Not many. It's unusual...and not advised. I don't even know if it's legal."

We sat quietly as the car idled. With the windows fogged up, all I could see were white streaks from the headlights coming down Columbus Avenue. The heat was on full blast, but it wasn't enough to keep us warm, and she crossed her arms, shivering slightly.

When I slid over to hug her, she hesitated at first then gave in, and for the next few minutes, we embraced awkwardly on the cold vinyl seat. From somewhere, perhaps her neck, I could smell the faint perfume that had faded over the course of a long workday. I kissed her chapped lips and looked into her eyes, and her expression slowly softened. It was a poignant moment in an unpoignant place, and we gripped each other as if something was trying to tear us apart.

"Let's get you home to bed," I said.

"Sounds like heaven."

CHAPTER 9

I WOKE UP RESTLESS AND COULDN'T STOP THINKING ABOUT WHAT RUTH had told me. It was Saturday morning, but I couldn't wait until Monday to investigate the woman who had fled the maternity ward. Ruth was already gone, shopping downtown with nurse friends who also had the day off. I jumped out of bed and called Harrigan, who agreed to a few hours of overtime for the sake of a lead. I had some tea and toast, put on yesterday's suit, and was out the door.

Harrigan rented an apartment in a three-story brick building on Ruthven Street in Roxbury, only three blocks from where I grew up. Unlike most officers his age, he was not married, and he lived alone. His elderly mother was a few streets away in a place that overlooked Franklin Park. With her island warmth and constant smile, she provided him with that dose of female companionship necessary to keep a man tame. He loved women but was a mama's boy at heart.

When I came down the street, he was waiting at the corner, a coffee in hand.

"Morning, Lieutenant," he said as he got in.

His eyes were bloodshot from the wind—his chapped skin gleamed from a fresh shave.

"What kind of perfume is that?" I joked.

I assumed his face was too numb to frown because he just rolled his eyes.

"They call it aftershave. You should try it sometime."

I hit the gas and we drove off, through the narrow streets of Roxbury, past boarded-up homes, abandoned buildings, and empty lots. Despite all the dilapidation, the area still made me sentimental.

"Blue Hill Ave. is that way," he said, pointing over his shoulder.

I hesitated, glanced over defensively.

"You gonna tell me how to drive in my own neighborhood?"

"Is it though?"

"It was," I mumbled.

I went down a side street, navigating by instinct and looking for a shortcut I knew from years before. But the further I went, the hazier the memories became, and I started to get lost.

"What makes you think the woman Ruth met was the victim?" he asked.

"Just a hunch. Why would a lady flee the maternity ward with her newborn?"

He blew on his coffee, took a sip.

"So she fled?"

"She may've skipped daisies out. I don't know."

We turned at the next crossroads and went over a shallow hill. When I looked ahead, I almost couldn't believe my eyes. There at the bottom was a huge crowd. Once again, I had ended up at St Kilda. The coincidence spooked me, and I thought of turning around, which would have been impossible with the snowbanks. I considered reversing too, but a car was behind me so I could only go straight.

"Damn it."

"The newspapers were right," Harrigan said.

As we approached the abbey, it looked like a parade, with twice as many people as before. Two officers in fur caps were blowing whistles and shouting orders in a futile effort to keep order. One was Sergeant Gerald Duggan, a six-foot-six giant with lanky arms and an overbite. His officers called him 'Sir,' his colleagues called him 'Jerry,' but his close friends called him 'Giraffe,' a nickname he got on the schoolyards of Charlestown due to his long neck and extraordinary height.

The moment Duggan saw us, he waved the Valiant through, and I pulled up to him.

"Hey, Giraffe," I said. "Got your hands full?"

He leaned over, put his elbows on the window.

"Full of shit maybe. What gives Brae? Or should I say *Lieutenant*?"

We had known each other since we were rookies and once even shared an apartment. It didn't matter how far up the department ladder I went because, in his eyes, we were always equals.

"How long's this gonna last?" I asked.

He stood up and looked around, eyeing the crowd with a mix of scorn and amazement.

"God knows," he said, winking at the irony. "Chief phoned the abbey, asked if we could clear the frost off the windows. The abbey declined."

"Who'd want the attention?"

"I'm sure they do," he said, nodding towards the hill. "This place was slated to close last fall. Archdiocese ordered it. Monks are on borrowed time. Squatters really."

"You're not much of a Christian."

"I'll be at Mass in the morning. Unless I can get more overtime, that is."

When the other cop called to him, he tapped his hands on the door and said, "Time's up. G'day, Gentlemen."

I put the car in gear and rolled through the crowd, watching all the faces. As we passed by the gates, I glanced over and saw masses of people trudging up the slope towards the shrine. The apparition was too far away to see, but I knew it was there.

"Watch it!" Harrigan yelled.

When I hit the brakes, we slid a couple of feet and stopped just in time. I looked ahead, and my entire body went numb. There, standing at my bumper, was Chester Sweeney's mother. Her eyes sagged, and she had the crooked expression of someone who was mentally ill. If she hadn't been so close, I wouldn't have recognized her at all.

We faced each other for ten seconds, and it felt like an hour.

"Are you alright, Lieutenant?"

Just as I went to roll down my window, she held up a bronze cross and mumbled something I couldn't hear. Then she turned away and vanished into the crowd.

"That was close," Harrigan said.

I took a napkin out of my coat and wiped the sweat off my forehead.

"Closer than you know."

CHAPTER 10

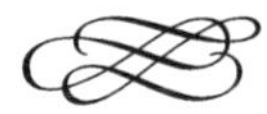

"Who was in charge Monday night?"

The woman behind the desk at the maternity ward got up and smoothed out her skirt. She was bone-thin, with red freckles and brown hair, a combination I had never seen.

"Um, I believe, um, Ms. Stuart is the ward nurse. Yes, she, um, works Mondays."

When she spoke, I heard a timid Irish brogue.

"Where's Ms. Stuart?" I asked.

She fidgeted with her hands; her eyes darted. It was obvious that we made her nervous.

"Can we speak with her, Madam?"

Harrigan's gentle baritone somehow put her at ease—he had that effect on people.

"Um, of course. Of course, you, um, can—"

The woman then went off down the corridor and disappeared around a corner. Seconds later she returned with another nurse who looked too young for such a senior position. Pretty and feminine, she approached with a dashing confidence that accentuated her good looks. She reminded me of Ruth, although they looked nothing alike.

"How can I help?" she said, extending a hand.

I still found it uncustomary for a lady, but I reached out and shook it anyway.

The four of us walked to a corner beside the main desk. Lowering my voice, I asked, "Did a woman leave here Monday night with a baby?"

Ms. Stuart glanced at the nurse, then said to me, "I don't mean to be smart, but lots of women leave here with babies."

"Right. Someone who left the ward unexpectedly...without authorization?"

She had the wary expression of someone caught in a lie.

"Yes," she said, pursing her lips. "There was a woman who fit that description. We aren't obliged to hold anyone. We can advise, but we can't detain them."

"Do you have the patient's name?" I asked.

She looked at the Irish nurse sharply and said, "Get the register from Monday."

The woman walked away and came back with a large three-ring binder. Ms. Stuart took it, opened it up, and began to thumb through the pages. As she scanned the columns, she mouthed the words to herself, and I noticed that her index finger trembled. In the background, newborns were shrieking, and I thought of Ruth.

"This is it, perhaps," she said, and we came in closer and formed a circle. "She was entered in as Brenda—no surname." She looked up from the binder and said, "We'll have to check with registration. They must have her information. It's policy."

Harrigan said, "And where is registration?"

"Second floor. But they're not open on weekends. They take the information downstairs, of course, but nothing's recorded 'til Monday."

I peered over to Harrigan and shook my head in frustration. Down the hall, I noticed some nurses watching, and when our eyes met, they all quickly looked away.

I faced Ms. Stuart and said, "Is it common for a woman to leave right after giving birth?"

She thought for a moment, looked at her colleague.

"Common? No. But as I said, we can only advise, we can't hold them—"

"I'm aware of that," I said. "Did you report it? Do you generally report these kinds of things?"

When she hesitated, it felt like a standoff. Her face got tense, and I could even detect a slight blush. It was clear that she didn't like my questions, and I didn't like her answers. Police work was like that—you tried to get the truth, and people always thought you were challenging their integrity.

"These things don't *generally* occur," she said finally, her chin raised. "Patients can be unpredictable."

To my left, a young nurse's assistant was waiting to speak with her. We had gotten about all we could, so I ended the conversation before things got heated. I reached into my pocket and took a business card from my wallet.

"Would you...please," I said, struggling to be polite, "check with registration on Monday and call me?"

Ms. Stuart swiped the card from my hand.

"Is that all, Officers?" she said coldly.

"That's all."

CHAPTER 11

WHEN I FIRST MET RUTH, SHE WAS THE CLOSEST THING TO SUNSHINE I had ever seen. She beamed with joy, shone with happiness. She would laugh if she tripped and cry at the sight of a rainbow. I thought it was Southern California naiveté combined with a dose of Hollywood melodrama, yet she was anything but a ditzy surfer girl. She had a true love for life, and an enthusiasm for living that made me ashamed to be a cynic. Maybe that was why it tormented me to see her depressed.

Sunday night, I decided to take her to dinner and to see the movie *Funny Girl*, which by its title seemed like a good remedy for the doldrums. As we drove down Washington Street, snow flurries swept over the hood, and my wipers struggled to keep up. It was bitter cold, and the streets were desolate.

When we reached Park Square, I found a spot in front of the Statler Hotel, something that would have been impossible most days. We walked down the sidewalk, headlong into the wind, and passed three prostitutes who stood shivering under an awning. We turned at the next corner and went into Sagansky's, a late-night diner that I had been going to for years.

I opened the door, and a bell jingled. We found an empty booth by the window and sat down. All I could smell was bacon fat and salty soup, and it made my stomach gurgle. A middle-aged waitress with cross-eyes and big hips came over, and we ordered ham dinners with potatoes and vegetables. Ruth asked for a glass of Chianti, but they only had Cabernet. By the time the woman left, Ruth had warmed up enough to take off her coat. As she rubbed her hands together, I noticed her nails were chipped from biting.

"Winter never seems to end," I said, but she didn't answer.

With her arms crossed, she gazed out the window with a dreamy detachment. On the sidewalk across the street, some hippies were sharing a joint and a bottle of something cheap. One of them had on a combat jacket, but I doubted he was a veteran.

"How're you feeling?" I asked.

"Okay, I guess. Like you said, *winter never seems to end.*"

"Something's wrong."

"I'm just tired."

"You aren't happy."

She peered up, her eyelashes fluttering.

"It's the drugs. They make me feel out of sorts. I'm okay."

The waitress returned with Ruth's wine and soda water for me. When she left, I said, "Something odd happened today." I waited until she was listening then continued, "This morning we passed a monastery—"

"St Kilda?"

"Yeah, how'd you know?"

"It's all over the news. Jesus and Mary in the window."

I smiled and said, "It's just frost."

"You're sure?"

With her lips pressed together, I didn't know if she was being cute or serious.

"I'm not sure of anything," I said with a sigh. "As we were leaving, a woman crossed my path. I almost hit her—"

"I always say you drive too fast."

"Would you let me finish?"

She smiled for the first time. In two minutes, she had drunk half the wine, and there was a glow on her face.

"It was the mother an old friend from childhood," I said.

The waitress came up and placed two steaming plates of food on the table. When she asked if we needed anything else, Ruth ordered another glass.

"I haven't seen her in twenty years," I continued, cutting into the ham. I lowered my voice and added, "Her son was my best friend... one of my best friends, I mean. There were three of us. Me, Russo, and Chesty."

"Chesty?"

"Chester...was his real name."

She put the fork down and listened curiously. It was the first time in days she had been interested in anything.

"Did you say hello?"

"No!" I said, and it sounded snappy. "I'm sorry, no. I didn't have a chance. She took off."

Before I could finish, the bell over the front door rang, and I lost my train of thought. I looked over and Sergeant Duggan walked in with two younger officers. They all wore long coats and earmuffs, and their faces were red from the cold. They kicked snow from their boots, dusted off their shoulders. When Duggan saw me, he came over, and the patrolmen continued towards the counter.

"Hey, Giraffe."

"Evening, Detective," he said, peeling off his gloves.

He introduced himself politely, and Ruth, chewing her food, put one hand over her mouth and waved with the other.

"Did you get to Mass this morning?" I asked.

He smirked and shook his head.

"Not with this overtime. That crowd at the convent is getting out of control."

"You mean *abbey*?"

"Right—abbey. There must've been three thousand people. Chief ordered us to block off the surrounding streets. TV stations were there and everything."

I knew he was a regular because when the waitress came over, she put her arm around his waist and surprised him. He grinned and ordered a Rueben and French fries.

"What's doin' tonight?" I asked.

He shook his head and looked around the diner.

"All the usual mischief. Hippies, junkies, queens, bar fights, assholes."

When he saw Ruth balk, he added, "Pardon my French."

"Don't worry, I'm used to it," she said.

The waitress returned again and put down a glass. Ruth had only eaten half her meal, but I knew she would finish all the wine.

"I should get going," Duggan said, and he bowed to Ruth. "It's been my pleasure."

She looked up, smiled pretty.

"Mine as well."

As I watched him walk away, I noticed a couple in the far corner. They were leaning over the table, holding hands and looking into each other's eyes like lovers. Although the overhead lamp was dim, I was sure it was Ms. Stuart, the ward nurse. The man had his back to me, but I could tell he was much older. Ruth waved her hand in front of my face to get my attention.

"I'm sorry," I said.

"Someone you know?"

"Maybe someone you know."

She peeked over and back quickly.

"Ugh! Queen bitch."

I couldn't help but chuckle.

"I met her yesterday," I said. "We went to see about the woman who left after giving birth."

She picked at her food, had some more wine. When I glanced over again, Ms. Stuart looked up, and I averted my eyes. I thought I saw her squint, but it may have been my imagination.

"Any news on the baby?"

If the question was hard for me to hear, it must have been harder for Ruth to ask. I shook my head no and looked down at my watch.

"We should get going. The movie starts in ten minutes."

She drank the rest of her wine and wiped her mouth. I left enough money for the bill and a tip, and we started to get up. I didn't know if it was paranoia or excessive caution, but I said, "Why don't you go first? I'll meet you outside."

"What? Why?"

"Things got a little tense with Stuart. It's probably better if she doesn't know I'm your husband."

"That's ridiculous. I don't care what that wench knows or doesn't."

Her feistiness was something to behold, but it wasn't always wise. We put on our coats, and she took my arm. As we walked towards the exit, I nodded goodbye to Duggan and the officers. The moment I opened the door, Ruth spun around and looked towards the back of the diner.

"Yoo-hoo, Ms. Stuart," she called out, standing on her tiptoes. "Don't be late for work tomorrow!"

I cringed. Ms. Stuart acknowledged the remark with a sour smile, and her companion turned around. When the light hit his face, I could finally see him clearly. Like I had guessed, he was much older than her, with a large nose and cold eyes. I nudged Ruth through the door, and we went back out into the cold.

"That wasn't funny," I said.

She swatted my chest playfully.

"Oh, c'mon. Lighten up."

THE SHOW GOT out at midnight, and although I didn't think it could get any colder, the temperature had dropped another five degrees. We walked quickly back to the car, arm in arm, and it took a few tries to start the engine. By the time we reached the first red light, Ruth was starting to doze off.

As we idled at the intersection, a solitary figure came around the corner and stopped at the curb to cross. The light changed, and the person peered out from the fur hood of his bomber jacket. Our eyes met, and I realized it was Teddy.

I tapped the horn and waved, but he couldn't see me. Ruth jumped up startled and looked at me with groggy eyes.

"What are you doing?" she asked.

"This boy came into The Armory last week, had some information. Roll down your window, please."

"He doesn't look like a boy."

Teddy glanced over suspiciously, and I could tell by his posture that he was prepared to run. When Ruth rolled down her window, I said, "Hey kid, need a lift?"

He must have recognized my voice because all at once his shoulders dropped, his body relaxed. With his hands buried in his pockets, he leaned into the window.

"Oh, hello, Sir," he said.

"Get in."

It wasn't an order, but he responded like it was. The whole exchange took twenty seconds, and by the time he got in the back seat, the light was red again. This time I blew it.

Ruth turned to him with a sweet smile.

"Teddy, my wife, Ruth," I said.

"Nice to meet you."

I looked in the rear-view mirror and asked, "Where're you going?"

"Home."

"Where's home?"

"Tyler Street."

"That's Chinatown. They let Koreans in?"

Ruth knew it was a joke, but she gave me a sharp look anyway. Gazing out the side window, Teddy shrugged his shoulders and said, "Anyone who's not *yang nom*."

"Yang nom?" I said with a chuckle. "I've heard that before."

"You have?"

"In the war. We were all *yang nom*."

"Not if you ask my uncle. He loves the Americans."

"Then he was on the right side."

"Have you lived here long?" Ruth asked.

"Since I was five."

"Must have been hard...leaving home."

"I don't remember much," he said. "This is my home. Korea is more like a dream."

I looked in the mirror again and waited until our eyes met.

"A bad dream, I'd say."

"No. Just a dream."

We drove in silence through the financial district then turned onto Atlantic Avenue. It was no longer snowing, but the harbor wind kicked up flakes, and I had to use the wipers to see. As we passed South Station, dozens of vagrants were huddled by the entrance doors. In the distance, I could see the neon lights of Chinatown, the one part of the city that never slept.

"You always walk home?"

"Mostly," Teddy said.

"Why?"

"It gives me time to think."

When I turned at Kneeland Street, things went from quiet to chaos. On both sides of the road, people scurried down the narrow sidewalks, going in and out of restaurants, darting into the street. There were more businesses than I could count—butcheries and fish markets, tearooms and newsstands. Although the signs were in Chinese, the exotic writing brought back memories of Korea.

"Turn here," Teddy said.

I hit my directional and took a sharp left down a street lined with brick row houses. The area was mostly residential with a few corner shops that had signs for cigarettes, milk, and meats in Mandarin.

"Tell me when," I said.

"Tell you when what?"

Leaning against the door, Teddy's face was hidden in the shadow, but I was sure he was grinning.

"Where's your house?"

"I don't live in a house. I have a flat." He slid to the middle of the seat and leaned forward between me and Ruth. "And you just passed it."

I put the Valiant in reverse and rolled back until he said stop. With no lights on, the building was like a murky wall of brick, and about the only thing that distinguished it from the other houses was a fire hydrant out front. While he zipped his jacket and pulled on his hood, an impatient taxi swerved around us. Teddy opened the back door, and the cold air rushed in.

"Nice to meet you, Miss," he said.

"Same to you, Teddy."

I reached my hand back to him, and he looked at it like I was passing him a grenade. But then he took it with a firm grip, and we shook.

"Thanks for the lift."

"Anytime."

The door closed with a whoosh, and I watched him scramble up the front steps and inside.

I drove through Chinatown and crossed into the industrial back roads of the South End. Here and there a delivery truck or stray driver would go by, but the area was mostly deserted.

While we waited at a red light, a homeless woman pushing a shopping cart crossed in front of us. I yawned, and when I opened my eyes, a truck sped through the intersection down Massachusetts Avenue. It happened in a flash—I could have missed it with a blink. But it was long enough for me to see it was a Dodge WC54, the same Army vehicle I knew from Korea. It had no military decals and was flat green. Even with my windows up, I could hear the raw drone of the six cylinders. It was straight gasoline, but for some reason, the sound always reminded me of a diesel.

I hesitated for a moment and looked at Ruth. Her head was tilted to one side—her eyes all but closed. She looked peaceful in her slumber, but the temptation was too much to resist so I cut the wheel and went after the truck.

The car bounced over the potholes, and she immediately woke up.

"Why're you driving so fast?" she said.

"I saw something."

She sat up straight, checked her seatbelt. Her voice began to rise.

"Something what?"

The truck must have been doing fifty because it was three or four blocks ahead, and I wasn't closing the gap. I pinned the gas and drove as straight as I could.

"Jody, slow down!" she cried.

"Hang on."

"There's ice, we're gonna slide—"

"Just hang on."

She grabbed my arm, but I wouldn't budge. We approached the intersection of Columbus Avenue, and all lights were green. Suddenly, a salt truck came out from a side street and got in front of me. I swerved to get around it, but the spreader was too wide. I craned my neck and watched the Dodge turn left at Symphony Hall, its red taillights fading around the corner. As we lumbered behind, tiny pellets of rock salt showered the hood and windshield. Finally, I pulled over in defeat.

"What the hell was that about?!"

"I'm sorry," I said, stumbling in embarrassment. "I saw a truck."

"What do you mean you saw a truck?"

"A green truck, from the war."

She shook her head in exasperation, ran her hand through her hair. Learning against the door, she gazed out the window, looking more sad than angry.

"I can't deal with this again," she said.

Her eyes began to well up, but she didn't cry. I put the car in gear, made a wide U-turn, and headed back home.

For the rest of the way, she didn't say a word, and I knew I probably deserved it. Flashbacks from Korea had caused almost as much turmoil in my life as the war itself, and I had spent years trying to squash those demons. She had seen the worst of it—the nightmares, the sweats, the panic, the psychosis. When she asked me to see a psychiatrist and I refused, it wasn't out of pride but fear that I would have to face the horror.

We got to Roslindale in ten minutes, which would have been a record in the daytime. As we drove up the hill towards our apartment, I stared ahead and mumbled, "I'm sorry."

"Don't be."

She put her hand on my thigh, and my body relaxed.

"I saw the truck."

"You still think about the war," she said, and it wasn't a question because she knew.

"Sometimes."

"It's okay to think about it."

I smiled but couldn't look over.

"I don't have a choice most of the time."

I backed into a spot in front of our house and turned off the engine.

"You know I love you."

My lips trembled; I started to choke up.

"Yeah," I said awkwardly, "of course."

CHAPTER 12

EVEN THOUGH I WAS A LIEUTENANT, I ALWAYS FELT SELF-CONSCIOUS walking into work on mornings I overslept. As I came up the stairs to the lobby, it seemed that a thousand eyes were watching. My head pounded, and my throat was dry. Two aspirins and a pot of coffee did nothing to relieve the booze-less hangover I had from being out too late.

I made it past reception, but the moment I turned down the corridor, I heard, "Jody!" I looked back and Sergeant Duggan was rushing towards me.

"You ever sleep, Giraffe?" I said.

I slowed to give him a chance to catch up.

"Turning in my time sheet, then going home."

"Don't let me hold you back."

He didn't smirk or smile, which was unusual for a man who thrived off sarcasm. I tried to keep walking, but he got in front of me and forced me to stop.

"I think the captain's got trouble."

He looked down at me with bloodshot eyes. His hair was damp, and he had sour breath from either too much coffee or not enough nourishment. Someone that tired and overworked wouldn't go out of his way for no reason.

"What kind of trouble?"

"Big trouble, maybe—"

"Get to it," I said impatiently.

He lowered his voice.

"One of my rookies—Petrucci. His girlfriend works upstairs." He glanced up and down the hallway as if to make sure no one could hear. "She told him that a captain on the third floor requested extended leave."

"Jackson?"

"He's been out a lot, right?"

I shrugged my shoulders.

"A few days," I said. "So what? Everyone's been sick."

When he drew closer, I stepped back and hit the wall. I had known him for years and had never seen him so worried about anything.

"This is different, Jody. The man is sick."

"Sick?"

"Real sick."

"What's real sick?"

"I don't know. Petrucci didn't know. But it's serious."

"Look," I said. "When you have more info, let me know."

Without another word, he patted me on the arm with a trembling smile and walked away. I watched as his tall frame lumbered down the corridor and faded around the corner.

I hurried to my office and slammed the door behind me like I was escaping an attacker. Out of breath, I unbuttoned my coat and was just about to take it off when I heard movement behind me, sensed that I wasn't alone.

"Good morning, Sir."

I spun around, and Teddy was sitting behind my desk.

"What the hell are you doing here?!" I snapped, and he instantly jumped up.

"I came to see you."

"Sit down," I said, but he continued to stand. "Who let you in?"

"The...the...big man," he stuttered.

With his casual clothes—a wool herringbone jacket, blue sweater, and khaki pants—he looked undeniably American.

"Sergeant Duggan?" I said.

"The black man."

"Harrigan. Look, kid—"

"I'm a man," he interrupted.

"Pardon?"

"I'm nineteen. I'm a man."

"Nineteen?" I said surprised, and I hung my coat on the rack. "Why do you people all look so young?"

"Why do *you people* all look so old?"

With my hands on my hips, I shook my head and looked down, stung by the comeback.

"Touché," I said.

He moved away from my desk, and I stepped over the clutter and sat down.

"Okay, you've got my attention."

"My uncle's gone."

"Gone? Whaddya mean *gone*?"

"He heard about the abbey...in Roxbury. When you dropped me off last night, I went in, and he was gone. I know he went there."

When the phone rang, I didn't answer, but stared at it thinking for a moment before asking, "What makes you so sure?"

Teddy averted his eyes.

"He's a Christian. He believes it's a sacred vision."

"You uncle is Christian?"

"A minister," he said with a nod. "*Was* a minister. When Kim Il-Sung took power, his church was burned down. He tried to flee to the South but was caught by the NKA. He spent five years in an internment camp."

"Explains a lot," I said, rubbing my chin.

"I know, he's a little *michin*, but he's a good man."

"Is that how he was injured? By the North Koreans?"

"He was more than injured, Sir. He was maimed."

As I leaned back in the chair, a cold draft came through the window. It was the second time I had thought about the war in as many days. The wall clock chimed 11 a.m., and we both looked over like something was supposed to happen.

"What did your parents say?"

Teddy looked down at the floor, spoke with a blend of shame and sadness.

"They were both killed…in the war."

I felt a lump in my throat—my eyes got unexpectedly teary.

"I'm sorry…" I said, struggling to conceal my emotion. "I'm sorry to hear that."

"Thanks. I don't remember them," he said. "Maybe my mother. I remember her face. I see her sometimes, in dreams. That's all I remember."

I smiled warmly.

"Don't ever forget that face."

When he finally looked up, I could tell he was touched by the advice, and it made me glad for saying it.

"I won't," he said.

The room went silent as I drifted into a state of poignant reflection. Our lives were separated by cultures and generations, but our scars had their origins in the same human conflict. When the radiator clanged, I snapped out of the daydream and spoke gently.

"So, what can I do?"

"Find him, please. Get him back. He'll listen to a cop."

I considered it for a moment, but I couldn't give him an answer. Homicide would only act on missing persons cases if there was evidence of wrongdoing. Otherwise, we would have spent all our time tracking down runaways or men who had abandoned their families. I was relieved when the door suddenly opened, and it was Harrigan.

"Look," I said to Teddy. "If I get a chance to go by the abbey, I'll see what I can find out. No promises."

A smile broke across his chin.

"Thank you, Sir."

"Be good."

He turned and headed for the door, politely acknowledging Harrigan before walking out. I sat quiet for a couple of minutes, tapping my fingers on the desk, and when I looked up Harrigan was standing with his arms crossed.

"You always let civilians in my office?" I said.

"I didn't know it was an office. I thought it was a storeroom."

I looked around at all the unpacked boxes and laughed to myself.

"I found him in the parking lot," Harrigan explained. "He was too scared to come in."

"Maybe you saved him from frostbite."

"Maybe you can save his uncle."

He stepped over a duffel bag and a crate to get to the leather chair beside me, the first time he had ever sat down uninvited.

"So he told you about the old man?" I said.

He just nodded.

"And you think I should look for him?"

He crossed one leg over the other, clasped his hands.

"Frankly, I do."

"And why?"

"For one…you just said you would."

"I need a better reason. I can't go searching for a demented chink on department time."

When he winced at the slur, I regretted using it.

"Secondly, he's the only witness we got."

I shifted in the chair and glanced out the window, thinking about the woman in the dumpster, the baby that might still be alive. I turned back to him and said, "That guy wouldn't know an ambulance from an AMC Ambassador."

"Remember what the captain said, *an unreliable witness is still a witness.*"

"Speaking of Jackson, is he here?"

Harrigan's expression changed.

"I'm afraid he's out today."

"Again?"

"Again."

There was a short but tense pause. When I finally went to speak, he blurted out, "I'm concerned for him..."

I tried again, but again he beat me to it.

"...and I believe there's something he's not telling us."

For someone as reserved as Harrigan, those two sentences—sudden and direct—were the equivalent of an outburst. I waited a few seconds then said, "And there's something I haven't told you."

His face dropped, and I recognized the same dread I felt when Duggan cornered me in the hall. Jackson was the bedrock of homicide, a respected leader who was more than a mentor, more than a colleague—he was a beloved friend. The thought that he might not be well was more terrifying than anything we had encountered in our careers.

"I've just learned that he requested extended leave—for illness."

"What? What kind of illness?" he said, his chest rising, "What's wrong with—"

"I don't—"

"We've got to find out—"

"I don't know, goddammit!"

I smacked my hand on the desk and he flinched. I seldom raised my voice to him, but some inner distress had overcome my self-control. I turned in the chair, so fast my knee hit the desk, and stared at the far wall fuming.

"I'm sorry," I said, my voice low and remorseful. "We'll know soon. Let's hope for no surprises."

He accepted the apology with a subtle nod. When he switched legs, crossing the right over the left, it somehow signaled that he was ready to move on.

"Speaking of surprises," he said.

"Good news or bad?"

"Depends on what side of the law you're on."

I loosened my tie a little and said, "Let's have it."

"We traced ownership of the dumpster to the Archdiocese of Boston."

As I listened, a tingle went up my back.

"That's an odd place," I said.

"They have offices in the adjacent building. Administrative, mostly."

"So you think Cardinal Cushing is killing women?"

He gave a bashful grin. Maybe because he was so well-mannered, he seemed to enjoy it when others were not.

"I don't think anything yet."

"Know what I think?" I said, and he waited for my answer. "I think it's a good reason to visit the abbey."

CHAPTER 13

ST KILDA WAS A MADHOUSE. WHAT STARTED AS A LOCAL CURIOSITY HAD, in less than two weeks, become a holy jamboree. People were camped out on the sidewalks, sitting on blankets, tarps, and milk crates. They brought coolers full of food, and I saw one group cooking over Bunsen burners. The place was beginning to look like a refugee camp.

They were from all walks of life—Orthodox priests in black cassocks, retirees in scally caps, and tradesmen on lunch break. A group of hippies danced in the snow barefoot, banging on tambourines and chanting. Children were playing between the parked cars, and an old man stood on the curb reading the King James Bible aloud. There were even street vendors peddling sausages and tea, and I thought I saw one selling souvenirs, although it might have been peanuts.

Two patrolmen stood by the front gates directing traffic. As we approached, they saw us and ordered people to move so we could enter. I waved thanks and turned into the property, starting up the long driveway to the abbey. I looked across to the hillside and there were more people than I had ever seen in one place. With one eye on the road, I scanned the crowd for Teddy's uncle but saw only an indistinguishable sea of winter coats, scarfs, and hats.

Soon we reached the top and parked. I got out and went up to the front door, where I rapped the bronze knocker. As I waited, Harrigan stepped over to the grass and looked out across the property. I reached in my pocket for a cigarette, and when I flicked the lighter, he looked back with a frown.

"What? I can't even smoke outside?" I exclaimed.

He didn't answer. I walked over and stood beside him, and together we gazed off into the distance. Standing at the crest of the hill, we could see all of Roxbury and beyond. Plumes of black smoke rose from the endless tenements; roofs and porches sagged under the heavy snow. In some ways, winter was like a long siege, and I wondered what sort of faith it took for people to leave their warm homes to come here. At that moment I prayed, at least for their sake, that it was all true.

"Ever see anything like it?" I said.

He shook his head.

"Never."

I went back to the door and knocked again, but still, there was no answer.

"Why don't you take a walk over," I said, nodding towards the crowd. "You might spot the old man. I'll look around here."

"It's a needle in a haystack."

"How hard can it be to find a chinaman?"

He shook his head and started across the grassy slope.

"Korean, Lieutenant," he said, his voice fading. "Get your prejudices straight."

I went down the side of the building, stepping carefully over the uneven ground. St Kilda was like a fortress, with plank doors, stone walls, and windows so small a child couldn't fit through. If it wasn't a monastery, it probably would have made a good prison.

Soon the ground tapered off, and I found myself walking along the edge of a steep embankment that dropped into a ravine. Every step was treacherous, and my feet were getting numb from the snow. At one point, I had to shimmy along with my back against the wall. I was ready to turn around when suddenly I came to an archway. I looked in and saw the courtyard where Russo, Sweeney, and I encountered the priest years before.

I stepped through and began to walk. Inside there was a perfect silence. All I heard was the sound of my breath, the crunch of my footsteps, some birds in the woods. When I reached the center, I stopped at the statue of Jesus with the three children. I thought about that Halloween night and, for some reason, remembered more about the incident now than in all previous years. I had never felt guilty about attacking the priest, but I always regretted letting Sweeney go back to him.

"Are you in prayer, Detective?"

I spun around to see Brother Emmanuel. He had one hand in his pocket, and the other was holding a cigarette. I was so surprised that I said the first thing that came to mind.

"You smoke?"

Peering out from his brown hood, he grinned and took a drag.

"We're not all saints, you know. Did I scare you?"

"I don't scare that easy."

"You jumped."

"Reflexes. From the war."

His face was red from the cold—there was frost at the tip of his beard.

"Come," he said. "Let's walk together. We can talk. It's too cold to be still."

I followed him across the quad, and we went under a covered walkway that encircled the cloister. He took another puff and glanced back.

"So, what brings you back?" he asked. "Soul searching?"

"There's an old man, a Korean man. He may be a witness in a murder case. His nephew thinks he might be here."

We stopped beside a pillar, and he turned to me.

"Here?"

"He's a religious man. He might have come to see the apparition."

Emmanuel rubbed his beard and looked down in thought.

"It will certainly be difficult to find him in that crowd," he said offhandedly. "But let us keep walking. I only gave you half the tour last time."

We went through an archway that led to another small courtyard. He pointed ahead and said, "That's our main building, built in 1845—"

"Year of the Famine."

"Sorry?"

"The Potato Famine, in Ireland," I said.

"Ah, of course. It wasn't the Irish though, I'm afraid. Church Of Scotland. That's where St Kilda comes from. The Archdiocese of Boston purchased it right before the First World War."

"Scots?"

"Scottish Protestants, originally. Yes."

"And the Archdiocese kept the name?"

"St Kilda is not a Saint," he said eagerly as if he enjoyed explaining the misconception. "It was the original home to some of the early benefactors. It's a remote island, eighty miles from the Scottish mainland. A tiny community lived there for centuries, separate from the rest of the world."

I thought about the isolation of the abbey.

"Sounds familiar," I said.

He raised his eyebrows, acknowledging the irony.

"The island is abandoned now. The last settlers were evacuated in the '30s."

"Is Father Vogt Scottish?"

"No, hardly."

We approached a short staircase that led to a utility door. I followed him through an old doorway which, aside from the front door, was the only wood I had seen so far in the abbey. We went into a corridor and there were brooms, mops, and other janitorial items along the walls. The floor was linoleum, and the walls were a modern brick so I assumed the space was a newer addition.

As we walked, a person holding a clipboard came out of a closet and almost knocked into us. It happened so fast I could have easily missed him. But when Emmanuel stopped and said, "Ah, Anthony," I looked at the man and was stunned. The years between childhood and now had changed much, but not the gangly figure of Anthony Vigliotti.

"Detective…my cousin, Tony…"

We eyed each other with that cold bravado all men have when they come across someone from their delinquent past. But despite what happened that Halloween, Vigliotti and I were never really enemies. And considering his long history of crime and trouble, I doubted he even remembered me. In the ethos of Boston street culture, one scrap was never grounds for a lifelong grudge.

Vigliotti and I stood facing each other. It wasn't a showdown, but more a moment of reflection as he tried to remember who I was and how he knew me. Then he extended his hand and we shook.

"There's a leak in the washroom," he said to Emmanuel, looking at the clipboard. "Might be some mold behind the cabinets. I'll check."

"Bless your heart. I'll need the keys to the tower."

Vigliotti reached in the pocket of his coveralls and handed him a key ring. Emmanuel made a slight bow and thanked his cousin. When Vigliotti turned to leave, our eyes met again but only for a second. He walked off and we continued down the hallway.

"Does he work here?" I said, still distracted by the encounter.

"Our custodian. He has been for many years…"

After the annex, we came to the main wing of the abbey and went down a long corridor.

"…He's responsible for maintenance, small repairs, etc. Knows… every…corner…of the abbey," he said, walking so fast that he was starting to lose his breath. "…He may have been the first one to discover the image. He was in the belfry clearing off icicles—"

"Does that mean he's blessed?"

If there was such a thing as a compassionate smirk, Emmanuel made one.

"If so, it's long overdue."

"Why is that?"

He clutched a handrail, and we descended a stone stairway.

"Let's just say his past is not unmarred," he said, glancing back between steps.

We came down to a wide-open area. On one side was a rounded wall made of granite blocks, fused together with old mortar. At the center, there was a stout door that looked like the entrance to a dungeon.

"Now I'll show you what you've been wanting to see."

"Don't make assumptions," I said.

"What would life be without assumptions."

His quick responses weren't sarcasm, but they were close enough that I could relate. I had always thought clergy were humorless cranks, and it was nice to see a human side.

He pushed back his hood and took out the key ring. He separated the many smaller ones until he was holding a large iron skeleton key. Rusty and primitive, it looked like a blacksmith had forged it during the American Revolution.

"This, of course, must remain secured."

"Enough keys for the Vatican," I joked.

"They're all important in their own way," he said, leaning into the wall, straining to turn the old lock. "We only have one for the tower, however."

When the bolt finally moved, the door swung inward, and the air shocked me. With no heating, the bell tower was as cold as outside, if not colder. He invited me to enter, and I squeezed through the gap.

As we ascended, I looked around in fascination at the ancient structure. The stairs were made of thick stone slabs, cantilevered into the sides like a medieval castle. A white, chalky substance dripped down the walls from the old grout. The smell of mold was almost suffocating.

We reached the first landing, where the huge front windows began. Brother Emmanuel stopped and looked up. I followed his gaze to the very top and saw, etched into the frost, Mary and the infant Jesus. It was no less clear up close than it was from a distance. Parts of the scene were vague, but the central image—the outline of the bodies, the detail on their faces—was a perfect depiction. A chill went through me that was not from the cold.

"Are you a believer, Detective?"

I hesitated to answer, continuing to look at the image. Then I turned around and said, "I believe that's a—" I almost said *damn* but stopped myself. "...darn good likeness."

He smiled.

"What I mean is...do you believe in miracles?"

"I don't believe in the impossible."

I dismissed the questions as mere banter, but he persisted.

"It doesn't have to be impossible to be a miracle."

"May be true," I said, looking back up at the window. "What happens when this melts?"

"Nothing is permanent."

"Now you sound like a Buddhist."

He laughed out loud for the first time.

"Don't let Father Vogt hear you say that. He accuses us all of lacking in Christian discipline."

"I've heard a lot about him," I said, although it wasn't true. "When can I meet him?"

"I'm afraid he's out at a meeting. But I can arrange it if you'd like."

"Another meeting? He's a regular politician."

"Well," he explained, "it's with the Archdiocese. They've been trying to close the abbey."

"Is he trying to stop it?"

His expression changed, and he spoke with hesitation.

"That's what he tells us."

"But he's opposed to the closing?"

"We all are, Detective," he said, shrugging his shoulders. "This is the only life we know. Most of us have been here since seminary. Our abbot arrived after the war—as a refugee."

I stepped closer to the window and glanced out. At the bottom, people were still pouring through the gates in a steady stream. I saw the faces of the hundreds of pilgrims as they plodded up the hill towards the tower, and I wondered if Teddy's uncle was among them. The shrine was only one story below, but standing behind the thick walls, I couldn't hear anything.

"They can't close it now."

"As I said, nothing is permanent," he said, then he lightened his tone. "Come, let me get you some tea before you go."

Just before I turned away, something in the distance caught my eye, and I stopped. When I looked closer, I observed a green truck rolling down the driveway towards the gate. I must have seemed anxious because Emmanuel looked over from the stairs and asked, "Something wrong?"

"A truck," I said, half-consciously.

I followed the vehicle as it drove out and turned onto the street. He came over beside me and looked out too.

"A truck?"

"A green truck. It just left. You can't see it now, it's behind the wall."

"A delivery, perhaps. Most of our necessities are delivered."

He headed back to the stairwell, and I followed. Something about the unevenness of the steps made descending more difficult than walking up, and at every point, I thought I was going to lose my balance.

When we reached the bottom, we ducked through the narrow opening, and I waited while he locked the door and double-checked it.

"Worried someone will get in?"

He raised an eye and said, "Evil thrives when good men do nothing."

"Leviticus?"

"No, Detective. Edmund Burke."

We proceeded down the hallway, past prayer rooms, dormitories, and alcoves. When we came out to the atrium, the wooden statue of Christ was hanging above. Its charred hands and legs reminded me of gruesome injuries I had seen in Korea, and I wondered why they hadn't repaired it. At the end of the corridor, I saw the front door and had the urge to leave and leave quickly.

"Thanks again," I said.

"Won't you have tea?"

"I can't. My partner is waiting."

With his hands together, Brother Emmanuel closed his eyes and bowed.

"Well then, I enjoyed our time together," he said.

"If you happen to see an elderly Oriental man on crutches, would you call me at headquarters?"

"If someone of that..." He averted his eyes, pulled the tip of his beard, searching for the right adjective, "...*inimitable* description crosses my path, I'll be sure and let you know."

I nodded farewell then continued down the hall and out the door. The change from dark to light confused my eyes, and, for a moment, I couldn't see. As the world slowly emerged, I saw Harrigan walking up the hill.

Leaving the strange solitude of the abbey was like coming out of a trance. I took out a cigarette, put it in my mouth, and held up my lighter. My mind drifted to thoughts of my childhood, the war, Ruth —and everything in between. In those few seconds, I contemplated my entire life, and I didn't know why.

"Are you alright, Lieutenant?"

I looked up, and Harrigan was standing in front of me.

"Of course," I said. "Why?"

"Because the cigarette is backwards."

I took it out of my mouth and realized the filter was facing out. Embarrassed by the mistake, I changed the subject.

"I saw the tower," I said. "One of the monks took me up."

"How's the window look from inside?"

I lit the cigarette and took a long, desperate drag.

"Pretty damn real."

I walked over to the grass and Harrigan followed, and together we stood looking out at the city.

"Lovely, isn't it?" I muttered.

"Everything's lovely from a distance, Lieutenant."

I flicked the butt and turned to him.

"Any sign of the old man?"

He shook his head no.

"Seems like all of Boston is down there," he said. "You could probably see more than me from the tower."

We walked over and got in the car. I turned around, and we drove slowly down the driveway.

"Hey," I said, suddenly remembering, "Did you see a truck leave?"

"A truck?"

"A truck. A green truck. It left about ten minutes ago."

"No. I didn't see a green truck."

As we neared the entrance, I slowed even more. Some people got out of the way, but most were too distracted, and I didn't want to hit anybody. I thought about using the horn but was afraid it might start a stampede.

When we got to the gates, I heard a voice and looked over to see a woman preaching on the lawn. There was a small crowd around her, and they all seemed captivated. Just before we drove out, she looked over and our eyes met. It was Sweeney's mother.

In a moment of panic, I hit the brake and gas at the same time, and the Valiant lurched.

"Lieutenant, what the hell are you doing?"

"I need to get out of here."

"You're gonna kill somebody!"

As I barreled out the entrance, people leaped out of the way, waved their arms, shouted for me to slow down. The traffic cops started to respond until they realized who we were. By some miracle, there were fewer pilgrims than earlier, and I had a clear path. I sped to the end of the road and stopped, shaken and out of breath.

"What in God's name was that about!" Harrigan yelled.

"I'm sorry."

He looked away and stared out the window angrily.

"Don't know," I said panting. "I got jumpy."

"Are you claustrophobic?"

"I don't think so—I don't know. I mean…no."

I put the car in park, and we idled for a few minutes in silence, recovering from the outburst. After we had both calmed down, he turned to me and said, “Who’s that woman? You saw her before. You had the same look. Who is she?”

“It’s a long story.”

He pulled up his sleeve to expose his watch.

“We have all afternoon.”

CHAPTER 14

SOMEHOW I ALWAYS KNEW THAT THE NIGHT CHESTER SWEENEY WENT back to help the priest was the end of my innocence. I woke up the next morning sore and bruised all over. There was blood on my pirate costume, and my plastic sword was gone. My head pounded from the rum, and I had trouble seeing because I scratched one of my eyes in the fight. I was fourteen but felt like I was forty.

I was probably fortunate in feeling old because no youth would have been able to handle the events which followed that horrific event. When Sweeney didn't show up for school the day after Halloween, we assumed he either got in trouble for what happened or that he was sick. But when he didn't show up the following week, Russo and I started to panic.

"He...e...e's out again, Jody..."

"I know!" I snapped.

We stood by the fence of the schoolyard at dismissal while throngs of students poured into the street. We were both nervous, but he almost couldn't speak.

"Maybe he's got the flu," I said.

"I...I...I hope so."

When a teacher approached, we instantly shut up. After she passed, I thought about Halloween night and wondered if the priest had turned Sweeney in to the police. If that happened, I thought, Sweeney might have confessed, and we would be arrested too. Assaulting a person was one thing, but harming a priest was an unthinkable crime, and the shame would have been as terrifying as the punishment. In the guilt-ridden culture of our parochial world, there was nothing worse.

I glanced around then spoke quietly.

"If anything happens, we say we weren't with him. It's our word against his."

"But—"

"Not a word! You hear me?"

I gave him a dark, threatening look, and he took a step back.

"Okay, Jody, I get it," he said with a pout. "We weren't with him."

"We weren't with Chesty on Halloween night."

Russo repeated it, and we shook hands. Those words would haunt me for the rest of my life.

TWO WEEKS WENT BY, and Chester Sweeney still had not returned to school. I was sitting in class on a Friday afternoon gazing out the window when there was a knock at the door. A school official walked in and whispered something to the teacher. When she looked over and called my name, I felt a lump in my throat.

With the whole class watching, the man escorted me out of the room and down the hall. We came to the main office, and I saw the principal sitting at her desk. Mrs. Halloran was a trim woman with thin lips, glasses, and a perpetual pompadour. She spoke in monotone and started every sentence with 'Now.'

She called for me, and I walked into the room to see two Boston Police officers and a priest. And there, seated before them like a man on trial, was Russo. I was so nervous I began to get dizzy, and I was momentarily relieved when Mrs. Halloran said, "Mr. Brae, please sit."

I took the chair beside Russo and sat down. When I looked over at him, he wouldn't look back.

"Now, I'm afraid I have some difficult news," she said, her eyes alternating between us and the men. "Chester Sweeney was found yesterday afternoon in the rail yard..." After a short but dramatic sigh, she added, "Dead."

The word echoed in my head over and over again. In the dramatic silence of the office, it was louder than anything I had ever heard. I gripped the arms of the chair and stared ahead in shock.

"Now," Mrs. Halloran continued, "I understand that you two are friends of the boy? Is that true?"

Russo and I nodded in unison.

"Do you know anyone who would want to hurt him?"

One of the officers walked over and got to the point.

"When was the last time you saw Chester Sweeney?"

"Two weeks ago," I said.

"Halloween," Russo blurted.

I cringed inside but maintained my composure. The man glanced over to Mrs. Halloran then looked at Russo.

"So you saw him Halloween?"

"N...n...not really Halloween, Sir," he said. "Halloween day."

I breathed a little easier with his answer.

"And where did you see him?"

"A...a...after school. In the schoolyard. I saw him in the schoolyard...a...a...after school."

With arms crossed, his nightstick gleaming, the officer nodded to his colleague. He knelt down and looked us both in the eyes.

"Now you boys swear you know nothing about what happened to your friend?"

We responded with nervous nods that were somehow convincing.

Okay," the cop said, and I couldn't believe the interrogation was over. "We'll get who did this. We'll lock 'em up for good."

I looked over to Russo, and this time he looked back.

"Now," Mrs. Halloran said, "I understand you boys are Catholics, which is why I've asked Father Francis from St. Patrick's to be here. He's available for counsel."

When we turned, the priest waved over with a toothless smile. I hadn't been to Mass since grade school, and Russo hadn't gone since I knew him. After what happened at the abbey, the vestments represented savagery and not succor, and the last thing we wanted was to confide in the clergy.

"Now, would you like to speak with him?"

We both hesitated as if considering the offer, then we quickly shook our heads no.

"Very well, then," she said, "Now, we've already called home…to explain." She tilted her head and smiled with a forced sympathy that was anything but genuine. "Again, we're so sorry."

The charade ended when the last bell rang. Mrs. Halloran dismissed us, and Russo and I walked out of the room like we had just escaped the gallows. We hadn't killed Sweeney, but our deceit made us feel like accomplices, and the guilt was crushing.

We left school under such a haze that I had no recollection of getting our coats and walking out. For the rest of the day, Russo and I wandered the streets of Roxbury with no destination. I should have been sad, but instead, I felt numb, and everywhere we went I had the strange sensation of walking in a dream. Eventually, it began to get dark and the temperature dropped. When we passed a drug store, Russo spoke for the first time in hours.

"Wanna split a chocolate bar?"

He reached in his pockets and pulled out a broken cigarette, a couple of nickels.

"Sure," I said.

When he came out of the shop, we crossed the street and sat on the corner by a large tree. Looking around, I realized it was the same place we encountered Vigliotti and his gang the night they chased us. And there in the gutter, mixed with the fragments of dead leaves, were the wrappers from Sweeney's candy. My heart sank.

"What's gonna happen, Jody?"

I shook my head and took a bite of chocolate, although I had no appetite.

"Should we have told them?" he pressed.

"I wish I knew."

CHAPTER 15

THE ADMINISTRATIVE OFFICES OF THE ARCHDIOCESE WERE ONLY TWO blocks from The Armory. It was so close that Harrigan and I didn't need the car, and it might have been the first time we ever walked to an investigation. When we got to the address, the only marker was a small sign beside the door that read *Property of Archdiocese of Boston*. There was no bell, so we opened it and went into a small foyer with a door and elevator. The walls were cracked and peeling—the parquet floor was worn down to the wood. By all appearances, the Archdiocese hadn't updated the building in years.

Harrigan raised an eyebrow and said, "Hardly the opulence of Rome."

"Boston ain't the Vatican."

I pressed the buzzer, but it didn't work so I knocked. We stood waiting and finally, the door opened, and a man appeared. He was short and bald, with beady eyes and glasses. In his shabby Argyle sweater and corduroy slacks, he looked like a washed-up accountant.

"May I help you?" he asked.

"I'm Detective Brae, this is Detective Harrigan. Boston Police. Mind if we ask some questions?"

He looked at Harrigan, who was holding out his badge.

"I guess I've been expecting this. Please, come in."

I glanced at Harrigan, and we followed him into a cluttered room that looked like it was part office, part storeroom. I saw a few walnut desks, typewriters, a file cabinet, and a Xerox machine that looked broken. On the opposite wall, there were stacks of folding chairs, boxes, and a large map of the city.

The man walked halfway across the room and turned around.

"Paul Frawley," he said, rolling up his sleeve. "Facilities Director for the Archdiocese. What can I do for you gentlemen?"

"You said you were expecting this?"

"It's about the young woman found out back, I presume?"

"How'd you hear about that?" Harrigan asked.

"It happened in my backyard. An awful tragedy. Any idea who did it?"

"Maybe," I said flatly. "What's the dumpster used for?"

"Trash, of course. We manage all properties of the Archdiocese—seminaries, parishes, schools, prayer centers, clinics—"

"St Kilda Abbey?" I said.

He stopped, and his expression changed.

"Certainly, St Kilda would fall under our jurisdiction."

"And who uses the dumpster?" Harrigan said.

"Just us. This building. All locations have their own."

"So you think someone randomly found it?"

He squinted as if considering the question.

"It's likely. We don't lock it. And the alleyway is accessible."

"Was anyone working here that night?" Harrigan asked, "Anyone who might have seen or heard something?"

"No one's here at night. This building is for storage. We stock toilet paper, cleaning supplies, paint. A janitor's paradise."

Frawley laughed, but we did not.

"Can we walk back to see the dumpster?"

"Of course," he said, "come..."

We headed back out into the foyer, and he hit the elevator button. There was a loud creak, some vibrations, and seconds later the doors opened. We went down one floor and came into a vast basement that had a low ceiling and no windows. As we walked, we passed cases of rock salt, barrels of commercial carpet cleaner, rubber mats, and unused mops and brooms. We turned at the end and continued through another room with tools and workbenches, eventually coming to a set of double doors. He lifted a 2X4 wooden barricade and pushed them open.

The first thing I smelled was garlic and peanut oil. When I looked across, I saw the back of the Lantern House Restaurant. Frawley leaned against the doorway while Harrigan and I walked over to the dumpster. I climbed up and peered in to see trash bags, boxes, tangled wire, a bent street sign, and some empty paint cans. Spread throughout the debris like brown lava was the sludge of kitchen waste. It would have been crawling with flies in summer, I thought.

"You say only your building uses this?"

"Supposed to be," Frawley called over. "The restaurants toss things in from time to time. I don't mind."

"Maybe people don't know it's private." I jumped down and dusted off my hands. "There's no warning—no name on it," I said.

"The Archdiocese doesn't like to advertise."

"Really? Why's that?"

He pulled some loose caulking from the doorjamb and tossed it in the dumpster.

"Truth be told, the Church has been losing influence for years. Since Vatican II, really. They own property all over the city—prime real estate. Developers have been chomping at the bit to get it..."

I listened closely but pretended to be only half-interested.

"...the politicians used to be on our side—not so much these days."

He stepped out from the doorway and looked up at the rusted fire escape. "This building is one giant violation. Could've been condemned years ago. They should've taken it down when they demolished Scollay Square."

"But it was overlooked?" Harrigan said.

"More than overlooked. It was exempt. I've been here for thirteen years and not one inspection."

Harrigan and I looked at each other. I heard something and turned to see a worker come out from the Lantern House kitchen. He eyed us suspiciously then reached under his smock for a cigarette.

"Thanks for your help," I said. "We'll take the scenic route back."

"Anytime officers. Glad I could help."

Frawley pulled the doors closed, and Harrigan and I wandered into the alleyway. We peered up the sides of the buildings, scanned the pot-holed ground, absorbing the crime scene. I felt a cold stare and glanced over to see the kitchen worker watching us. I looked away and then back, but when he wouldn't stop staring, I decided to walk over. The moment I approached, he mumbled something under his breath.

"Pardon?" I said.

"Gijeok."

Seated on a crate, his elbows on his knees, the man shook his head.

"Gijeok."

"What's he saying?"

"Don't know," I said to Harrigan. I looked at the man, raised my voice, and said, "What is it?"

He just gazed ahead, repeating the word like a mantra. Suddenly the door opened, and an Asian man stepped out with a wide grin. He was dressed like a dandy, with a pinstripe suit, silk tie, and burgundy loafers.

"Hello, hello," he said. "You police?"

I looked at Harrigan with a sarcastic frown.

"We're detectives. Is this your place?"

"Yes, yes, my place. And you're welcome here."

With his accent, fancy clothes, and overly friendly personality, he was like a foreigner trying to impersonate an American.

"Gijeok," the kitchen worker said, and we all looked over to him.

Before I could ask what it meant, Johnny grabbed the man by the arm and pulled him up. Yelling in words I couldn't understand, he shoved the employee towards the kitchen door. The man covered his head and scurried back inside.

"These guys," Johnny said with a pretentious sneer. "They want to talk more than work, eh?"

"What was he saying? What's *Gee-zuck?*"

He straightened out his jacket, fixed his tie.

"Gijeok. It means…ah, how would I say?…like…a miracle."

"Miracle? What miracle?"

Harrigan came to my side and we both listened.

"They talk nonsense. An old guy, on crutches. He went to the vision, in Roxbury. Now he walks without crutches."

He shrugged his shoulders, rolled his eyes.

"Maybe I should go too, eh? Then I'll be able to fly."

He started to laugh, but Harrigan interrupted, "Have you seen him walk…without crutches?"

"Magic is for peasants, my friends." He raised his arm towards the restaurant like he was introducing a circus act. "The only miracle is I stay open with workers like these."

"Tell me, is Teddy here?" I asked.

"Teddy, Teddy, Teddy," he said, rubbing his chin, thinking. "I have so many workers. Is he the boy?"

"He's a man," I said, and he looked at me confused. "He's nineteen."

"Ah, yes, that's especially true because he had to go to the board, so he's not coming to work."

My face dropped.

"Board? What board?"

"For the draft—draft board—he got called." Johnny started to sing '*You're in the Army now*,' until he realized I wasn't amused. "Yes, my friends," he continued, "sad to say. He's a good boy…man. Even if his uncle is *din*." He spun his finger at his temple and mimicked the face of a crazy person.

"Do me a favor?" I said.

"Any favor for police."

"I'm Detective Brae—this is Harrigan. If the old man shows up, call me at headquarters."

I nodded in the direction of our building, although it wasn't visible from the alleyway.

"And…" I added as an afterthought, "if Teddy comes back, have him come see me. Please."

Johnny put one hand on his abdomen and made a slight bow.

"As you wish, my friend."

When Harrigan and I started to walk away, he called out, "Your young friend is off to war. Make him into a real American, eh?"

The remark was probably meant to be more lighthearted than literal, but somehow it angered me. I gritted my teeth and looked back over my shoulder.

"He already is."

CHAPTER 16

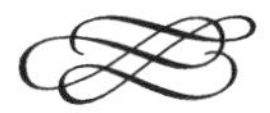

THE GOSSIP I FEARED WAS CIRCULATING THROUGH THE DEPARTMENT finally came to a head when three patrolmen cornered me and asked about the captain. There had been other inquiries too, off-handed comments and inferences, in the hallways and even the lavatory. Much of the concern was genuine—I didn't doubt that everyone loved Jackson. Yet I found myself responding with guarded suspicion. People probably thought I was being tight-lipped out of loyalty, but the truth was I had no answers. And if anybody knew what was wrong with the captain, it should have been me.

When I passed his office Thursday morning, I noticed a light on and assumed it was the sun coming through the windows. But when I walked over and put my ear against the door, I heard humming and knew he was in. I went to knock but suddenly refrained, overcome by a sudden and paralyzing dread. Even with no one watching, I felt embarrassed.

I took a deep breath and tried again.

"Enter."

I opened the door and peered in to see him working at his desk.

"Morning Capt.," I said.

He mumbled something that may have been a greeting, then

continued what he was doing. As I sat down, I glanced over and his appearance was chilling. He was already a slight man, but he had lost ten pounds and his face was pale and gaunt. His shoulders hunched—his arms were limp. Everything about him seemed to have changed in a week.

When he finally looked up, he acknowledged me with a curt smile. He coughed into his fist and handed me a folder across the desk. Inside was a report from the medical examiner, flawlessly typed and neatly stapled.

"Is this our femme fatale?" I joked, but he didn't answer.

There was a tap at the door, and we both turned to see Harrigan, dressed in a gray suit, briefcase in hand. As usual, he waited for Jackson to invite him in. Once he sat, he took out a notepad and pen and faced us with businesslike aplomb.

"It would seem," Jackson began, "that we not only have a dead woman, but also a living child." He adjusted his glasses, and his fingers were trembling. "That is my hope, at least."

I tried to get Harrigan's attention, but he wouldn't look over.

"What's the cause of death?" I asked.

"Broken neck—a clean break. You can read the report yourself."

He clasped his hands and looked across to both of us.

"Now what've you got for me?"

"We think she delivered at BCH," I said, and I could hear my voice wavering. "We...we met with the lead nurse of the maternity ward... last Saturday."

Jackson coughed again.

"And?"

"And she confirmed a woman *did* leave prematurely, with a child, the Monday prior."

The captain's eyes narrowed as he listened. I shifted in the chair and looked again to Harrigan, but again he ignored me. "Registration was closed," I added, "I'm expecting a call—"

"Expecting?" he snapped, and it made me flinch. "We don't *expect* anything in this business, Lieutenant. You need to go there today. This is a murder investigation, not a cereal sweepstakes."

The statement was corny, but somehow it made sense.

"Yes, Sir. Today."

He looked away in frustration, his white eyebrows twitching.

"Have we checked the missing person's docket?" he asked.

When Harrigan and I both said *yes* at the same time, he raised his voice and said, "...and the store owners? Staff? Vagrants? Someone must have seen something!"

There was a tense silence, and I stared down at the floor.

"What else?" he said, nearly yelling. "I can't do everyone's job, Detectives." The words felt like a lashing. "The autopsy was ready last Friday," he said, tapping his finger hard on the desk, "Why wasn't it reviewed?" When neither of us replied, he raised his arms and said, "Do you have anything for me?!"

I glanced over to Harrigan for the third time, and he finally looked back.

"W...we know the dumpster is owned by the Archdiocese. They have a building that backs up to the alleyway."

"There could be a link," Harrigan said softly, "Maybe an employee of the Church."

I nodded in agreement.

"Whoever it was," I said, "they knew there was a dumpster there. It wasn't sitting on the side of a road. It was a hundred yards off Cambridge Street. Hardly wide enough for a car, never mind an ambulance."

Jackson turned back to us, and I saw the fleshly yellow of his eyes.

"Speaking of," he said. "Whatever happened to the Chinese boy and his father?"

"Korean," Harrigan corrected.

"And it's his uncle," I said.

The captain acknowledged the mistake with a nod.

Harrigan, as prepared as always, said, "I contacted all the ambulance firms. No one was in the area...until the call came in, of course."

Jackson was silent. We sat in the stillness of the room while the world seemed to buzz around us. Everywhere I could hear muted voices, the tap of footsteps, phones ringing. After about a minute, the captain spoke, and his voice was calm again.

"What bothers me most," he continued, "is not the murder, but the child. Above all, we need to find that child. Call the state wards, the private orphanages, charities. Find out if a newborn was dropped off."

I went to give him back the report, but he put his hands out, insisting I keep it.

"Now get to work. I have an appointment. I'll be out the rest of the day. If you need anything, leave a note with the secretary."

Harrigan closed his notebook, put the pen in his coat pocket, and got up. I followed him to the door, and we were just about to exit when the captain called out.

"Detective."

Harrigan looked too, but when he realized Jackson meant me, he left.

"Sir?"

"A moment, please."

I walked over to the desk.

"Is everything alright?" he asked.

He took off his glasses and wiped them with a napkin. When I saw his face without them, he looked clinically exhausted.

"Alright?" I replied. "Of course, I mean, well—"

"You have a possible identification and you don't follow up with the hospital. Why?"

"An oversight. I'm sorry."

He got up with the shakiness of an elderly man and came around the desk. As he did, I noticed his leather belt was at the last notch and there was still some slack. I kept my hands ready in case he stumbled, but he continued steady and walked right up to me.

"We don't make oversights," he said. "Tell me what's wrong."

I drifted back an inch or two, strangely uneasy and unable to look him in the eye.

"It's Ruth."

"You two having trouble?"

He spoke with a warm and fatherly sympathy.

"No. I mean, not really. Maybe. In a way—"

"You don't have to tell me."

I hesitated for a moment. I had only ever been straight with him, and the circumstances, however personal, required total honesty.

"She...she has," I said, "depression. Bad depression."

He pursed his lips, stared down at the floor. When I saw the top of his head, his scalp was dry, his white hair thin and brittle. He thought for a few seconds and then looked back up at me.

"Is she getting help?"

"Not yet," I said, and a surge of emotion came over me. "Truth is, we've been trying to have a child." He gave me a slow and understanding nod. "It's affecting her. Bad."

"I'm sorry."

"Thank you."

He gazed into my eyes more intensely than he ever had before.

"These things are not always in our control."

"She's taking fertility drugs."

"It's not up to us," he said, looking towards the ceiling. He wasn't religious, but somehow I always knew he had faith.

"I never figured you for a believer."

"We have to believe in something," he said, "or else life is just vanity." He covered his mouth and coughed. "You take care of Ruth. If you need time, let me know. I can always put someone else on the case."

"Not necessary, but I appreciate it."

With a wide, soothing smile, he patted my arm. Then he turned around and lumbered back to the desk.

"Capt.," I called out.

When he looked over, I stiffened up.

"I...I'd like to know what's wrong."

"I'm sick, Jody," he said, and my heart skipped. "It's obvious, I'm sure."

The fact that he called me by my first name—something he never did—said much about his condition. When he didn't elaborate, I was disappointed but not surprised. The captain's life was so private that it bordered on mysterious. About the only thing anyone knew for certain was that he was born in Cornish, Maine and that he wasn't married.

After a short pause, I asked, "How sick, Sir?"

When he responded, the words seemed to hang in the air.

"Sicker than I wish to be."

CHAPTER 17

SOME DAYS IT FELT LIKE I WAS AT CITY HOSPITAL MORE THAN THE Armory. When Harrigan and I arrived, there must have been a shift change because a flood of nurses was coming out the front doors. We parked behind an ambulance and went into the lobby. As we turned down the first corridor towards the records department, a man came barreling around the corner and we almost collided.

"Hey, watch it, wise guy!"

When I looked, it was Doctor Ansell.

"Pardon, Doc."

Because I only ever saw him in a lab coat, I practically didn't recognize him in a suit.

"This is serendipitous," he said, taking off his hat.

"How's that?"

"Got a call this morning, kid." He lowered his voice and glanced around. "That broad from the dumpster—her uncle's coming to claim the body." He took out his pocket watch and looked at it. "Be down in The Crypt in 30 minutes."

I looked to Harrigan, and he nodded coolly.

"We'll be there in twenty."

Harrigan and I hurried to the end of the hallway and turned into an alcove with a single door. When I knocked, I heard the tap of heels. The door opened slightly, and a short, middle-aged woman peered out. With fat cheeks, thick glasses, and a gold cross around her neck, she reminded me of a nun.

"May I help you?" she said.

"Detective Joe Brae. This is Detective Harrigan."

Harrigan went for his badge, but I already had mine out.

"We have some questions about a registrant."

She opened the door a little more and looked out to the hallway. After a short hesitation, she said, "Come in, come in."

Aside from a small desk, the room was almost entirely file cabinets. They ran from floor to ceiling and extended all the way to the back wall. She wobbled over to them and said, "Now, when was she admitted?"

When I looked at Harrigan, he was already eyeing me.

"I didn't say it was a woman," I said.

I couldn't see her face, but I sensed that she was flustered.

"Right, right, I'm sorry. I assumed—"

"Probably the 29th," I said. "Maybe a day earlier. Maternity ward."

"So it *has* to be a woman," she joked, but I didn't laugh.

We followed her down one of the aisles, and she knelt and pulled open a large drawer. She flipped through the files with a clerical precision, scanning the tabs.

"Name?" she said.

"We don't know."

She turned her neck and said, "Well, how, I mean—"

"The patient left without telling anybody. With her child."

"That helps a bit."

Harrigan and I remained silent while she searched. The tons of paper acted like insulation and made the room uncomfortably warm.

"Well," she sighed, struggling to get back up. She came over and showed us a black ledger. "I'm looking at the discharge roll from that day." She pointed to a column with dates, times, and initials. "If there's no release time, it usually means the patient was transferred to another ward..."

I followed the column from Monday, the 29th, and read off the names to myself. I had never considered how many women gave birth each day. As my mind drifted, I saw the faces of the endless newborns, giggling and crying, and I thought of Ruth. When I snapped out of the daydream, my eyes were on a single name: *Brenda Mardini.*

"This," I said, abruptly. "Here."

Harrigan looked over my shoulder and examined the entry. Aside from the registration date, all the other information was blank: date of birth, address, guardian, etc.

I looked at the woman.

"Just a name?" I said.

She blinked a few times then spoke with a stuttering uncertainty.

"I don't know. I mean...I'm just the record keeper. But, um, I've seen it before. Not a lot, but before, yes. She could've been homeless—"

"You mean, could *be* homeless."

"Of course, that's right. Or maybe had, um, no identification. If she was in labor, we... we're morally obliged to help."

When I looked over to Harrigan, he was straight-faced. He tapped his hand on his watch, and I knew we had to go see Doctor Ansell. I handed the woman the book and looked around.

"How secure is this place?" I asked.

She straightened her back, seeming almost offended.

"Like Fort Knox."

CHAPTER 18

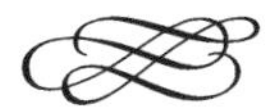

When we knocked at The Crypt, I expected Ansell but got his bumbling intern Mayonnaise instead.

"Is the doctor available?" I asked.

Peeking through the crack of the door, he looked at me and Harrigan. With his oxford shirt, wool sweater, and medical coat, he took himself too seriously, and I understood why Ansell ridiculed him.

"Let me check," he answered.

As he glanced back, I pushed through, and Harrigan and I whisked by him. He puffed up indignantly but didn't try to stop us.

On the far wall, the mortuary door was slightly open so I went over and looked in. It was a long room with high ceilings and no windows, and along the walls were rows of corpse compartments. At the back, Ansell and three men were standing in a circle talking. I forced a cough to get their attention then entered.

"Lieutenant," the doctor said, looking over. "This is Mr. Sid Mardini."

He was an older man, close to seventy with broad shoulders and a full head of white hair. He wasn't tall, but he had the bearing of someone who should've been. As we shook, our eyes locked, and I realized it was the man I had seen with Ms. Stuart at Sagansky's diner. If he recognized me, he didn't let on.

"Pleased to make your acquaintance," he said.

His voice was gravelly, and he spoke with the force of someone used to giving orders.

On his left and right were two younger men, about my age, with thick necks and long overcoats. I didn't trust them for a minute.

Ansell said, "We were, ah, just ready to make an identification, kid. Stay if you'd like." He looked to Mardini and added, "If that's okay."

"The more the merrier."

"You think..." I said, stumbling, "You believe this to be your daughter?"

His expression went cold—he looked at me with a piercing gaze.

"Daughter? No. Niece? Unfortunately, yes. But we'll see."

His answer was unusually blunt, but depending on how close they were, it might have been appropriate.

Mardini turned to Ansell.

"Let's get this done," he said.

The doctor unlatched the chamber door, and the clank of metal echoed across the room. He pulled out the tray, and it made a long rumble. Standing back, I peered between the men and saw the shiny plastic of the body bag. Ansell took it halfway out, adjusted his glasses, and leaned forward. As he began to undo the zipper, I remained still and watched.

She was a glittering young thing, no more than twenty-five, with hair that was blacker than black. Her eyes were stuck in a sideways glance that was somehow seductive even in death. She wore dark lipstick and light rouge, and she had on faux diamond earrings that glittered in the dull haze of the mortuary lamps. I cringed and averted my eyes. Viewing the dead, especially someone so young, was something I never got used to.

The identification took only a few seconds, and I knew it was over when I heard the zipper close. One of the men patted Mardini's back and mumbled something. The old man nodded twice and turned away emotionless.

"I'll just need an affidavit," the doctor said.

"Get me a pen."

Mardini marched towards the door like the whole affair was an inconvenience, and his entourage followed. We all went back into the office, where Harrigan was waiting with the intern. Ansell opened a cabinet and thumbed through it until he found the file. He placed it on the desk and handed Mardini a pen. The old man leaned over, scanned the fine print, and proceeded to write.

"I've got some questions," I said, "if you have a few minutes."

Still crouched, he glanced back at me annoyed.

"What makes you think I have a few minutes?"

The remark caught me off guard, and I spoke with a politeness he didn't deserve.

"Please. When you have time. We need to talk."

With Harrigan standing behind me, I saw the other two men align themselves with Mardini. There was an unexpected tension that even the doctor seemed to notice. For those few seconds, I felt like there was going to be trouble, but it might have just been my own paranoia.

Finally, Mardini stood up straight and faced me with his hands on his hips.

"Okay. You wanna interrupt me in my time of grief? Let's talk."

I fumbled to respond.

"It doesn't have to be now."

He flared his arms and said, "You have my attention—*now*."

Harrigan took out his notepad and pen.

"Did your niece—"

"...Brenda," Mardini interrupted.

"I'm sorry, Brenda," I said, clearing my throat. "When was the last time you saw her?"

"Maybe a month ago. I don't know."

"Did she have any enemies?"

"Not a one."

"Anyone you can think of who might've wanted to harm her?"

He scoffed and said, "A twenty-six-year-old woman? Hardly."

When I felt his associates glaring, I didn't give them the satisfaction of looking back.

"Is..." I said, hesitating. "*Was* she married?"

"No."

With each question, his answers grew more hostile. I didn't want to push him, and it wasn't out of courtesy for his loss. I had an unusual reluctance that I couldn't explain, and I almost felt intimidated. When he stared, I looked away; when he moved slightly towards me, I stepped slightly back.

"Did you know?" I continued but then stopped. Bringing up the child might have been too much.

"Did I know what?!" he barked.

"Did you know…she was missing?"

Mardini frowned.

"What kind of question is that? I reported her." He looked side to side at his acquaintances and said to me, "You have any suspects or you expecting me to provide them?"

"Not yet, Sir."

"Anything? Have you made any progress?"

His questions were like a continuation of Jackson's earlier grilling, and I started to falter. When Harrigan noticed, he stepped in and said, "We might have a witness."

Mardini's whole body pivoted, and he faced Harrigan like he suddenly realized he was there.

"An old man," I explained. "He might have seen a vehicle…" I was going to say *dump* but caught myself just in time. "…drop her off."

Mardini's expression went flat, then he squinted in surprise. The other two men were similarly struck, and their eyes darted between us and Mardini. Even Ansell, always one for intrigue, seemed to perk up at the revelation.

"This man," Mardini said, in a softer, more conciliatory tone. "He saw them put Brenda in the…" He stopped, struggling to finish the sentence, to say the word, "…the dumpster?"

"No. But he may have seen the vehicle," I said.

"He was nearby," Harrigan added.

"Urinating."

"He saw a vehicle pull out of the alleyway."

Standing behind Mardini and the others, Ansell gave me a sharp look.

"Who is he? A worker?" Mardini asked.

"No. An old Chinese man."

"Korean, actually," Harrigan said.

"He stops by the Lantern House to see friends. A strange old duck. But the only witness we have."

When I looked over to the doctor a second time, he just stared back with a disappointed frown. Something about Mardini had cajoled us into talking, and even as we did, I knew we had said too much. I felt like a rookie all over again.

"And this man, what's his name?"

Yet even under the spell of Mardini's strange charisma, there were limits, and I couldn't believe his nerve. It wasn't often we were asked specifics about a witness, even by friends or relatives of a victim.

"I'm afraid we can't tell you that," I said.

He tried to stare me down, but I stood firm and wouldn't look away. In the next room, the intern dropped something, and we all turned. The noise was enough to break the tension, and I was relieved that it did.

"Very well then," Mardini said, ending the conversation, "Any more questions, come see me."

He nodded to his men, and they all headed for the door. Before they walked out, I called over, "We're gonna find who did this."

It sounded like a cliché from an episode of Hawaiian Eye. And I might have regretted the remark if Mardini hadn't turned around and said, "If you don't, I will."

The door shut, and the office went quiet. It was a peculiar silence, one that went beyond the mere absence of sound. The encounter with Mardini had created more questions than it answered, and the three of us stood around wondering. Ansell was the first to speak when he yelled, "Mayonnaise!"

The intern hurried out from the other room, his glasses askew and struggling to balance a tray of vials.

"Take lunch."

"I already ate."

"Eat again. You're as thin as a stick for chrissakes."

"Yes, Sir," he said, and he left to get his things.

The doctor went over to his desk, where he took a half-finished cigar from the ashtray and lit it. When he turned around, his smock was open, and his paunch bulged through his shirt.

"I don't like that guy," he said.

"You don't like anyone."

He smirked and flicked an ash.

"True. But I especially don't like liars."

"How do you mean liars?"

He went to speak but stopped when the intern came out. Fumbling to put on his coat, the young man paused, and we all looked over at him. Probably sensing that he was unwelcome, he scurried across the room and left. Once the door was shut, Ansell continued, "That broad is not his niece."

"That's a strong statement."

"I've seen thousands of identifications, kid," he said, waving the cigar, speaking with his hands. "That's NOT his niece."

"He didn't seem particularly moved," Harrigan said.

"That's because he's an arrogant bastard."

"He should be," Ansell said. "He owns one of the biggest development companies in the city, *Peabody and Forbes*."

"Sounds more like a law firm."

"A lawyer?" I said to Harrigan. "He wasn't that arrogant."

"It wasn't his demeanor," the doctor said. "I've seen fathers identify daughters—cold as ice. Women identify husbands—no emotion. Everyone reacts differently, for different reasons. But this guy Mardini…he didn't mention a baby. No one forgets children—nobody. Not even the most callous sons of bitches. It's unnatural. When did he say the last time he saw his niece was?"

"A few weeks."

"A month," Harrigan said. "He said a month."

"There you have it, gentlemen," Ansell said. "He saw her a month ago and didn't know she was knocked up?"

CHAPTER 19

NOTHING SEEMED RIGHT. MAYBE IT WAS THE SOUL-NUMBING CHILL OF winter, but I felt detached from everyone and everything. The days dragged on like a long and bitter flu; the world had lost all color. The mere act of breathing was a struggle. I might have been concerned if I hadn't experienced that same malaise before. During the war, I had gone months in an emotional coma that dampened my senses and smothered my spirit. At the time, it seemed like an easier way to live until I discovered that anything which kills pain also kills joy.

It was strange that the thing which put me over the edge was not Jackson's illness or Ruth's depression or the general pathetic state of the world. It was the news that Teddy had been drafted, that a young man was being sent off to fight in a conflict which half the country opposed. In my time, it was different. And although people weren't happy about going to Korea after five years of peace, Truman made us all feel like heroes. Vietnam was a war that no one could win.

I opened the door, and Ruth was laying on the couch in a white robe, her feet curled beneath her.

"Hello," she said, not turning to look at me.

In one hand, she held a wine glass, and in the other Life Magazine. There was a half-empty bottle of cheap Merlot on the coffee table.

"How're you feeling?" I asked.

I put my coat on the coat rack and loosened my tie.

"Fine."

I walked over and sat down to take off my shoes. The Jonathan Winter Show was on the television, but the volume was low. She peered over for the first time, looking up from the magazine just long enough to catch my eye. Even without makeup, she was beautiful.

"There's chicken in the fridge," she said. "You can reheat it."

"Thanks. I had something earlier."

I went into the bedroom and put my wallet and watch on the bureau, my .38 in the top drawer. When I came back out, she had refilled her glass, and the bottle was almost gone. I sat on the couch by her feet and stared at the screen, watching the antics but unable to hear. The tension in the room was subtle, but it was real.

After a few minutes of silence, she took a sip and said, "How was work?"

"Long."

"Isn't it always?"

"Not on Fridays."

"Then you'll be glad tomorrow is Saturday."

I leaned back into the pillow and yawned. She flipped a page in the magazine and said, "I heard you were at the hospital today."

"Your spies are everywhere."

She looked over, and her eyes were glassy.

"C'mon Jody, everyone knows you," she said.

"That's part of the problem."

I stretched my arms and looked up at the ceiling.

"Ruth," I said, and she turned. "I need a favor."

When she raised her eyes, I couldn't tell whether she was being cute or dismissive.

"Can you pull a record?"

She leaned forward and rested her glass on the table. She put down the magazine and shifted on the couch to face me.

"A record?" she said, "That's confidential. It's illegal."

Her words were sharp, her voice bitter.

"Jesus, Ruth—"

"Don't Jesus me." She got up and stood over me. "You come home late every night, say a few words then go to sleep..."

As I watched her get upset, I felt my own fury building. I rose from the couch and braced for an argument. My knee hit the table and the glass fell over, sending red wine over the rug and floor.

"Oh, there you go!" she shouted. "I'm sure that was an accident."

"You know it was!"

"Or some hidden sign, right? I'm drinking too much? Not taking my pills on time?"

When she started to cry, I tried to calm her, but it was too late for apologies.

"I don't care about your drinking. Or your pills for that matter."

"But you want a child, and I'm the one who bears the brunt!"

"And you don't? This was our choice. If I could—"

"What?!" she screamed, tears coming down her cheeks. "What? If you could give birth, you would?" She shook her finger at me and said, "Well, believe me, Jody, I'd let you because this is hell..."

I stepped back and let her vent.

"...and then," she went on, "I have to worry about your sanity too?"

"What are you talking about?"

She stomped her foot on the floor.

"What am I talking about? I'm talking about the flashbacks, the imaginary war you're still fighting."

I put my hand to my forehead, rolled my eyes.

"Oh, for God's sake. That's ridiculous and you know it."

"Ridiculous? You don't hear yourself in your sleep. Sergeant this, captain that. The line, the mortars—" I went towards her, but she backed away. "How about last summer in Newburyport? Someone sets off firecrackers and you're the one that explodes!"

"There were kids around. Someone could've been hurt."

"The only one who almost got hurt was the guy who lit them. You jumped a mile, went at him...like a maniac. He wasn't the only one scared, let me tell you."

I lowered my voice, somewhat ashamed, and said, "I wasn't gonna hurt him."

"And what about the truck last week? What was that all about? Ten o'clock at night, you chase after a phantom truck from the war? And almost get us killed?"

I dropped my arms, looked down, and shook my head. Whether any of her points were fair, accurate, or true, I was in no condition to assess. I went towards the door and grabbed my coat.

"What?" she said, rushing over. "Now you're gonna leave? Is that what a soldier does?"

"I need some fresh air."

When I reached for the doorknob, she unleashed her final shot.

"Maybe you can stop by the hospital, find some third-shift bitch to pull a record, help with your investigation—"

I spun around and looked at her defeated.

"Ruth, it's not for the investigation. It's the captain. I think he's dying."

CHAPTER 20

As I drove through the dark city streets, the pleas of Ruth's anguished voice rang in my ears. I honestly believed she was sorry, but I had to get out of the house.

The restaurants along Boylston Street were still open, and the sidewalks were quiet except for a few stragglers. A group of rowdy young men, maybe fraternity brothers, were pushing a friend's car out of the snow. On the corner of Dartmouth Street, a girl in a pink petticoat waited alone for a taxi.

Soon I passed the Prudential Building—the largest skyscraper in Boston. It soared into the night and seemed to touch the stars. I drove by the Public Gardens and Boston Common and then into the Combat Zone. The neon of the strip joints and dive bars reminded me of seedy sections of Kyoto, Japan I had visited while on R&R during the war. Here, it was the only part of town that was always busy—debauchery never rested. On Essex Street, I passed a veterans' homeless shelter, a five-story tenement wedged between a peep-show and a liquor mart.

I eventually drifted towards Chinatown and into its network of small lanes. There were cars parked along both sides, and the roads were narrow enough to make a coachman nervous. On almost every block, workers were unloading produce and seafood from trucks, making it hard to pass. Caught in the flow of the sluggish traffic, I smoked one cigarette after another and watched all the nighthawks.

At the corner of Kneeland Street, a young woman in rolled-up jeans and a suede jacket was swaddling a baby beside a phone booth. She could have been a drifter or a drug addict, and the figure of the infant made me think of the child that was missing. Distracted, I didn't notice the green light until someone behind me beeped. I punched the gas and sped across the intersection, into a residential neighborhood of row houses and brick buildings.

I had gone a half block before realizing it was Teddy's street. There were hardly any lights on in the houses, and the sidewalks were empty. If it hadn't been so desolate, I might not have noticed two Asian men standing behind a parked car. One was slight, but the other was as big as Harrigan. They both wore scally caps and long, black leather coats with the collars up. I held my breath, stared ahead, and drove to the next corner.

I may have been exhausted, but I wasn't delusional. Judging from their position, they were directly across from Teddy's house. Anyone who hadn't been in combat or who wasn't a cop might have thought me paranoid. But those experiences had given me something more precious than reason and logic—they had given me instinct. And my gut told me something wasn't right.

I went around the corner and parked. I reached in the glove compartment for the Beretta .32 I kept for convenience, then I quietly opened the door. When I came around the corner, I thought for a moment that they were gone. But as I got closer, I discerned their outlines in the shadows. I crossed the street and went towards them, my heart pounding and jittery with adrenaline.

I noticed someone coming down the opposite sidewalk. I couldn't see his face, but I recognized the gait. The two men looked across and started walking toward the person, fanning out as they went. But when they heard my footsteps, they turned around, surprised. I knew then what was about to happen.

"Hey guys," I said, walking right up to them. "Which way to Shanghai?"

Without a thought, I swung my leg and booted the larger guy in the groin. As he crouched over, the other one smashed me in the right eye.

"Teddy, run!"

I stepped back and threw some wild punches that all missed. The big man tried to get me in a headlock, but I slipped out of it. There were no words—no threats. The only sounds were muffled grunts and shoes sliding on the snowy pavement.

All my weight was on one foot when I hit some ice and slipped backward. Lying flat on the cobblestone, I tried to cover up as they kicked me in the ribs, back, and head. I flailed and rolled but couldn't get up. I was starting to get dizzy and disoriented. A minute or two more and I would have ended up in intensive care or worse. I had to make a decision. I reached in my belt, grabbed the Beretta, and pointed it in the air. Then I pulled the trigger until the chamber was empty.

Instantly, the men scattered. The sound of the shots broke the quiet of the night. Porch lights went on, people looked out from second-story windows. Somewhere a dog barked. I got up unsteady and limped after them. When I saw the men turn the corner, I ran into the street, and a taxi almost clipped me. I darted down an alleyway, hoping to head them off, and stumbled out onto Harrison Ave. The street was empty—they were nowhere in sight. The only person I saw was an elderly Chinese man out for a stroll.

I tucked the .32 into my belt and leaned against a car to catch my breath. As I inspected the bump at the crown of my head, I heard a rumble and watched a vehicle pull out two blocks away and speed towards Kneeland Street. It was too far away to catch, but not too far away to see. And when I looked, the hair on the back of my neck stood up.

It was a green Dodge WC54.

CHAPTER 21

"YOU SAW THE BOY?"

"Pretty sure it was him."

"Pretty sure?"

"Very sure."

The captain leaned back in the chair thinking. I had caused a lot of chaos for a Friday night while off-duty, and there wasn't much evidence to back my story. The assailants got away, and Teddy was nowhere to be found. About the only thing certain was that my accuracy was awful because BCI found slugs in as varying places as a gutter, a mailbox, and a billboard down the street. I was only trying to scare them, but I could have killed them.

"It happened so fast," I said.

Jackson chuckled then started to cough.

"These things often do."

He looked over towards the window and started to hum a familiar tune. In his silhouette, I saw that his arms hung limply from his shoulders, and his chest was sunken in. I hated the silence because I could hear him wheeze.

"Why were you in Chinatown at that hour?" he asked.

I looked down and sighed.

"I had an argument."

"With Ruth?" he guessed, lowering his voice. He started to hack again but quickly got control. "You know I'm sorry to hear that."

"I had to get out of the house."

When he shifted in the chair, he winced from some ache or discomfort.

"I ended up on Teddy's street," I continued. "I don't know why I was there." I was sore all over; I couldn't think clearly. I felt like someone recounting sober the questionable things he had done while drunk. "He's been on my mind since I heard he got drafted."

Jackson lurched forward, as spry as he used to be, and blurted, "That boy's been selected for the draft?"

"He's a man, actually. He's nineteen."

"Damn war," he said, shaking his head. "Why in God's name would someone put a hit on him?"

"His uncle is the sole witness in the case, for one. And he's missing."

"What do you mean *missing*?"

"Teddy came to see me last week. He said when he got home from work, his uncle was gone. He thinks he went to St Kilda."

There was a knock at the door, and we both turned. Harrigan peered in and Jackson said 'enter.' He walked across the floor in a clean suit and freshly shined shoes. In one hand was his briefcase, in the other a tangerine. He was the only person I knew who would eat citrus in winter, something I attributed to his childhood in the tropics.

"Morning, Captain," he said, opening the briefcase and taking out a notebook. "I called the Department of Social Services, The Home for Little Wanders, Catholic Charities, all the regional orphanages." When he had finished running down the list, he looked up.

"Nothing checks out," he said.

"No infants?"

"Plenty of infants. But private agencies are by referral. They don't receive abandonment cases..." The term *abandonment* was harsh but accurate. "...Those are for the Department of Social

Services, churches…" He glanced aside to me and said, "…and hospitals."

"We don't even know if the baby's alive," I said, and I immediately regretted it. Giving up on a child was like giving up on humanity. I quickly changed my attitude and added, "But if it is, we'll find it."

The phone rang, but the captain didn't answer.

"We get the murderer, we get the infant," he said. "That I'm sure of."

I looked at Harrigan, he looked at Jackson, and the captain looked back to me. It was a round-robin epiphany that not only solidified our priorities but also our principles. Jackson took out a pencil and scribbled some notes, and Harrigan did the same. Still sore from the scuffle, I reached in my pocket for two aspirins and swallowed them dry.

There was a tap on the door, and it creaked open. We looked over to see the brunette secretary I had been running into everywhere. She could have been a hundred women because each time I saw her, she was dressed differently and had a new hairstyle.

"There's a call…" she said, and Jackson went for his phone. "…for Lieutenant Brae." When she said my name, it seemed like she curtsied, but it was probably my imagination. Ruth and I hadn't slept together since our argument the week before, and that short break was enough to send my libido into overdrive.

"Put it through, dear."

The young woman smiled and left. Moments later, the phone rang again, and Jackson picked up. When he gave me the receiver, his hand was trembling, and I was sure that Harrigan noticed it too.

"Hello."

"Detective Brae," someone said.

"This is Brae."

"It's Brother Emmanuel from the St Kilda Abbey. I may have seen the Asian man you're looking for."

I nodded to Harrigan and the captain, who sat waiting in suspense.

"Is that so?"

"Yes," he said. "An hour ago, by the bell tower, an elderly man, looked Chinese, with crutches, sitting cross-legged in front of the shrine—" He spoke nervously, his voice low and almost muted. "If you want to see him, I advise you come quick—"

"I'll leave now."

"And one thing, please."

"Okay."

"Don't tell anyone here I told you."

CHAPTER 22

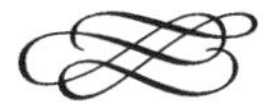

The back streets of Roxbury were intricate enough to stump a mapmaker. I spent the first eighteen years of my life there and still felt like a stranger some days. As we rushed to the abbey, I drove down dead-ends, up one-ways, circled the same block twice, and once even ended up in a school parking lot. I couldn't ignore the mystical irony that I had stumbled upon St Kilda several times by accident yet couldn't find it when I wanted to.

"Right..." Harrigan said.

I realized then that he knew my old neighborhood better than me. I swallowed my pride and cut the wheel.

"...Now go left at the end."

We came to a familiar crossroads, where the road descended to the entrance of St Kilda. When I saw the crowd, I knew our trip there would have been easier if we just rolled down the windows and followed the roar. There were enough people to fill Fenway Park and more. Both sides of the street were lined with automobiles, many double-parked, and one neighbor was clever enough to charge for parking in his driveway.

"This should be interesting," I mumbled.

Harrigan didn't answer. He put on his sunglasses, buttoned his coat, and prepared to head into the storm. With traffic backed up, we got as far as we could, and I pulled into the only empty space, which was in front of a fire hydrant. It may have been a mob, I thought, but it was a religious mob, and drivers obeyed the law.

We got out and merged with the procession, following the abbey wall towards the gates. Out front, there were a dozen cops, but keeping order was impossible, and they just looked around dumbstruck. If it wasn't for the overtime they were getting, I might have even pitied them. The media was encamped across from the entrance, and reporters were asking people questions.

"Brae!"

I turned to see 'Giraffe' Duggan, his head rising above the mob like a man treading water. He pushed through and came over with a walkie-talkie in hand.

"Jesus," he said, leaning down. "How's that cheek?"

"Worse than it looks."

"I heard what happened. Any idea who the bastards were?"

I shook my head.

"Not yet," I said.

Probably sensing that I didn't want to talk about it, he looked around and said, "Isn't this nuts?"

"More than nuts. And you wanted the overtime?"

"It's no joke," he said. "Someone's gonna get hurt."

I heard sirens at the far end of the street, and we turned to see an ambulance crawling towards us.

"It ain't the Watts Riots."

"That it ain't," he said. "But it could turn on a dime. You know that, Jody. A few troublemakers—a few hippies, some clowns from SDS. Then whadda we do? The chief wants us to keep order but look at this."

As I stood there, bodies rubbed against me, slithered through and around us. I had the creepy sensation of wading in murky water while a school of fish passed by.

"And what about the old people?" he went on in a rare moment of compassion. "A lady passed out from dehydration this morning. She was praying at the tower for two days straight."

As he said it, three elderly women in bonnets and winter coats walked by holding hands. The ambulance was right behind them, and when Duggan saw it, he raised his arms and directed it through.

"Have you seen an old Oriental?"

Distracted, he glanced back and said, "An old Oriental what?"

Harrigan grinned, the first sign of emotion since we arrived.

"Oriental man," I said. I held my hand out to what I thought was about five feet. "Maybe this high. Walks with crutches."

A man strayed into the path of the ambulance, and Duggan shouted at him to move. Then there was a call on the radio—someone needed assistance. Overwhelmed by it all, he looked around and said, "Jody, are you fuckin' kidding me?"

Harrigan and I left him and headed towards the gate. We entered the abbey, and instead of taking the driveway, we started up the lawn. Most of the snow was gone from the constant trampling, and the ground was wet and squishy. Walking among the pilgrims, I experienced an anonymity I hadn't known in years. And considering that it attracted people of all races and backgrounds, I wouldn't have been surprised if Harrigan felt the same way.

There were hundreds of campsites on the hill and the whole way up we had to step around tents and sleeping bags. Some people were cooking, others sat on blankets talking. As we neared the top, the ground became steeper, and our shoes sank in the mud. I knew Harrigan wasn't happy about it, but he seldom complained.

Soon we reached the summit and stood before the bell tower. It was stunningly quiet. The only sounds were the birds and the wind, the only voices the whispers of pilgrims in prayer. Harrigan and I turned around at the same time and looked up to the windows. With the morning glare, I had to put my hand to my forehead and squint, but once I saw the vision of Mary and Jesus, I couldn't take my eyes off it.

We began to wander, scanning the faces and searching for Teddy's uncle. At Harrigan's suggestion, we split up and went in separate directions. I walked around for another few minutes before stepping aside to smoke. As I took out the pack, my eyes swept the main abbey building in the distance, and there was someone in the doorway—watching. I turned away from the wind to light a cigarette and when I looked back, he was gone.

I went back into the crowd and continued the search. But by now I was more interested in who he was, and every few seconds I glanced over to the door. I was so preoccupied that I wasn't looking and bumped into someone.

"Pardon me," I said.

When I looked, it was Sweeney's mother. I almost jumped out of my skin. She stared back in a dull stupor, her head tilted, her eyes distant. At that moment, the sunlight hit her in such a way that, for the first time in years, I saw Chester, and it terrified me.

As I slowly backed away, she held up her wooden cross and muttered something I couldn't hear. I spun around and ran away from the tower, across the grass and towards the abbey building. By the time I reached the front door, I was sweating, confused, and Harrigan was nowhere to be found.

"May I help you?"

I turned around and saw a man peering through the half-opened door. Dressed in a brown tunic, he looked like all the other monks, except he was the size of a sumo wrestler. His hands were as big as my head, his shoulders spanned the width of the doorway. He was probably close to seventy, but I still would have had trouble taking him down.

"Um, is…is Brother Emmanuel here?"

"He's in prayer."

He spoke in a stern monotone that was either rude or direct. I showed him my badge and said, "Detective Jody Brae—"

"I know who you are."

I gave him a cold stare.

"Is that so?"

"Brother Emmanuel told me you were here last week. I'm the abbot, Reinhardt Vogt."

"My pleasure," I said, but it wasn't sincere. "We're looking for an old Korean man. He walks on crutches."

"There's no one here by that description."

"Not here," I said, and I looked towards the tower. "Over there. His nephew reported him missing, said he might be here."

His expression changed subtly, but enough for me to notice. With a large forehead and fat jowls, he was a hard man to read. He looked past me to some pilgrims that were coming in our direction. "Come," he said. "Let us speak inside."

I followed him through the doorway and into the corridor.

"Absurd, all of it," he complained.

"You don't believe it?"

"An accident of physics, nothing more."

We came into the atrium, where the damaged figure of Christ hung from the ceiling.

"There're probably ten thousand people who would disagree," I said.

We stopped at a small bench that had a brass plaque with the name of some donor or benefactor. He invited me to sit, but I declined.

"Listen, Mr.—"

"Detective Brae."

"Brae," he said, putting a finger on his chin. "I don't know why you're looking for this man or why you were here last week. But I can tell you that this...how should we call it?...*situation* will soon be rectified—"

"Rectified how?"

"Removed—the image wiped clean."

"Why haven't you done it yet then, if it's only frost?"

Vogt smirked.

"We're awaiting approval from the Archdiocese. They ordered a temporary halt. Normal procedure for such things. It must be formally discredited. Had it been up to me, it would be gone already."

"What about the pilgrims?"

He paused and smiled at me with phony sympathy. Like all men his size, he sweated constantly, and when he moved closer, I could smell body odor.

"Illusions are no measure of faith, Detective Brae. The people will return to their homes, we'll be left in peace, and the city will be better for it."

I looked around the atrium in thought. The floor was polished tile, the walls mahogany paneling. With the many portraits of former clergy, the room felt like a cross between a museum and a memorial.

"There're rumors this place is closing," I said.

He frowned dismissively.

"We live under persistent rumor, unfortunately. The Archdiocese has been threatening to close it for thirty years."

"But *you* haven't been here that long."

"No. No, I have not," he said, gazing up at the statue. "I came at end of the war—a refugee. According to the Church, it was a *transfer* or some other euphemism."

"And you brought that with you?"

"Ah, another rumor," he exclaimed, trying to be lighthearted. "Unfortunately, that one is true."

"Why's it *unfortunate?*"

He looked me dead in the eye and said, "You cannot imagine what that relic has been through. I pulled it from a burning cathedral in Berlin." He chuckled nervously. "Allied bombers, a direct hit." As I stood straight-faced and listening, he was quick to add, "No bitterness, of course. What America did was save us from ourselves."

"By that, you mean the Nazis?"

He made the restrained scowl of someone who is offended but doesn't wish to show it.

"Germany is much more than Nazism, my friend. We don't call all Americans slave-owners—"

"Because we weren't."

"We are many people, many creeds, many ideologies. I'm Prussian, my grandfather was Bavarian. I could barely understand him. Germany is a land of small kingdoms, nothing more—a patchwork of clans and cultures, with ancient rivalries, long and violent histories."

I looked at him with a dark smile.

"Sounds like Boston."

"Detective Brae?"

We both turned to see someone approaching from the end of the hallway.

"*Brahzah* Emmanuel," the abbot said, and I detected, for the first time, an accent. I would have expected him to be relieved by the interruption, but he wasn't. Emmanuel walked into the atrium, bowed reverently to Vogt, and said to me, "What brings you back?"

I looked at him awkwardly and replied, "I...I just wanted to check on the situation."

"Well, I'm glad you're here. I...we owe you and your department some thanks."

"It's not often we're thanked."

"We got a call from Police Chief McNamara yesterday," he said, his hands clasped behind his back. "He's going to continue to provide assistance until the Archdiocese makes a decision about the apparition."

"Quite kind, indeed," Vogt said.

"I'm not sure the taxpayers would agree."

"It won't be much longer," the abbot remarked. "Two, three days—"

"Unless, of course, it's declared a miracle," Emmanuel said.

Vogt huffed.

"You see, Detective Brae, the brother and I are of a different mind about what has occurred."

With the abbot on one side and Emmanuel on the other, I felt like a mediator in a holy dispute. I stepped back and said, "Listen, whether it's real or not doesn't change the consequences. You've got a helluva crowd out there..." I regretted using the word *hell*, but neither man seemed to care. "As long as people are law-abiding and things stay orderly, it's not a problem. The publicity might do this place some good."

There was a sudden lull in the conversation. Vogt looked down at Emmanuel, and Emmanuel looked up to him, but somehow their eyes didn't meet. In the awkward quiet of the moment, I remembered Harrigan and realized he was probably looking for me.

"Well," I sighed. "I must be leaving."

"I'll see you to the door," Emmanuel said, but Vogt intervened. "No, thank you, *Brahzah* Emmanuel. I know you're preparing for Vespers. I'll see the gentleman out."

Emmanuel put his hands together and made a quick bow. He pulled on his hood, turned around, and quietly walked away.

Vogt escorted me back down the hallway and we stopped at the door. When he opened it, I saw his face clearly for the first time, and it made me uneasy. To my surprise, he extended his arm and we shook. His large hand engulfed mine, and the more he squeezed, the more I squeezed back. As far as cordial goodbyes went, it might have been the most hostile I ever had.

"Come see us again, Mr. Brae."

"I'm sure I will."

Once I stepped out, the door slammed shut, and the bolt locked.

To avoid the crowd, I took the driveway down. When I came out to the street, the shift had changed, and Duggan was gone. Several reporters stood by a news truck, drinking coffee with gloves on, waiting for the next broadcast. A Salvation Army van was parked on the sidewalk, its workers handing out blankets and hot food. The spectacle was fast becoming a humanitarian crisis, and I wouldn't have been surprised if the Governor called out the National Guard.

When I finally got back to the Valiant, I was relieved to find Harrigan sitting in the passenger seat.

"Sorry," I said, opening the door. "I was in the abbey, lost track of time."

"It's easy to do here, Lieutenant."

I started the engine and rubbed my hands together to restore some feeling.

"Any sign of him?" I asked.

He gave me a troubled, almost distressed look.

"A sign? Yes," he said. "Him? No."

I looked at him confused, and he nodded over his shoulder. When

I turned, there were crutches lying on the back seat. Etched into the wood, like the markings on an Indian totem, were hundreds of Korean symbols, a chronicle of the old man's life.

"Where the hell did you find those?" I said.

"Would you believe at the tower?"

With the engine idling, I gripped the wheel and looked ahead.

"I'd believe anything at this point."

"There were others too. Crutches, braces, a wheelchair."

"Some kind of healing shrine?" I said sarcastically.

"Apparently so."

As we drove by the abbey gates, I looked over to the bell tower and saw its long shadow looming over the hill.

"This place is no Lourdes."

CHAPTER 23

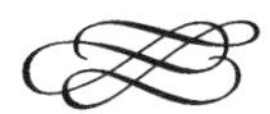

RUTH AND I HADN'T SPOKEN IN ALMOST A WEEK. WE COULD HAVE blamed it on our schedules because she worked two doubles over the weekend to cover for a coworker. But the past few nights I had come home to find her already asleep, which either meant she was unusually tired or that something was wrong.

The concern I had for her since she began feeling depressed was slowly turning to panic, and I didn't know what to do. So I had someone secretly check in on her at work—I asked the dispatchers to look out for any calls from my home address. It may have seemed excessive, but sometimes surveillance and control were the only forms of protection I knew.

As I came to the top of Roslindale Ave., I peered up to the third floor, and the lights were on. She was still up. I reached to the passenger seat for the dozen red roses I had purchased in haste from a vendor at Park Street Station. The only reason I remembered it was Valentine's Day was because the brunette secretary at the front desk mentioned she had no Cupid.

I walked up the front steps, picking off the dead petals, propping up the bunch. I went through the foyer and up the stairs, reaching for my keys with one hand. I was at the top landing and ready to unlock the door when it swung open.

"Happy Valentine's Day."

"Oh, they're gorgeous," she cried with a girlish flair.

She had on a pink babydoll dress, and her hair was blown-out and full. The skimpy outfit was the best reconciliation I could have hoped for, and it was almost worth the quarrel. I had the urge to maul her there and then, but I refrained and stepped into the apartment. As she tiptoed over to the table to put down the flowers, I noticed that her feet were bare. Then, in a move I couldn't have predicted in a fantasy, she took my hand and dragged me into the bedroom.

The window shades were down, and two candles were flickering on the dresser. I thought I heard soft music, but there was no radio in the room so it must have been my imagination. While I watched, she sat at the edge of the bed and faced me. She untied her nightgown to expose her bra and abdomen. Then she leaned back, put one knee up, and eyed me seductively. I was no prude, but there was something awkward about jumping into bed after a week of stubborn silence.

My desires were stronger than my misgivings, however. I knelt down, brought her towards me, and we began to kiss. I unsnapped her bra and her breasts popped out. She unbuttoned my slacks, and the coolness of her hand against me sent a chill through my body.

"What a pleasant homecoming," I said.

She tore off my shirt.

"If you want a baby, you need to fuck me."

The words were as crass as they were erotic, and they fueled the lustful urge that was there—always. She pulled me over the bed until I was on top of her. We worked so clumsily to bring our bodies together that it took longer than usual, and by the time I was inside, I thought I was going to explode. For those next few moments, the only sounds were the twanging of bed springs and the groans of our mutual ecstasy.

When it was over, I fell on my back and lay staring at the ceiling. Fatigue came over me like a heavy anesthetic, and I had to fight to stay awake. She cuddled close on her side and twirled my hair. Her body was warm, her breath sweet. The curve of her hip under the sheet rose like a hill against the flatlands of the mattress.

"You know I love you," she said.

I put my hand on her knee.

"I do, of course."

"I'm sorry about last Friday."

"Me too."

The shadows on the ceiling formed shapes and objects. I recalled as a child staring at the darkness and seeing things that weren't there. Now, as then, I looked off into the void and dreamed. I was only startled from the spell when I felt the mattress shudder and realized she was sobbing.

"What is it?" I said, sitting up. "What's wrong?"

She just gazed ahead, her arms folded into her chest, her feet curled. I rubbed her shoulder, but she didn't respond.

"Ruth, please."

She lifted her head off the pillow. Seconds passed before she was able to look at me.

"I pulled the medical record for you," she said.

I fell back to the bed and again gazed at the ceiling.

"You were right," she said. "So right. And I'm so sorry."

I said nothing. Then in one thundering word, she confirmed for me the horror that I had suspected all along.

"Cancer."

Finally hearing it brought some perverse relief—I didn't have to wonder anymore.

"How bad?"

"Bad, Jody," she said, her voice cracking. "Incurable. It's everywhere. He's—"

I gripped the sheets with my fists.

"No. Please don't."

"I'm sorry. And I'm sorry I got angry."

She then sank into a fit of soft but uncontrollable crying. There were so many tears it was like she wept for us both. More than anything I wanted to turn over and hug her, but I couldn't move. I experienced an overpowering paralysis that affected my brain as well as my body. I thought nothing, I felt nothing. In those few moments, the totality of my life and career lay exposed before me like a journey without end. The universe seemed empty, vacuous, meaningless. If I hadn't had her to cling to, I might have slipped into the abyss.

CHAPTER 24

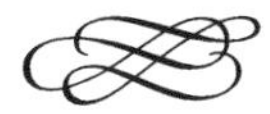

THE VALIANT WAS ALMOST OUT OF GAS AS HARRIGAN AND I SAT IN Thursday morning traffic. Commuters waited at trolley stops shivering; on the sidewalks, people trudged headlong into the wind, squinting and teary-eyed. The sky may have been clear, the sun may have been shining, but the bitter cold stole any joy the cloudless day could have given.

"You seem out of sorts."

I looked at Harrigan.

"I was born out of sorts," I said.

I punched the horn in frustration and tried to get around a slow driver. It took us ten minutes to go a mile, and by the time we got to the intersection of Massachusetts Avenue, I was ready to get out and walk to work. Rather than risk running empty, I cut the wheel right, bounced over a curb, and drove two blocks to a service station on Tremont Street. While the attendant filled it, we sat quietly and gazed out at the morning madness.

I was watching a jogger go by when, suddenly, a vehicle passed behind him and broke my focus. My entire body got tense when I realized it was the green Dodge WC54.

"Son of a bitch," I said to myself, turning the key. This time it wasn't getting away.

"Lieutenant, what are you doing?"

In a lapse of coordination, I hit the gas pedal before putting it in gear. The engine revved, the tires chirped, and we shot forward. As we screeched out of the lot, I heard the fuel hose snap and knew the nozzle was still in the car.

"Dammit," Harrigan said, punching the dash. "What in Jehovah's name are you up to?!"

Whenever he got angry, his latent Caribbean accent came out, and he used phrases he wouldn't normally say.

"Hang on," I shouted. "I saw the truck."

"What truck?"

"The green truck. The one from the abbey."

I watched the tail of the vehicle turn left at the next intersection. As I raced ahead to close the gap, the signal turned red, and I went through it. Harrigan reached under the steering column and hit the siren switch.

"If you're in pursuit, have the decency to make it known," he said.

I ignored the dig and concentrated on the road, determined not to lose the phantom truck. It only went a half block up Shawmut Ave. before veering right and slowing down. With the sirens blaring, I came up beside and motioned for the driver to halt. Confused, he rolled down his window and I yelled, "Pull the fuck over!"

He hit the brakes and stopped in front of Blackstone Park.

"You better have a reason for this," Harrigan said.

As I reached for the door handle, I turned to him.

"I'll find one."

I thought he was going to wait, but as I walked over to the truck, I heard his footsteps behind me. When I approached the driver's window, I was fuming and didn't know why.

"License and registration," I said, showing my badge.

He was a lanky middle-aged man, with a long neck and protruding Adam's apple. He must have been tall because his head almost touched the top of the cabin.

"What did I do, officer?" he asked politely.

He handed me the documents, and I pretended to review them.

"You, um, blew a red light."

"It was green," he said nervously. "I—"

"You must be colorblind."

I looked over at Harrigan.

"Wasn't it red?" I said.

The driver and I waited for a reply.

"Beats me," he said, shrugging his shoulders. "I'm colorblind."

The man looked to him and then to me like he wasn't sure if it was a joke, a setup, or just bad police work. I took a step back and ran my eyes along the length of the vehicle. I had been right all along—it was a Dodge WC-54, the all-purpose Army truck I saw everywhere in Korea.

"Who owns this vehicle?" I asked.

"Peabody and Forbes. I work for them. Says right there."

He reached out the window and pointed to a line on the registration.

"Peabody and Forbes?" I said. "Sid Mardini?"

"Yes, Sir."

I paused for a moment thinking.

"Two weeks ago I saw you at the monastery."

"Monastery?"

"St Kilda Abbey, in Roxbury. I saw this truck."

Squinting in the sun, the man looked at me dumbfounded.

"I'm sorry, Sir. We have a whole fleet of these."

"A fleet?"

He nodded.

"Mr. Mardini got them from the War Department years ago."

I glanced over at Harrigan, who kept his distance but was listening.

"What are they for?"

"For?" he said with a friendly smile. "Well, they're work trucks. We transport supplies and such...to building sites."

I folded up the registration and handed it to him along with his license. I smacked the side of the truck twice and said, "Don't let me catch you speeding again."

"Thanks, officer," he replied, and Harrigan looked away with a reluctant grin.

I walked back to the Valiant, thinking about the Dodge with a mixture of nostalgia and regret. Many were the nights I sat in its cold cabin, bouncing over the rocky terrain of the Korean mountains. If any analogy could have explained the way I felt, it was that the WC54 was not a friend, but it was a close acquaintance. Before I drove away, I took one last look in the rear-view and shook my head.

We went north along Albany Street towards downtown, and for those first few minutes, Harrigan said nothing. I knew he had more questions than I had answers, and I appreciated the courtesy of his silence. But by the time we reached the Boston Common, the grace period was over, and I would have to talk.

"That lorry," he said. "What's your obsession with it? Is it about the war?"

I knew he was perceptive, but sometimes he surprised even me. I pointed behind with my thumb and said, "That…that has nothing to do with the war."

"It's an old Army vehicle, am I right?"

We came to a red light, and I turned to him.

"Right," I said. "But you know why I stopped him?"

Harrigan stared at me but didn't answer.

"Because those trucks were used as ambulances."

CHAPTER 25

CHESTER SWEENEY WAS THE RIDDLE I LEFT UNSOLVED. WE HAD BEEN friends since kindergarten and maybe before—I was never really sure. His presence stretched back to that haze of first memories where everything was vague and unformed. Simply put, I never recalled him not being there. Along with Al Russo, he was the only true friend I had, and the bond we had was forged by the pain and wonder of our impoverished youth. Russo, Sweeney, and I were a brotherhood of three, bound by scraped-knee blood and stickball honor.

In the months following Chesty's death, Russo and I never talked about what happened at St Kilda. In some way, we wanted to believe his death was an accident. We clung to that remote prospect that he had left the abbey and wandered in the dark, lost and drunk, until he stumbled down the embankment of the train tracks and cracked his skull. No one ever told us how he died so we never asked. With his humble background and crazy mother, it was as if the world didn't care that he was gone. Few of the kids in school ever talked about him —there was never a memorial service. When, a year later, my English teacher was kind enough to ask if I wanted to write a paper about our friendship, she mistakenly called him *Feeney*.

In the end, Russo and I were the only ones who could keep

Sweeney's memory alive. Maybe it was the shock of seeing our friend forgotten, but whenever we got drunk, we celebrated his life in bizarre ways. One night we roamed the streets with felt tip markers, scribbling CHESTY WAS HERE on every street sign, mailbox, and store window we could find. Another time we painted his name in large letters across the side of Egleston Station. We even re-carved the names that, years earlier, we had cut into a large oak tree in Franklin Park. But over time, the rain washed away the ink, the station was painted over, and the tree was cut down due to fungus.

With every trace of him gone, all that remained was our guilt. It wasn't because we left him at the abbey, but that we didn't tell the police or school officials what happened. At a time when the Church dominated all matters big and small, beating up a priest was like striking God himself. The afternoon Mrs. Halloran called us into her office, we had an impossible choice—confess everything and face the consequences or say nothing and face ourselves. We had chosen the easier way.

Russo and I may have tried our darnedest to memorialize Sweeney, but we never spoke about that night at St Kilda. And like all things left unresolved, the issue simmered under the surface of our friendship until it finally boiled over.

On a cold winter night a year after Sweeney's death, Russo and I went to a rocky cliff called Whisky Point. Hidden behind triple-deckers and covered by trees and brush, it was the only undeveloped land in Roxbury and had long been a gathering place for hobos, delinquents, and runaways.

Russo had stolen a case of Pabst Blue Ribbon from the liquor store he worked at, and I bought some cheap cigarettes. Together, we scaled the snowy path up the hill, climbing on our hands and knees as we neared the summit. Although it was steep, we managed to drink and smoke the entire way, and eventually, we stumbled onto the ledge. Russo and I had been there a hundred times, but the view was something that always enthralled. He stepped over to the edge of the cliff and looked out to the city.

"Amazing."

I sat down on the rock and opened another can.

"Ever see anything like it?"

"Yeah," I said sarcastically. "When we were here two weeks ago."

He leaped across the rock, from one high point to another, circling a fire pit filled with ash and broken bottles. Even when drunk, he was as skittish as a colt and could never be still.

"Take a seat, will ya?" I said.

When he finally sat down, his leg was rattling, and he wouldn't shut up. He tilted his head back, took a slug of beer, and looked at the stars.

"Ever wonder if Chesty is up there?"

"Up where?"

"Up there," he said, turning to me. "You know, heaven."

I ignored the question and got up to piss. I had only walked a few feet when he mumbled, "You shouldn't have let him go back—"

I stopped and turned around.

"What'd you say?"

"I said...*You shouldn't have let Chesty go back.*"

I stormed over, and he jumped up and threw his beer can. I got as close to him as I could in the darkness and stared into his face. I was always taller than him, but in the past year he had caught up.

"Drop dead! You were the one who was gonna let him go. I tried to stop him."

"N...n...no you didn't, Jody," he said, stuttering from rage and not fear. "I did—"

"Take it back, you stinkin' bum!"

Our eyes were locked, our jaws tense. In all our years of friendship, I had been his protector and to have him challenge me was a betrayal.

"A...a...and you...you told me not to say anything to Mrs. Halloran. W...w...we should've told the cops."

"And get thrown in jail for beating up a priest?"

"He was the one that would be in jail, Jody. You and I both know he k...k...k—"

But before he could say it, I dropped my beer and socked him in the mouth. He stumbled back but didn't fall. He shook off the pain and charged, tackling me over the rock. We wrestled on the ground for a few seconds, and I got on top of him. When I punched him in the eye, he kneed me in the balls, and I keeled over stunned. He then got me in a headlock and dragged me around in circles. Snot ran down my face; my lip was starting to swell.

The moment I was ready to give up, I curled my feet around his leg and tripped him. He fell backward, and I jumped on top. Sitting on his chest, I dug my elbow into his mouth and watched his eyes bulge. It was the first time I discovered that having the power to kill someone was just as satisfying as doing it. When he started to choke, I grunted once and let go. He rolled over on the rock and lay face-down, panting and beaten.

It was the last time either one of us questioned our role in the death of Chester Sweeney.

CHAPTER 26

THE STATLER BUILDING IN PARK SQUARE WAS ONE OF THE MOST prestigious addresses in the city. The triangular, fourteen-story structure was at the junction of the Back Bay and downtown, overlooking the Public Gardens. Harrigan and I walked into the elegant lobby with the apprehension of uninvited guests. Boston was far from the class-bound tinderbox of my youth, but as a blue-collar son of Roxbury, there were still some places I wasn't comfortable. And as we walked across the polished floor to the elevator bank, I was sure the concierge was watching us. It almost made me proud to know that, in some areas of society, Harrigan and I were both black.

Once inside the elevator, I pressed fourteen and we went up. The doors opened to a long corridor lined with offices, law practices and financial consultants, white-shoe investment firms and commercial insurance agencies. As distinguished as a social register, they bore the names of the city's first families, entrenched like royalty into the highest echelons of business might. A burgundy runner spanned the length of the hallway; the walls had silk wallpaper. There were oil paintings, prints, gilded mirrors, and, at regular intervals, pedestal ashtrays.

We read off the companies, one after another until we got to the last door. There I squinted to see the small writing on a bronze plaque: *Peabody & Forbes, Building Construction*. I looked at Harrigan then knocked, unsure whether we should go straight in or wait. But when no one answered, I opened the door and we stepped into a small reception area with a desk, white couch, and end tables with Tiffany lamps. I heard footsteps and a woman came out from the back room in a tight-fitting skirt, her hair in a bun.

"May I help you?" she asked.

Her face was flush like someone who was busy or overworked. Under one arm she held a brown folder.

"We're here to see Sid Mardini," I said.

She arched her back and spoke haughtily.

"Do you have an appointment?"

I went to take out my badge but decided we would catch more flies with honey than with vinegar. So I made a sheepish smile and said, "I'm sorry, we don't."

She changed her posture and blinked, flabbergasted that anyone would be so bold. Walking into a firm like *Peabody and Forbes* and expecting to see the owner was an indication of either impudence or importance. In those few tense seconds, I hoped she would assume the latter.

"Okay," she said, finally. "Let me see."

She started to turn around then paused.

"And your names?"

"Jody Brae."

She went down the hallway and disappeared behind a row of walnut file cabinets. When I looked at Harrigan, he was as still as a wax figure. Moments later, I saw the woman waving for us in the distance.

"Gentlemen, please come."

We followed her down the hallway, where she turned and continued to walk. We passed several empty offices and a small conference room. Except for the hum of a refrigerator in the employee kitchen, the floor was completely quiet, and no one was around. It was Friday afternoon, but it might as well have been Sunday morning because the place was deserted.

At the end, we reached a corner office and the woman stopped. She motioned for us to enter and left without another word. When I went in, Sid Mardini was sitting squat behind a large desk. Wearing suit suspenders over a white t-shirt, he looked more like a bookie than a business owner. His forearms were hairy, his gut bulged. He looked up with a flat expression that was neither welcoming nor hostile.

"Detectives. Please sit."

When he didn't get up to shake, Harrigan and I nodded and took the leather armchairs by his desk. Throughout my life and career, I thought, I was always facing someone across a desk.

"Well," he said, rubbing his hands together. "You were able to find me I see."

"You're not a hard man to find."

"I usually am. You got lucky. I'm working on a big deal—"

"And where's that?"

The twitch in his eye told me he was not used to people interrupting him.

"When it happens, you'll read about it in the Record American," he said, squinting ironically. "They seem to take a special interest in what I do."

"Which is what exactly?" Harrigan asked.

"We're a construction firm. We buy things. We build things. We tear things down."

He pivoted in the chair, just enough so he could see out the window. The view was magnificent, the office overlooking all of Back Bay and the South End. The highlands of Roxbury rose in the distance, and I thought I saw the bell tower of St Kilda, although it was probably a church steeple.

"You see," he went on, "ever since I was a boy, I liked to make stuff." He gazed out the window and drifted into nostalgic reflection. "When I was three it was sandcastles—when I was eight it was forts." He turned sharply and looked at both of us. "I bought my first property at sixteen. An abandoned brick building. North Grove Street."

"The West End?"

He smiled and said, "That's right. The land that time forgot. Born and raised there, my friend. Watched it get blasted to smithereens ten years ago. Didn't that break my heart?"

Scars ran deep for residents of the old West End, a ten-block neighborhood of tenements and row houses that was leveled in the late fifties to make room for expensive high-rises.

"You weren't in on the action?"

"No," he scoffed. "Not a bit. My own mother still lived there. Many of my friends, too."

"With a name like Mardini, I would've guessed the North End."

Harrigan glimpsed over to me, trying to follow the back and forth of our insiders' chatter. He may have lived in Boston since age six, but that didn't make him a Bostonian.

"North End?" he said. "We had Italians in the West End too." He leaned forward and looked me straight in the eye. *"But I wasn't one of them."*

With a deep, guttural laugh, he said, "Full-blooded Armenian, my friend. And the rage to prove it. Ha, ha!"

He nodded to the far wall, and Harrigan and I craned our necks to see a framed portrait of a priest in a red headdress and black vestments. Around his neck was a gold Byzantine cross. For some reason, I thought of Chester Sweeney.

"Ignatius Bedros XVI Batanian," Mardini boasted, "Our patriarch."

"You don't seem like a praying man."

"I'm like most men. I pray when I have to, but never when I should."

When he slapped his hands on the desk with a roar, Harrigan and I couldn't help but laugh too. As with any interview, the small talk was a dress rehearsal for the hard questions to come. And I enjoyed the light conversation that much more because I knew it wouldn't last.

Mardini's tone turned suddenly serious.

"You got some news for me?"

When he looked at me, his expression was cordial but somehow threatening—just like at The Crypt.

"We do," I said, and I knew the lie made Harrigan uneasy.

A grin crept across Mardini's chin.

"Then how about giving me the bastard's name, eh?" He laughed aloud and shook his head. "No, don't. I don't need that on my conscience. I'll murder him." When he swept his hand in the air, I couldn't tell what weapon he was mimicking. "Like in the old West End, you killed a young woman, gettin' pinched for it was a blessing! You got caught by the wise guys, they'd pull your teeth out with pliers, cut off your prick and shove it up your ass."

"Fortunately, we have the rule of law."

"This is true," he said. "And a good thing."

"How close were you to your niece?"

He stopped and gave me a sideways glance. His temples pulsated; there was sweat around his ears.

"Close?" he asked. He looked down and lowered his voice. "No, we weren't close. That's the truth. My brother Frank's child, only child." When he looked up, he said, "She was trouble from early on. Not a bad girl. Just...how should I say?...emotional."

"You didn't see her much?"

"She stopped by—"

"Stopped by here?" Harrigan asked.

"No," he said, holding out his hands, "She stopped by my house sometimes. Usually in a jam. Needed cash."

"When was the last time you saw her?"

"I thought I already told you that," he said coolly, and the outburst caught me off guard. "At the coroner. Do you guys take notes?" I glanced over at Harrigan. "I probably saw her a month ago."

"Right, sorry. Was there anything unusual about her? Anything changed?"

Mardini frowned.

"No, not that I could tell. Besides, what would anything *then* have to do with *now*?"

I could tell his courtesy was wearing thin.

"There could've been precipitating events."

"A serial killer?"

"I'm afraid we can't say. It's too early."

"Too early? She was found three weeks ago for chrissakes."

"These things take time," Harrigan chimed in. "We wish it weren't so."

Mardini pursed his lip and looked over at him. Harrigan never said much, but his ability to calm things with a few words was as much a gift as it was a skill.

"Very well," Mardini said with a sigh. "What else do you need to know?"

He leaned back in the chair and hooked his thumbs around his suspenders. Somewhere in the office a phone was ringing and wouldn't stop.

"I want to make sure you don't have any suspicions," I said.

"Like what? Like I know who killed my niece?"

When I nodded, he said, "Believe me, son, if I did, he'd be pushing up daisies now."

I smiled wryly, acknowledging the remark for both its humor and its truthfulness. Then I paused, hoping it would prompt him to say more. But he didn't. A man like Mardini only divulged what he wanted to, and two detectives on the snoop wouldn't be able to coax him. A timer might as well have gone off because the conversation was over.

"Let me give you gentlemen a short tour on the way out."

He strained to rise from the chair, the weight of his gut acting as an anchor. Harrigan and I stood up and followed him to the door. As we passed the portrait on the wall, Mardini kissed his hand and gestured to the Patriarch.

We went out to the hallway, and he stopped at a framed photograph showing a complex of yellow brick apartment buildings. It took a moment, but I realized it was Columbia Point, a massive public housing project between South Boston and Quincy. With a freeway on one side and a city dump on the other, hundreds of families lived there in isolated poverty.

"This," he said, "was one of our first big ventures."

"Columbia Point."

"That's right. Fifteen hundred units for the poor. God bless 'em."

We continued down the corridor, past empty offices, and came to another image of a similar place, only this one was next to a public park.

"Franklin Field."

"The very same," Mardini said, turning to me. "You born and bred in Boston?"

I nodded.

"Roxbury Memorial, class of '47."

He touched my shoulder and looked up with a warm grin.

"A child of the ghetto, like me, eh?"

I didn't like his hand on me, but I didn't make it obvious.

"Wouldn't have wanted to grow up anywhere else."

"That's what I like to hear," he said, glancing back to Harrigan. "Pride. Can't put a price on that."

As we walked back, he pointed out all the prominent projects his firm had been involved in. It was a spectacular portfolio of urban improvement, and the developments ranged from modern housing to renovated slums. Judging from the pictures, Peabody and Forbes was responsible for half the new construction in the city.

We were almost at the door to the waiting room when I saw a photograph above a file cabinet. In it were several men, including Mardini, the former mayor Collins and Ed Logue, head of the Boston Redevelopment Authority. They were standing at a job site in white hardhats, shovels in their hands, smiling at the camera for a public relations photo. Right beside Mardini and almost out-of-view was Johnny, the owner of the Lantern House Restaurant. The moment I realized it was him, I quickly looked away and kept walking.

We entered the front room, where the secretary was sitting at the desk stapling documents. She looked up but didn't say anything, and Mardini led us to the door.

"Always so quiet on Fridays?" I said.

"Don't be impressed by the wallpaper and millwork. This is a glorified file room. My men are usually out meeting with investors, contractors, et cetera."

I looked at him and joked, "So we don't get to meet Mr. Peabody and Mr. Forbes?"

"Pure window dressing, my friend. Forty years ago you wouldn't get far with a name like Mardini."

As he held the door open for us, I said, "And how about these days?"

"It takes me anywhere I need to go."

CHAPTER 27

When I awoke Friday morning, a shadowy pre-dawn light filled the room like a dreamscape. Ruth was facing away from me, but I could tell she was awake and staring at the wall. She had her arms wrapped around the blanket, her legs curled up. I knew something was wrong.

"Ruth, what is it?"

She didn't answer. I snuggled close, put my hand on her hip, and asked again. After a short silence, she finally said, "You know Ms. Stuart, the ward nurse?"

"The one we saw at Sagansky's?"

"She's married."

"I figured so."

"That wasn't her husband. Can you believe she was with someone who wasn't her husband?"

She spoke wistfully; there was sadness in her voice. I got out of bed and went to the closet to get dressed.

"He's also one of the biggest developers in Boston."

She raised her head off the pillow and looked over.

"Sid Mardini, of Peabody & Forbes," I explained. "I met with him yesterday."

"Why?"

"Remember the woman that was found in the dumpster?"

"How could I forget?"

"It's his niece, so he says."

"You don't believe him?"

I pulled on my trousers, ran a belt through the loops.

"I don't know," I said. "Something's not right."

"There's a lot that's not right."

As I buttoned my shirt, she lay still and gazed blankly into the darkness. In the quiet of the morning, I began to notice sounds—a neighbor moving around below, a cold engine sputtering to start, a dog barking. The great symphony of humanity was starting to perform.

"Do you love me, Jody?"

I stepped over to the bed, knelt down, and rubbed her shoulder.

"Of course, I do. More than anything."

"What's wrong with this world?"

She spoke with a trance-like wonder, in a voice that was not entirely her own. I looked into her eyes but couldn't make contact.

"You have to get up for work," I said tenderly.

"Not today. I can't."

I stood up and looked at her concerned. She had called in sick the day before, and I feared she was losing her ability to function. I didn't know much about depression, but I knew about shellshock, and the battle of the mind was a solitary one. I leaned over and kissed the top of her head.

"Get some rest," I said. "Will you be okay?"

"I'll be okay."

"Promise?"

"Promise."

I left the apartment in such distress that my tie was loose, my shoes were untied, and my .38 was hanging from my pants pocket. As I waited for the Valiant to warm up, I smoked one cigarette after another and stared through the windshield. Watching Ruth suffer and Jackson deteriorate sent me into a quiet despair, and for the first time in my life, I felt helpless. It was hard to understand how I could have spent fifteen months in combat and fifteen years on the force, only to succumb to sentiment. I was able to handle a thousand goddamn deaths, but not one heartbreak.

Maybe I needed my own miracle because I gravitated, almost subconsciously, towards St Kilda. It was not even 8 a.m., and people were trudging along the sidewalks, congregating at the entrance, climbing the hill to the apparition. The news vans hadn't arrived yet, but some young journalists, eager for an early scoop, waited with cameras hanging from their necks. A half-dozen cops stood around sipping coffee and yawning in the morning chill.

Just over the wall, I could see the top of the bell tower, piercing the tree line like a castle turret. Someone beeped, and I looked behind to see a bus, filled with people and marked by the name of some tour company. The miracle was fast becoming Disneyland for the devout. I slammed the shifter into drive and sped off.

I got to The Armory at eight-thirty and circled three times before finding a spot. I tied my shoes, fixed my tie, and then got out. The slush from the previous day had frozen overnight, and a work crew was spreading rock salt. As I crossed the open lot, the harbor wind ripped through my overcoat, blasted my face. By the time I reached the front steps, I was too numb to even shiver.

"Lieutenant!"

Looking back, I saw Harrigan approaching so I waited for him in the shelter of the doorway.

"You're late," I joked.

"As are you."

"Got here before you."

He brushed by me with a frown, and we walked inside together. We passed reception and continued down the corridor, stopping at a water bubbler. Noticing the captain's light was on and surprised he was in on a Friday, I went over and tapped on the door. Moments later, he said 'enter,' and there was a feebleness in his voice that I hadn't heard before. Grasping the doorknob, I hesitated and looked at Harrigan, wishing I hadn't knocked at all.

I opened the door and went in.

"Detectives," Jackson said. "Perfect timing."

He was standing at the window, staring out at the parking lot and watching the morning activity. He had on a pressed shirt and tie, and there was a navy jacket draped over the chair. I hadn't seen him wear a suit in months, and the formalness conjured strange thoughts of how he would look at his own wake.

"Have a seat, please."

Harrigan and I quickly sat, but the captain walked slowly towards his desk and lowered himself into the chair. He adjusted his glasses, cleared his throat, and said, "I just came from a meeting with McNamara." After a suspenseful pause, he looked up and continued, "He's decided to act on the situation at the St Kilda Abbey."

I glanced over to Harrigan.

"What do you mean *act on...?*" I asked.

"Well," he said, with some regret, "the crowd is becoming a public safety hazard. It's likely they'll be asked to vacate the premises. The chief is in discussions with the Archdiocese to determine the 'how' and 'when' and to come up with a contingency plan in case there're any problems."

"You mean like a riot?" I said, and it wasn't sarcasm.

When he sighed, it caused him to cough.

"I'm not saying I agree. But something has to be done. Apparently, the property is in the process of being sold."

"Sold?"

"It's been underway for months."

"They haven't told the monks. I spoke with one—Brother Emmanuel. He has no idea."

"The abbot is well-aware," Jackson said, and a tingle went up my back. "He doesn't support the idea of a miracle."

"Looks real to me."

"That may be true, but—"

"Who's he to say?" I said, getting heated. "There're thousands of people who believe."

"You're right, Lieutenant. It's not for him to say..."

His tone got stern. He may have sympathized, but he wouldn't tolerate any dissent.

"...But it *is* for the Archdiocese to say," he went on. "It's their property. It's their purview. Again, I'm not saying I agree. But something must be done. It can't continue."

He began to hack again, this time in heavy, dry thrusts. When his face got deep red, I worried he might choke.

"I'm sorry," he said.

Sitting sideways in the chair, he was almost too ashamed to face us. Terminal cancer was like a battle without an enemy. And for a man who spent his life fighting external threats, being destroyed from within was probably particularly humiliating.

"The point is, I'm tied up next week. McNamara has requested some undercovers to be on-scene to look for agitators and troublemakers. Nothing heavy-handed. Just to monitor the crowd."

"I thought we were past that," I said.

When he finally looked over, it was with a rueful grin.

"Right. I'm no great fan of unjustified surveillance. His idea, not mine. Now, let us move on to the dumpster case."

"Yesterday we paid a visit to Sid Mardini, the victim's uncle."

His eyes widened.

"Go on."

I went to respond, but Harrigan beat me to it.

"He didn't seem much moved by her death."

"Were they close?" Jackson asked.

"He said not, but that wasn't what bothered me."

The captain made a gargling sound like he was trying to suppress a cough. I looked at Harrigan and added, "He admitted seeing his niece within the last month but made no mention of a pregnancy."

"She would have been near term," Harrigan said. "It would have been quite apparent."

The wall clock struck noon and we all stopped talking. Jackson's eyebrow twitched, my foot tapped, and Harrigan, for the first time ever, shifted anxiously in his seat. We were restless in different ways, but all for the same reasons. In the past, the sounds of the captain would have eased any tense silence. I realized only then that he no longer hummed.

"What do you know about Sid Mardini?" I asked.

"Just what I read in the newspapers," he said with a wink. "A bit of a rogue, but his company has helped transform this city." He looked specifically at Harrigan and reflected, "You may be too young to remember, but thirty years ago Boston was a dying seaport. Now look at it…" He waved dramatically towards the window. "…Construction everywhere, a new city hall. They just broke ground on a 60-story tower in Back Bay. It'll be the tallest in New England. Everything has improved."

"And a lot of hearts were broken in the process."

He stopped and stared at me with a tenuous sympathy. He may have shared my views, but he didn't share my outrage.

"I agree," he said. "The West End was no model of compassionate urban planning."

"Apparently not, if even Mardini was against it."

Jackson frowned and sat up straight.

"Against it? Hardly. He may have dodged public criticism, but not the profit. His firm made millions off that project. Much of the deal he put together behind closed doors—"

CHAPTER 28

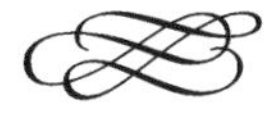

RUTH WAS GETTING WORSE. SHE STAYED IN BED THE ENTIRE WEEKEND, getting up only to use the bathroom or make tea. She insisted she was sick, but she had no fever or other symptoms, and whenever I tried to talk with her, she just asked me to leave her alone. More than once I tried calling City Hospital, but each time I hung up. Her depression was as paralyzing for me as it was for her.

"It's six o'clock," I said, crouching over the bed.

"I'm tired."

"You have to eat something."

"I can't."

"Let's go eat. Someplace casual. Please."

With her back to me, I couldn't see her expression, but I could tell she was considering it.

"We'll be back in an hour," I said.

"You think I'm crazy."

I didn't know if it was a question or statement.

"Not at all."

Finally, she rolled over and looked at me. Her eyes were bloodshot, glassy, encrusted. Her face had the puffy paleness of someone who had been in darkness for too long.

"I stopped taking the drugs," she said.

I wanted to ask why, but I already knew the answer. So I concealed my disappointment and said, "We can deal with that later."

"I know you want a baby. And I do too. I swear."

Her voice was shaky; she was on the verge of tears.

"Don't worry about anything," I said, rubbing her back. "We'll get through this, I promise. You need to keep moving. Laying here all day and night just makes it worse."

When she looked away, I knew she was in a tug-of-war between two urges—to stay in bed and suffer or to get up and try to heal. I kept my hand firmly on her, hoping that somehow my strength would transmit to her. After a minute of silence, she glanced up with a timid smile, and I knew she was willing to go. I had never been more proud of her.

Even in the throes of her depression, Ruth was not one to just pick up and leave. So while she showered and put on makeup, I sat in the living room staring at the TV. I was craving a cigarette, the only thing that ever seemed to take the edge off, but she hated the stench, and I wasn't about to do anything to upset her. But my mind raced, and I was so restless that the mere act of being still was painful.

When I got up to get a glass of water, she walked in dressed like an angel. Her hair was curled, and she had on a pink turtleneck, plaid skirt, and knee-high brown leather boots I had never seen her wear before.

"You look…stunning," I said.

She smiled and walked over to the table to get her pocketbook. She took my arm, and together we went down the stairs and into the night.

By the time we reached Victoria's Diner, it was eight o'clock and the place was packed. Situated off a dark stretch of Massachusetts Avenue in an industrial no-man's-land between South Boston and Roxbury, it was the busiest restaurant no one had ever heard of. The owner didn't advertise, and it never made the tourists brochures. The food was simple but fresh, and the fanciest thing on the menu was a steak Béarnaise that they always seemed to be out of. The diner was open from dawn to late, and its clientele ranged from parolees to politicians.

The owner must have recognized me as a cop because the moment we walked in, he whispered something to the hostess, and we got a table by the front window. Ruth took off her coat and sat in the chair, peering around curiously.

A scrawny waitress with bleached hair came over.

"Good evening, what can I get ya?" she said.

She was gruff but friendly, and when she smiled, I noticed she was missing some teeth.

"White wine," Ruth quickly answered. "Any type."

"Soda water," I said. "Any specials?"

The woman looked over her shoulder and squinted to read the chalkboard.

"Lasagna with garlic bread."

Ruth and I looked at each other at the same time.

"Okay," I said, and Ruth nodded. "We'll have that."

We sat silently, enjoying the cozy warmth, happy just to be out together. In the background, the jukebox was playing the Everly Brothers, and it reminded me of my days as a rookie. British Rock had yet to infiltrate this little corner of society, and most customers wanted the simple melodies of the past.

"You're twiddling your thumbs," she said.

I looked down and saw that I was.

"It keeps my hands warm."

A younger waitress brought over our drinks and put them on the table. When she left, Ruth said, "I'm causing you distress."

"That's absurd," I scoffed. I leaned back in the seat and crossed my arms. "I was distressed way before I met you."

While I had hoped for a laugh, all I got was a smile, and that was enough.

"How's Captain Jackson?" she asked.

I took a deep breath.

"He's lost a ton of weight. But seems to be carrying on."

She looked down at the table sadly.

"Don't expect it to last. He'll probably decline fast."

"I'll take it as it comes."

I must have shifted because the grip of my .38 dug into my underarm, and I winced.

"I shouldn't have done it," she said.

"What do you mean?"

"I shouldn't have gone into his medical record."

When I leaned forward to take her hand, I underestimated the distance and hit her glass. I looked her straight in the eye, lowered my voice, and said, "I asked you to. I needed to know. Harrigan needed to know."

The waitress came over with the food, and we stopped talking. I took my knife and fork and started to eat.

"I'm sorry," she said. "I know I'm a basket case."

"Don't say that."

"I am. You don't deserve this."

The continuous apologies and self-pity were starting to irritate me. I wanted it to stop. Without looking up, I took a slow bite and said, "Ruth, please. Enough."

"I don't know what's wrong with me."

She dropped her utensils and sat back in the chair. It wasn't an outburst, but it was obvious enough that a couple at the next table looked over. I reached across the table, gently took her wrists, and waited for her to look at me.

"We'll get through this. Whatever it is. You're strong. You're tough. Remember when you threw the ashtray at me?"

With a cute grin, she said, "I was drunk."

"But you were right. And remember you got in an argument with a cabbie because he was blocking a wheelchair ramp?"

She nodded.

"That's you. You're a fighter."

Even with all the noise in the restaurant, the space around us seemed to fill with a poignant calm, and we gazed at each other like the first time we met. Sometimes silence communicated more than words, and I could see that she was feeling better. When the young waitress passed by, I stopped her and ordered another water. I turned to Ruth and said, "Want more wine?"

She looked up at the lady, her eyes red, lashes fluttering.

"Sure, why not."

BY THE TIME we were finished, Ruth was as tipsy as I wanted her to be. I paid the bill, and we got up to leave. As we passed the hostess station, the owner thanked us with a wide smile. I put my arm around Ruth's waist, and we pushed through the glass doors and went back into the night.

When we got into the Valiant, the vinyl seats were stiff from the cold. I took her hand, and we waited while the heat came on. Her hair was a mess and her makeup smudged, but her raw beauty counted for much more than elegance. The wine had calmed her body and her mind, and I saw in her face that feminine glow which had first captivated me. She slid over and put her head against my chest. When she looked up, our lips met, and we kissed in the dark. By the force of her passion, I knew it could have gone further, but we were parked on a main road, and I was too old for sexual acrobatics.

"That warmed me up," she said, finally pulling away.

"The wine or the foreplay."

She smiled bashfully.

"Both."

I pulled out, and we headed south along Massachusetts Avenue. It was a quiet Sunday evening, windless and starlit, but the temperature was cold enough to scare an Eskimo. It reminded me of those brutal nights on the Korean front when piss would freeze before it hit the ground.

At the next red light, I looked over, and she was out. To give her time to sleep and to let the wine wear off, I drove aimlessly through Roxbury, past Dudley Square and down Blue Hill Avenue. Except for a few takeout restaurants, everything was closed. The streets were dark and desolate. I continued for almost an hour, wending dreamily through the back roads of my old neighborhood. Before I knew it and not by coincidence, I found myself approaching St Kilda.

When I looked ahead to the entrance, something was not right. There were a half dozen police cruisers parked in front of the gate with their sirens flashing. I turned the wheel and pressed the gas, and the slight, but sudden acceleration woke Ruth up.

"Where are we? What're you doing?" she said, rubbing her eyes.

"Hold on, love."

A few pilgrims hovered in the shadows, but most of the daytime crowd was gone, and the abbey was stunningly calm. I rolled down the window and called out to the first cop I saw.

"What's going on?"

A young officer looked over then came towards us with a flashlight.

"Evening, Detective."

When he crouched down to the window, he peered across to Ruth with an awkward smile.

"Did you get a call?" he said.

"A call?"

"A man was found unresponsive in the tower. A monk, I guess. About an hour ago."

I heard more sirens, and we all turned to see an ambulance coming from the other end of the street.

"Let me by," I said, and the patrolman snapped to.

"Yes, Sir."

He waved the flashlight, and one of the cruisers backed away from the gates. As we started to roll, Ruth clutched my arm and said, "No. Please."

I stopped the car and turned to her.

"You won't?—"

"No," she said. "I can't deal with this."

"You can wait in the car. It won't be long."

"Please. I can't. I'm sorry."

The officer was in the middle of the street, holding off the other vehicles, waiting for me to move.

I put the Valiant into park.

"Here. Take the car," I said. "Are you still drunk?"

She made a tired frown.

"I never was."

"Okay. Drive carefully. Go straight to bed. I'll be home in a bit."

I leaned across the seat, held the back of her head, and kissed her above the eyes. As I reached for the door handle, she said, "How'll you get home?"

I looked out the window at all the patrol cars.

"I'm sure I can get a lift."

I started to get out, but she pulled me back. She put her hands on my cheeks and kissed me so intensely that when she finally let go, I was aroused.

"See you in a bit," I whispered, gasping.

"Be safe."

"I will."

CHAPTER 29

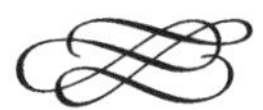

I WALKED THROUGH THE GATES OF ST KILDA AND STARTED UP THE LONG driveway. On the hill to my left, I was amazed to see hundreds of burning candles and lanterns. Everywhere were the dark shapes of tents, shanties, and other temporary dwellings. There wasn't much movement, and the only sounds were quiet voices and the crackling of campfires. Somewhere somebody was strumming a guitar.

With a pound of lasagna in my stomach, I was sluggish so I stopped halfway to rest. Suddenly, a vehicle turned into the entrance below and sped up the hill, its headlights blazing a path in the dark. I heard the low rumble of eight cylinders; the lights were too high to be a car. When it came around the bend, I knew it was a truck. I stood in the road and waved my arms, but it just seemed to speed up. The engine rattled, the white lights glared, and the front grille came at me like a comet. A second before it would have hit me, I jumped out of the way and fell back into a tree.

In the confusion of the moment, I reached for my pistol and had it out. Realizing I was unhurt and unthreatened, I shoved it back in the holster and scurried up the last leg of the driveway. I got to the turn-around by the front door of the abbey and saw the coroner's van parked beside a police cruiser. I ran straight up to it.

"What the hell was that for?!" I yelled.

As Ansell got out, he turned to me with the poise of a deaf man and simply smiled. I walked with him to the back, where he opened a hatch to get his things. I pressed for a response until finally he looked up and said, "Don't get so excited, kid. This place is tense enough as it is."

"You almost ran me down for chrissakes!"

"Wrong place to be blaspheming, son. But you're the Christian—you deal with the consequences." He threw a leather satchel over one shoulder and picked up a gray medical box. "I didn't see you. I can barely see in the day, never mind at night. Legally blind, we call it." As he walked away, I put my hands on my hips and shook my head, still rattled from the near-miss. Then I followed him to the front door.

"Hitchcock couldn't make this shit up," he grumbled. "A body in a tower...on a winter night...in a monastery."

"It's an abbey."

Just as he reached for the handle, the door opened, and we were both startled.

"Jody," a voice said. I looked over to see Sergeant Duggan emerge from the shadows, so tall he had to crouch. "You're a sight for sore eyes. We called for a detective an hour ago."

"I was just..." I said, hesitantly, "passing by."

"Glad you were."

Ansell's eyebrows twitched with impatience, and he squeezed between the two of us.

"While you guys jerk each other off, I'm gonna go see about the stiff."

Duggan rolled his eyes, and we followed the doctor down the corridor. The lighted sconces along the walls created the eerie sensation of walking in a tomb. We passed through the large atrium, where the damaged statue of Christ loomed overhead. We continued down the adjacent hallway towards the bell tower, passing dozens of arched doorways and a chapel.

Ansell proceeded with his head down, neither curious nor impressed by the strange and Gothic atmosphere. The easy answer was he didn't care because he was a Jew, but that was only part of the story. With the exception of horse racing and Yahtzee, he was indifferent to almost everything, and the mystique of Christian monasticism did nothing to intrigue him.

We came to the wooden stairs that led down to the tower entrance, and I saw a small crowd in the dark. An officer was guarding the door, and there were several monks dressed in brown robes and sandals. When my eyes adjusted to the dim light, I noticed a large man among them, his bearing so distinct that I immediately knew it was Father Vogt. His face was tense, his forehead wrinkled. The snot that dripped from his nose might have been from a cold, but it seemed more from distress.

As I came down the stairs, he stepped clumsily forward and bowed.

"D...deeetective," he said. "This is beyond belief!"

He reached out his hand, but I didn't shake it. I approached the group with a cool and professional detachment, making eye contact with everyone at once. Then I looked at the officer.

"What's occurred here?"

He was a young cop—they all looked young—with a buzz cut and the crooked smile of youthful bluster. But when I spoke, he stepped forward respectfully and said, "One of the residents, Sir, was found unresponsive." He pointed to the tower door and added, "In there, on the landing. Reported at 9:17—"

"Deeetective," Vogt interrupted.

The first time we met, I had barely noticed the faint accent of his gutter German, but now it grated on my ears. Without pivoting, I glanced over and snapped, "You'll have your turn to talk."

His politeness turned to indignation, and he glared back like a pompous schoolboy after a scolding.

"It's one of the priests," Duggan said. "No vitals. He's dead."

Vogt huffed.

"A monk," he said. "I'm the only priest in this commune."

I was ready to tell him to shut up when Ansell barged through.

"You men can debate ecclesiastical classifications later. We've got work to do."

The monks parted to let him by, and he opened the tower door and ducked in. I went next, and Duggan and the other officer followed. The space was totally black, and I was glad to see that Duggan and Ansell had flashlights. We climbed up single file, clinging to the iron handrail, our footsteps echoing as we went. Despite his age, the doctor got to the landing first, and he laid down his equipment.

"Tough place for a nap," I heard him say.

I reached the last step, and my eyes went instantly to the massive windows. But when I looked to the top pane, the image was gone. I gasped. Then I realized it was just behind the shadows. I was relieved.

"Brae!"

I was startled and turned around to see Duggan and the other cop standing in the corner. Ansell was on his knees, crouched over the victim and examining the body. Embarrassed by the momentary spell, I hurried over.

"Any signs of foul play?" I asked.

Ansell turned to answer, and I froze when I saw the face of Brother Emmanuel. I must have mumbled something too because Duggan said, "Jody, you know this guy?"

"I...," I tried to speak, but couldn't form the words. The only thing I could say with any confidence was, "Yes."

The doctor stood up.

"I can tell you it's a broken neck," he said, then he looked up the stairwell towards the second landing. "Perhaps a fall."

"You sure?"

"I'm not sure about anything, kid. I'll have to get him under the light, see if there're any contusions. If he fell from up there, there'll be bruising, other injuries."

Ansell finished up, and we got the body loaded on a stretcher. He walked ahead while Duggan, the other cop, and I carried the sheeted corpse down the tower stairs. As we came out, Father Vogt and the monks were waiting in the hallway. The men were visibly upset, and I understood the pain of seeing a comrade killed. Two more officers were standing by to assist, and Duggan ordered them to take our places.

"Who wants to tell me what happened?" I said.

Father Vogt came forward and walked straight up to me.

"I believe we should discuss this in private," he said.

Our eyes locked in a standoff of mutual contempt. It was obvious we didn't like each other, but no one there could have possibly known why. Looking at Vogt, I announced, "Gentlemen, I'm sorry for your loss. Go about your business, please. We'll keep you informed."

When I turned, two dozen eyes were staring back from under heavy brown hoods. Vogt made a quick, forceful nod, and the men started to move. They walked solemnly, two in a row down the hallway until they faded out of view. I stood with my arms crossed, stone-faced and glaring at Vogt.

"Let's hear it."

"Shall we go into the vestry?" he asked, peering over to Officer Duggan.

"Here's just fine."

Vogt appeared shaken from the incident, and he was eager to talk alone. But my trust in him was about equal to my respect for him, which was to say non-existent.

"This is terrible—"

"Who found the body?" I said flatly.

"Unfortunately, I did. We had finished evening prayers. I was in the sacristy tidying up. I heard somebody. When I looked out, I saw Anthony at the end of the hall. It was unusual, he is never here at night—it's not permitted." He spoke fast, his chest heaving under his cloak. I could smell his breath, and it was awful. "So I followed him. He went out the annex. When I passed the bell tower, I saw the door open. I went in and walked up to check on the vision—"

"And you found Brother Emmanuel?"

He closed his eyes and shuddered.

"It was horrid."

"What about Vigliotti?" I asked, and he seemed surprised I knew his last name.

"Gone, Detective. Totally and utterly gone."

Officer Duggan was no longer hovering in the background but now standing beside us.

"Are you implying that Vigliotti had something to do with his death?" I asked.

Vogt waved his index finger in the air.

"Not something. Everything. I'm sure of it."

"How're you sure?"

"He's a bad man, Mr. Brae," he said, pronouncing my name like *brie*. "Quite a wily rascal." The corny phrase was just another indication that he was foreign-born. When I looked at Duggan, we both struggled to keep from laughing. "Check for yourself. He was a criminal once."

"What's his past have to do with now?"

He hesitated then said, "I believe he's been stealing from the abbey for years. Things have gone missing, chalices, crosses."

"Did you ever file a report?"

"No," he said, and when he shook his head, beads of sweat went flying. "There was no proof. The clergy loved him, beguiled by his charm. I was never such a fool."

I heard footsteps and looked to see Harrigan coming down the hallway.

"Lieutenant," he called out as he approached. Leaving Duggan and Vogt behind, I met him halfway, and we stopped by a holy water font. Cold air emanated from his coat; his brown cheeks were chapped.

"One of the monks was found dead in the bell tower," I said.

"I heard. What'd the coroner say?"

"Looks like a neck break."

"An accident?"

"Not according to him," I said, tilting my head towards Vogt. "Said he saw the handyman leaving."

"And Doctor Ansell?

"Not sure yet. He said it could've been from a fall."

"You believe him?"

I looked Harrigan in the eye and said, "I don't believe anyone. But if he says it, we have to look into it."

We heard voices and turned to see two more patrolmen coming. It was obvious that the cops were getting antsy. When they walked up, they weren't looking for details—they wanted a decision. I didn't have the power to declare it an accident or a homicide, but I could set the course of action. With Ansell's uncertainty and Father Vogt's story about Vigliotti, the status had been determined for me. I looked at one of the men and said, "We need this place dusted ASAP."

The officer took the order, turned around, and marched off.

As Vogt stood watching, I whisked by him and went over to the tower entrance. To my surprise, the old key was still in the door, firmly stuck in the corroded mechanism. I crouched down and yelled to ensure no one was inside. Then I pulled it shut and twisted the key until it locked.

I called out to Harrigan, Duggan, the patrolmen—anyone who was listening.

"This must stay secure."

Father Vogt stepped forward, his eyes bulging.

"But this thing is to be expunged next Monday." His refusal to describe it as an image, vision, or even a picture showed the extent of his skepticism. "We need to get inside to do so."

"Expunged?" I said.

"Indeed. The Archdiocese has ordered it so. These people must be evacuated too."

As we stared at each other, I considered the consequences of cleaning the glass and destroying the miracle. I saw the faces of the many pilgrims, poor and defenseless, plodding through the snow. For once I sided with the pious.

"Not my problem."

"This is unacceptable! I must have access to that tower."

When I shook my head, he came closer like he wanted to challenge me. His face was bright red; his teeth were clenched. My instincts told me that if there hadn't been two other cops in the room, he might have tried something stupid.

As a final taunt, which wasn't my style, I held up the rusted key then snapped my hand shut. I shoved it in my pocket and said, "Don't go far. We'll need a witness statement."

EMERGENCY LIGHTS WERE STILL FLASHING by the time Harrigan and I reached the bottom of the driveway. Two men from the Bureau of Criminal Investigations were idling at the entrance, chatting with the detail officers, in no hurry to get to the scene. When they noticed us, one of them waved, and I walked over to the car.

"You'll need this," I said, handing him the key. The man behind the wheel looked up with a fat smile, his fedora tipped back.

"Thanks, Lieutenant," he said. "We'll take good care."

BCI were a crusty bunch—men who worked late hours and were either divorced or never married. Many of them were drunks, and I could smell liquor on the agent's breath. But theirs was a brutal job, so I didn't blame them.

"Leave those with the front office or Captain Jackson."

As I turned to go, he said, "How's the old man doing?"

The question struck me as bold, although I knew he didn't mean it that way. The street seemed to go silent as everyone waited for my reply. The man peered up from the driver's seat; the officers nearby stopped talking and looked over. The universal concern should have made me grateful, but instead, it made me bitter.

"Still on the right side of the ground," I snickered.

I walked off and headed towards Harrigan, who was waiting beside his car in the shadow of the abbey wall. I realized then that, if he hadn't shown up, I would have had to beg some street cop for a lift home.

Someone called my name, and I turned around to see Duggan.

"I heard they're planning to clear this place next Monday," he said.

Like all patrolmen, he was trying to pry for information, and like all detectives, I had to be vague.

"To be honest, I don't care if they nuke it."

"What's your take on tonight?" he asked.

"Wanna know what my mind tells me or my gut?"

"Whichever is full at the moment," he said, and we both chuckled. When I looked over his shoulder, Harrigan was watching from thirty feet away. I took out a pack of cigarettes and handed one to Duggan. After lighting his, I took a drag and said, "It was a hit."

"You're sure of that?"

I stared through the entrance and up the dark hill, where the embers of dying fires and candlelight shimmered like distant stars. It was beautiful really, and who could deny it? I recalled a similar cold night many years before when Russo, Chester, and I had climbed the roof of a vacant building to watch the moon. Those simple days were so far gone that I wondered if they ever really existed.

I flicked my cigarette in the snow and it made a hiss. Then I gave Duggan a grim look.

"As sure as shit."

CHAPTER 30

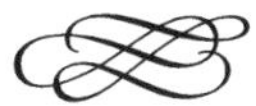

RUTH FINALLY WENT BACK TO WORK. WHEN I AWOKE MONDAY morning and she was gone, I jumped up and flew into a panic. I was just ready to go in the kitchen and call headquarters when I looked over to the closet and saw that one of her uniforms was missing. Laying on the bed, rubbing my eyes, and breathing heavy, I felt like I had just escaped death. I didn't know if the decision meant that she was better, but it certainly meant she wasn't getting worse.

By the time I got to The Armory, it was close to 10 a.m. I hurried down the corridor and was relieved to see the captain's light on. When I got to the door, I stopped and took a few seconds to relax and gather my thoughts. There was sweat on my forehead; my shirt was untucked. I smoothed out my jacket and ran my fingers through my hair, but it still felt tousled. Finally, I opened the door.

"Lieutenant."

When I looked in, Harrigan was sitting across from Jackson. The moment I entered, the captain started to cough, and the noise sent a chill up my spine. It was a dreadful hack, one that began in the throat and ended somewhere near his abdomen. I sat down, and Harrigan acknowledged me with a nod. Once the fit was over, Jackson wiped his mouth with a handkerchief and looked up.

"We were just discussing the incident at the abbey," he said.

"You mean the murder?"

It was supposed to be sarcasm, but nobody laughed.

"Is that your impression?"

I glanced over to Harrigan, who sat up straight, his gray suit perfectly pressed.

"According to the abbot," I said. "He saw someone leave the tower."

"Yes, Detective Harrigan has told me. A handyman?"

"More than a handyman." When I noticed Jackson starting to cough again, I waited. "He's a criminal. Anthony Vigliotti."

"And what are his crimes?"

Harrigan chimed in.

"I pulled his file this morning. Assault, larceny, witness intimidation, armed robbery—the man has a record going back to '42."

The captain acknowledged the fact and said, "And recently? What's he done recently?"

Harrigan looked over at me uncomfortably.

"Well, Sir. Nothing recently. Last conviction was, I believe, sometime in the mid-fifties."

"Seems odd," Jackson said, adjusting his glasses. "Is he in custody?"

"Not yet. He left before the body was discovered. But I got his address."

"Get on that, gentlemen. No time to waste. The monastery..." he said, and I almost corrected him with *abbey*, "...will be cleared a week from today."

"What do you mean *cleared*?" I asked, then I softened the interruption by adding, "Sir."

He coughed suddenly, and it seemed to knock the wind out of him. "Pardon me," he continued, blinking. "Good question, Lieutenant. McNamara called me over the weekend—it's been finalized. Next Monday the Archdiocese will remove the ice from the tower window, and we're responsible for expelling the trespassers. The chief has called in extra manpower."

"Trespassers?"

He must have sensed my indignation because he said, "I know, it's not the most humane solution. But we're not advocates...and the Archdiocese is not obligated. It's their property. It's gonna be a messy job. And if this is a homicide, it's gonna complicate things." He reached towards a manila folder on the desk and tapped it with his fingers. "Crime lab came back with nothing. Clean. Not even a hair."

"A tidy killer."

"No crime is perfect," he said. "And we're still waiting on the prints."

"Prints?"

He opened the report and skimmed the first page.

"Yes, here. Apparently, they pulled some prints off a metal railing."

"Then that's gonna make me a suspect," I joked.

"Well, you should've wiped them."

When he smiled, Harrigan and I smiled back. The fact that he still had his humor meant that he still had some life left in him.

There was an awkward lull as we sat waiting for the captain to dismiss us. Back when he was well, the three of us would spend whole afternoons debating evidence, logistics, witness accounts. Now our discussions seemed to peter out in under an hour. Jackson still had the will, but he had none of the energy.

Finally, he gave us a meek salute, and we both got up to go. As we exited the building, Harrigan walked with a stunned silence I had never seen before. I realized then that, throughout our years as partners, there had never been an opportunity to pity him.

We got in the Valiant and pulled out into the street. When I rolled down the window for a cigarette, he didn't object, another sign that something was wrong. He sat expressionless, completely unreadable, yet somehow I could tell he was sad. We were stuck in traffic on Park Street when a tour guide dressed like Ben Franklin walked by, and I didn't ridicule him. When the light changed, we both spoke at the same time.

"I think something's severely wrong with—"

"The captain's dying."

Harrigan's expression was so bizarre I thought he didn't hear me.

"Did you just say?"

I nodded.

"I did. I'm sorry. I found out last Wednesday."

He took a deep breath and looked straight ahead.

CHAPTER 31

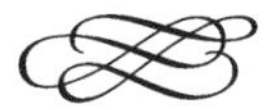

HARRIGAN AND I GOT TO CITY HOSPITAL AT NOON, AND IT WAS BUSIER than I had ever seen it. Automobiles lined up at the curb, and others idled on the driveway, waiting for a spot. I drove by the main entrance and continued around to the side lot, where we parked beside a dumpster. We went in the back door, down a set of stairs, and into the long, dark corridor that led to The Crypt. When we came around the last corner, the door at the end was half-open.

I stuck my head in and saw the doctor and his incompetent assistant standing at the desk. They turned in unison and looked over like we were interrupting a medical operation.

"Detectives," Ansell said, squinting through his glasses. I smelled smoke but didn't see a cigar.

"I'm here about the autopsy."

He put down the clipboard he was holding.

"Autopsy? You mean from the monastery?" he said.

"The abbey."

"Need more time, kid. The body hasn't been here twelve hours. I'm no miracle worker."

Harrigan stepped by me and said, "We think he was murdered—"

"And I don't think that's my problem."

Mayonnaise looked nervously at the doctor then decided to go into the other room. Harrigan and I walked over to Ansell.

"Please. I know you're busy. Can you give us anything? We've got some conflicting events here. The chief plans to disperse the crowd at the abbey in a week."

Ansell looked away, and I sensed that he was embarrassed by his rudeness. "Come. Let's talk." He looked past me to Harrigan and said, "Detective, I'm sorry. Accept my apology."

"Of course."

"Do me a favor, please." He reached in the pocket of his lab coat and pulled out a few crumpled bills. "I'm hungry. Your partner and I... we need to chat. Would you get some coffee, some sandwiches? Anything you want."

Harrigan looked down as the doctor pressed the money into his hand. Then he turned to me as if for permission, and I nodded. Without a word, he pocketed the bills and walked out the door.

In the back room, I could hear the assistant working, and there was soft music playing. Ansell motioned for me to follow, and we went towards the mortuary. Considering the temperature outside, I didn't expect to be uncomfortable, but when we entered the chamber, the frigid air hit me like an electric shock.

"Don't you get cold in here?" I asked.

We went halfway across the room before he answered.

"Never. Even if I did, I prefer solitude to comfort. That's what three months in the Italian Alps will do to you."

He looked around at the rows of corpse compartments stacked against the walls. Marked with only numbers, the anonymous secrecy made me wonder—were they empty or were they not? Above us, two utility lamps dangled from the ceiling and cast a bleak, yellow haze across the room. As we stood facing each other, the steam from our breaths collided.

"Listen, kid," he began. "I've heard some hard news. But I ain't gonna say it. Hear no evil—speak no evil. That's what my mother used to say." His glasses magnified his eyes, and I felt the intensity of his glare. "You can tell me if you want. Or you don't have to—your choice. But I want you to know I understand what you're going through."

His words made me suddenly emotional. Doctor Ansell wasn't the easiest person to deal with, but I wasn't surprised that his were the first condolences I received.

"You mean Captain Jackson?"

He nodded and said, "The very same."

"He's dying."

"I know."

I couldn't ignore the irony of discussing the captain's fate in a morgue. Ansell put his hand on my shoulder, and I trembled. "I know you love the man. I'll be honest—me and him don't exactly see eye to eye. But that don't mean I don't care. You gotta keep it together—you're the only hope for a lot of people."

I thought I felt a tear, but it was only an itch, and I was relieved not to be losing my composure.

"You're a good egg," I said.

"I'll take that as a compliment, kid, much as I hate them."

"You don't like eggs?"

"Ich!" he said, sticking out his tongue with exaggerated disgust. "They make me nauseous...or *nauseated,* which is the proper term." When he drifted towards the corpses, I knew he wanted to show me Brother Emmanuel. "But enough about eggs. If there's anything you need, name it."

"There's one thing," I said, and he stopped. "It's Ruth. She's got problems."

His expression softened.

"What kind of problems?"

"She's depressed."

"Depressed? What's got her depressed, son?"

The fact that he used *son* instead of *kid* was a measure of his concern, and his sympathy.

"I don't know. We've been...been trying to have a child. Not much luck."

He rubbed his chin, stared down in thought.

"Hmm, that's a tough thing for a woman." Then he looked at me and pointed. "And for a man. There's no shame in it. I know what she's feeling."

"You do?"

"Sure I do, kid. My wife couldn't have children so we adopted. My son Marvin, he's no Jew. He looks like Doris Day for chrissakes." As I laughed, he went on, "There wasn't much that could be done back then. They'd tell you to drink chicken broth, chew garlic gloves, sleep with your ass in the air. What'd they know? At least today there're drugs."

"That might be the problem."

"What's she taking'?"

"Clomi—"

"Clomifene?"

When I nodded, he said, "Don't know much about it. Fairly new stuff. Stimulates ovulation."

"It's doing more than that."

"Want me to ask around upstairs?"

"Sure."

"You're sure?"

"Damn sure."

He gave me a warm, almost fatherly smile then patted me on the back. We heard some movement and turned to see Harrigan peek in.

"Detective," the doctor said.

"Sorry, am I interrupting?"

"Not at all. Just getting ready to see the stiff."

"Come join us," I said, waving him in.

Ansell walked over to a compartment in the middle row and waited for us to gather around him.

"Now, I'm not done with the paperwork," he said, turning a steel lever. "But I can tell you..." The latch released with a clang. "...this guy didn't fall."

"You're certain?"

He looked at me, panting slightly from the exertion. "Let me rephrase that: he *may* have fallen. But not from the landing of a stairwell."

He grabbed the metal tray and slowly rolled it out of the chamber. The white sheet was so taut it formed eerily to every contour of the body like the canvas around a mummy. I held my breath in fear of that awful odor of death, which after the war took me years to forget.

Harrigan stood behind and watched over my shoulder as the doctor untied the covering and folded it back. I gasped when I saw the lifeless face of Brother Emmanuel laying with arms stiff by his side. His eyes were closed, his mouth shut, yet somehow, he had the expression of a person in mid-conversation. The ends of his fork beard were gray and curled, probably still growing postmortem.

"Look," Ansell said, grabbing the head and forcing it to one side. There was a muted creak that I thought was the spine but was probably tendons and ligaments. "No contusions—no major indications of trauma." He ran his hands along the cranium, kneading the hair with his fingers. "No blood, no swelling anywhere."

"How'd he break his neck?"

He let go of the corpse, and the head bounced against the tray.

"That's your job, kid," he said, wiping both hands on his coat. "I can only tell you it wasn't from a high-velocity impact."

"Someone did it?" Harrigan asked, and Ansell turned to him.

"You said it, not me."

When I looked at Harrigan, he stared back.

"He'd have to be strong," the doctor added, "I knew guys in the service that could snap a Kraut's neck in a half-second."

We heard a forced cough and looked over to see the intern.

"What is it Mayonnaise?"

"Um, Doctor, a, um—"

"Speak, for chrissakes."

"You have a call."

Ansell gave a quick, irritated nod, and the man was gone. He put back the sheet, slid the tray inside, and locked the compartment. Harrigan and I followed him across the floor, and we all returned to the office, where it was thirty degrees warmer. On the doctor's desk were three cups of coffee and a brown paper bag.

"What've we got here?" he wondered, looking inside.

"Egg salad sandwiches."

He winced and handed the bag to me. Then he took one of the coffees and headed over to the lab to take the call. As he disappeared through the doorway, he mumbled, "Tell your partner how I feel about eggs."

Harrigan looked at me and said, "How's he feel about eggs?"

"They *nauseate* him."

HARRIGAN and I left the hospital in silence. He was putting up a strong front but mainly because we were busy, and work was a wonderful distraction for the brokenhearted. We went out the back, stepping over puddles and wading through slush. As we approached the dumpster beside the Valiant, I heard some shouting and stopped. I peered around and saw a woman standing in the parking lot and facing a black car. She was beyond furious, pointing at the windshield, cursing and screaming.

When the car door opened and a man got out, I figured it just was another lovers' spat. I grimaced at Harrigan, and we started to go, but he quickly stopped me.

"See who it is, Lieutenant?"

I looked carefully and realized it was Sid Mardini. He approached the lady like he was going to either hug or hit her. Harrigan and I stayed back and observed, but if Mardini got aggressive, we were ready to intervene. When something he said made her react, the woman turned away exasperated, and it was Ms. Stuart. Mardini grabbed both her arms, forced her to listen. I could hear his low, threatening voice from twenty yards away.

Suddenly, she tore one of her hands free, slapped him across the face, and marched off. Mardini started to follow but then stopped. He wasn't a man used to chasing after what he wanted—he expected it to come to him.

When he ran back to the car and got in, I said, "Watch him!" and Harrigan and I came out from the corner. I thought he was going after Ms. Stuart, but instead, he drove to the exit and screeched out of the lot.

"What the hell was that all about?" I said to myself.

"Quite an odd pair."

I looked at Harrigan and said, "I gotta tell Ruth about this."

We left the car in the side lot and walked around to the hospital entrance. Things were less busy than when we had first arrived, with only a few ambulances and a utility truck parked out front. While Harrigan waited outside, I went through the doors and into the lobby. I walked over to the counter, where a fleet of receptionists was fielding calls, picking up and slamming receivers with the fury of switch operators. It took three minutes before anyone was free, and the moment one was, I blurted, "Can you call the 4th floor, ask for Ruth?"

The lady barely acknowledged me, but instead took the phone and dialed. As I waited, I scanned the lobby anxiously on the odd chance that Ruth was passing through. The receptionist hung up and said, "Ruth Brae has gone for the day."

"Gone? Whaddya mean gone?"

"Gone means not here, Sir."

I ignored the sarcasm and left. I walked outside and Harrigan was standing by a police cruiser, talking through the window. As I approached, I saw that it was Sergeant Duggan.

"That was fast," Harrigan said.

"She's not here."

"Where is she?"

"Don't know," I said, still surprised. "Maybe on break."

"Is this her break time?"

I pursed my lips and said, "Nope."

I bent down and looked in at Duggan, who was reclined in the driver's seat, a cup of coffee in hand.

"You look agitated, Jody."

"I'm always agitated. And you look comfortable."

"I'm always comfortable," he said, and we both chuckled. "Got a cigarette?"

I reached in my coat and gave him one from a crumpled pack. When he asked for a light, I said, "Want me to smoke it for you too?"

He frowned, and I held out the lighter for him.

"What're you doing here?" I asked.

"A woman collapsed at the abbey. Ambulance just brought her in. Dehydration, most likely."

"That's awful."

"It's only the beginning," he said. "There're too many people in one place. Must be five thousand today."

"Any trouble?"

He shrugged his shoulders, took a long drag.

"No trouble, but plenty of problems," he said. "Red Cross arrived today, food and water to the elderly, all that good shit."

I looked sideways at Harrigan, then nodded for us to go.

"Don't let your compassion kill you, Giraffe," I said.

He flicked the ash and gave a dry laugh.

"We don't get paid for compassion."

CHAPTER 32

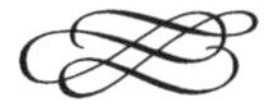

HARRIGAN AND I SAT IN THE BOOTH AT VICTORIA'S DINER, SIMMERING under a tenuous silence, eating without enthusiasm. Our choice of entrees couldn't have emphasized more our different backgrounds: he had liver and onions, and I had a tuna melt. About the only habit we shared in common was a love for Dr. Pepper, which we each drank in plenty and always on ice. Our partnership didn't work in spite of our difference but as a result of them. Maybe I was feeling sentimental because I had never felt more grateful to have him on my side.

"How's Ruth?"

"Pardon?" I said, surprised by the question. "Ruth? She's okay. She's fine."

He took a last bite, finished his drink.

"Is that true?"

When I looked up, our eyes met, and all formality was gone.

"No."

"She's a lovely woman—you're a lucky man."

His style was so understated it made me almost self-conscious.

"Thanks. She's depressed."

The waitress came over and dropped the bill on the table.

"We've been…trying to," I said, stumbling, "…trying to have a child."

"That's a wonderful thing."

"Haven't had much luck."

As I reached for the bill, he snapped it up.

"My mother used to say, *what's not today, will be tomorrow*."

He could express more with a few words than most people could with a dissertation. I smiled warmly and said, "Let's go find Vigliotti."

He placed some bills on the table and we left. The break had done us both good, and he even smiled once or twice. We hopped in the car and raced toward downtown.

Soon we reached the North End, a dense Italian ghetto that was one square mile and bordered the waterfront. Hanover Street ran through the middle and was lined with Neapolitan cafés, Sicilian cheese shops, butchers, and tailors. Automobiles were double-parked everywhere, and traffic flowed in a slow but steady stream like the canals of Venice. Young men in chinos and leather jackets loitered in doorways, congregated on stoops. I felt their stares as we passed by.

I took a left on Prince Street and drove a few blocks. The narrow roads were narrower from the snow, and the driving was treacherous. I turned onto Margaret Street, a tiny lane no wider than a footpath, and we rolled slowly past the tenements. All the flower boxes were barren; figurines of Mary and other Saints hung in the windows. When we reached number 16, I looked at Harrigan and said, "You sure this is it?"

"You were the one who got the address, Lieutenant."

"Right."

With no place to park, I left the Valiant in the street and turned off the engine. The space was so tight my door bumped against the building, and I had to squeeze to get out. Harrigan came around to my side, and we walked through the main door into a cramped foyer. On the peeling beige wall was a directory of names: Coppola, Longo, Bozzella, Natale, Vigliotti. I pressed the last buzzer and waited.

A door opened at the top of the stairwell, and a woman shouted down.

"Hello!?"

I looked up, and she was leaning over the railing.

"Whaddya want?" she said.

"Are you related to Anthony Vigliotti?"

"Who are you?"

"Ma'am, can we talk?"

"About what? Whaddya wanna talk about?"

I looked at Harrigan and rolled my eyes.

"We need to talk with your son."

"My son? My son died fifteen years ago. So you can't talk to him, right?"

The back and forth could have gone on for hours, and I was losing my patience. Without a summons, it was impossible to question someone who didn't want to give answers. I shook my head and motioned to Harrigan to leave. Suddenly, the foyer door opened, and a man stepped in with two bags of groceries. Cradled in his arms, they blocked his face, and we couldn't see him.

As I went to hold the door, he pivoted, and I saw that it was Vigliotti. Instantly, his expression dropped. He shoved the groceries at me and ran out the door. The bags ripped open and stuff went everywhere. In the small space, Harrigan and I stumbled over each other, slipping on cans of peas and rolls of toilet paper.

Once outside, I looked up and down the sidewalk, still stunned from the encounter.

"Over there, Lieutenant," Harrigan said, pointing towards the end of the street.

With my eyes fixed on Vigliotti's green jacket, I ran after him, and Harrigan stayed close behind. When we got to the next corner, he was still two blocks ahead, but we were closing the gap. The ground was slippery, the sidewalks were unshoveled in sections, and the parked cars were so close together we couldn't get between them. It was like an obstacle course.

Harrigan and I turned at the next corner and stopped. When we looked, we saw Vigliotti running wildly down a long but gradual hill, his legs and arms flailing. I hunched forward exhausted and even Harrigan, five years younger, was out of breath.

"Are you alright, Lieutenant?"

"Sure," I said. "Let's walk for a bit."

We started down the hill after him, walking fast but not running. The figure of Vigliotti was still visible in the distance, and our only hope now was that he, too, ran out of steam. But it didn't happen that way.

"Lieutenant!"

When Harrigan shouted, I looked to the intersection below, and there were two cars stopped in the middle of the street with their doors open. There had been no screech—no loud horn, yet someone was lying in the road. By the time we got to Commercial Street, a small crowd had gathered, and I saw the green of Vigliotti's jacket. Harrigan took out his badge and held it up, and the pedestrians moved out of the way.

Flat on his back, Vigliotti's eyes were wide open, and he was staring at the sky. When I knelt down, he moaned.

"Why'd you run?" I said to myself.

He gave me a sideways glance and tried to talk, but all that came out was bloody saliva. An ambulance must have been nearby because I was surprised to see two medics coming over with a stretcher. While Vigliotti faded in and out of consciousness, I offered him words of encouragement I wasn't sure he deserved. Finally, I went to stand up, and he grabbed my arm. As he labored to speak, I put my ear to his mouth, and he whispered something unclear, "Mar—"

CHAPTER 33

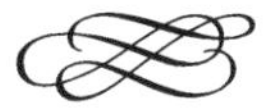

VIGLIOTTI'S AUNT KNEW ABOUT THE ACCIDENT MINUTES AFTER IT happened. In a place where everyone watched out for everyone, the eyes of the neighborhood were on every street corner, in every public park. When we returned to 16 Margaret Street, we expected her to chase us away with pots and pans. Instead, Martina Vigliotti invited us up to her apartment with a sad kindness. She made tea, put out some Italian cookies, and we sat on the sofa of her small living room.

"I'm sorry I was rude," she said. "I'm not usually rude."

Her voice quivered; her eyes were teary.

"We understand."

She was over sixty, with broad shoulders and jet-black hair that had no grays. With her plump breasts and round figure, she had the peasant beauty of a working-class housewife, and I was sure she had turned heads in her day.

"Tony was scared, I was scared for him," she said. "I'm overprotective, always have been. It's my nature. But he wouldn't have anything to do with that monk's death."

"We didn't say he did," I said. "We just needed to talk to him."

"Who was he scared of, Ma'am?" Harrigan asked.

"Don't know. He'd been acting strange in the past few weeks. I felt like something was wrong. He came home late last night upset. I thought it was the girlfriend, they're always fighting. He grabbed some things, said he was sleeping at the garage—"

"The garage?" I said.

"He works a few nights a week at a motorcycle garage on Hanover Street. Mostly guys he grew up with. It's more like a social club, especially in winter. They hang around, have beers, chew the fat..." She rolled her eyes. "...And God knows what else, those boys."

I sipped my tea and asked gently, "He likes motorcycles, does he?"

"All his friends have them, must be an Army thing. Since he came back from the war"

"Korea?"

"Yes, yes, he went to Korea, was a paratrooper, got the purple medal and everything. It changed him; he was never the same." I glanced over to Harrigan, but he was too busy listening. "He got into trouble after the war. His mother died while he was over there. His father—my husband's brother—died when he was a boy. I ain't saying that was the cause, but he got involved with some bad people, did some bad things."

"It's never easy coming home."

"Thank God he found God," she said, and I couldn't tell if she was being smart.

"He's religious?"

"Yep," she said, touching the tiny gold cross on her neck. "He came back to the Church, finally. Became a completely different man. Which is why he loves working at St Kilda. He loves that abbey. He would never..."

As she stared off dreamily, I looked around the apartment. It had the familiar modesty of any blue-collar home, with a Sears Roebuck sofa, mismatched end tables, and an RCA console television that was probably ten years old. The curtains were handmade, and the floral wallpaper had water stains near the ceiling. In the corner, a curio held figurines, a decorative kettle, and framed family pictures.

I looked towards the windows and saw that it was starting to get dark.

"Well," I said with a sigh, "we need to get going."

When I stood up, Harrigan and Mrs. Vigliotti did the same.

She smoothed out her dress and looked at me.

"When do you think we'll know about Tony? When can I see him?"

"I would call the hospital in an hour or two unless you hear from them sooner."

"Let's hope that doesn't happen."

We made our way to the door, and I saw it had three locks. As we stepped out to the landing, she lingered in the doorway like she didn't want us to go. I didn't ask if she was married because I didn't want to know, but she seemed like a lonely soul.

"I hope I was helpful," she said with a nervous smile.

"You were."

"Call me if you have any more questions."

I turned to leave then stopped.

"Oh," I said, and her eyes flickered. "What exactly does Tony do at the garage?"

"He paints gasoline tanks," she said, with a bashful pride. "Illustrations and drawings. He's an artist."

CHAPTER 34

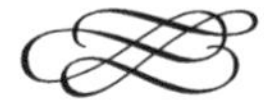

When we got back to The Armory, rush hour was over, and it was dark. I pulled into the front lot and stopped to let Harrigan out.

"Get some rest," I said.

He pulled on his gloves, turned up his collar.

"I don't know if I can, Lieutenant."

"That's an order."

He was too upset to laugh or even smile. He got out, and I watched him lumber towards his car like a man who just found out his wife had cheated on him.

I drove through the night with the heat on full force. Fatigue and anxiety were like weak insulation, and I couldn't seem to get warm. When I got home, I looked up to the third floor, and the lights were on. I was so eager to get in that I slipped on the icy steps but grabbed the railing just in time. Then I walked into the vestibule and realized Ruth hadn't gotten the mail.

I plodded up the stairs and opened the apartment door. At first, I didn't see her, then I looked over to the couch, and she was lying on her side, curled in a ball. I could hear whimpering; her little body shook. I dropped the mail and ran to her side.

"What's wrong?!"

I tried to rotate her, but she wouldn't budge. Her face was a tangled mess of hair, tears, and mascara.

"Tell me, tell me what's wrong," I said softly.

Each time she began to speak, her words were lost in a throaty exasperation.

"I don't…I got…I'm…I'm in big trouble."

"Trouble? What trouble?"

On the coffee table, there was a bottle of wine, a half-filled glass, and a Woman's Day magazine. I leaned close to her ear and whispered, "Ruth, please—"

When she finally lifted her head, the pillow had makeup stains. She looked at me with tormented eyes and said, "I...I got called into my supervisor this morning—"

"Go on."

I listened and nodded, not taking my eyes off her.

"And…and…she asked me about the record. About Captain Jackson's record. If I had viewed it."

"What did you say?"

She frowned then looked away with a pout.

"*Yes*, of course. What was I gonna say? I'm not going to lie."

She wiped her eyes and leaned up on one elbow.

"Ms. Stuart said…she said I was…I was suspended pending further review."

She started to cry again but stopped. She had no more tears—her despondency had exhausted itself. Sorrow was a stubborn thing, but it couldn't go on forever. I got her to sit up, and we snuggled close in quiet reflection, gazing off in separate directions. We were both ashamed but for different reasons.

"How'd they know?"

"I don't know," she moaned. "All the nurses snoop. Two weeks ago, Johnny Havlicek was on the floor, everyone wanted to know why."

"Why?"

She made a sour smile.

"A hernia," she said. "There's much worse that goes on, believe me. But Ms. Stuart hates me."

"She seemed cordial at Sagansky's that night."

"That's the problem. I think she was worried I saw her with that man."

"Sid Mardini?" I said. "I saw them together at the hospital this afternoon. They were arguing in the parking lot. It was pretty ugly."

She looked away with a guilty stubbornness that suggested she knew more.

"Did you tell anybody we saw them at the diner?" I asked.

Her hesitation was confirmation enough, but I sat silent and waited for her to respond.

"Maybe a few of the nurses," she mumbled. When I rolled my eyes, she raised her voice and said, "I wasn't the only one. Lots of people know."

"Ruth, you didn't."

"I'm sorry. The bitch is cheating on her husband. You want me to pretend?—"

"Don't trust anybody!" I snapped, and her face dropped. With my arm around her, I felt her back muscles tighten. It was cynical advice from a hardened soul, and I regretted giving it. She may have been feisty, but deep down she had an innocence I cherished and never wanted to see tainted.

"I didn't mean that," I said. "I'm sorry. But did anyone see you look at the record?"

"No. I mean, yes. The woman who works there, of course."

I thought about the day Harrigan and I went looking for information on the murder victim. All they recorded was a first name—they allowed the woman to flee right after giving birth. A department that sloppy had no business reprimanding Ruth.

"I don't want to lose my job," she said.

"You won't."

She leaned into my chest and stared off at nothing. When I was sure she had calmed down, I helped her to her feet, and we walked slowly to the bedroom arm in arm. She started to undress, and I reached for the lamp on the bureau. Beside a framed picture of her and her father was the refill bottle of her fertility pills, unused and unopened. Whether she read my expression or heard my thoughts, I didn't know. But she looked over and said, "You're mad I stopped taking them."

"No," I said, but it wasn't completely true.

"They do something to me."

"I know."

In the pale light of the room, she stood in front of the closet, naked and watching. The shadows beneath her breasts, her feminine curves —they tempted me with a seductive passion. Despite my headache, hunger, and exhaustion, I was instantly aroused. I turned away and put my wallet and keys on the dresser, worried I might have misread her cues. She tiptoed up behind me, and I felt her hands on my waist, her nipples against my back. I froze.

"You're not doing this for me, I hope," I said.

"This is for us."

She began to undo my belt.

"But you're tired."

"I'm always tired."

I shut off the light and turned around. With eyes closed, I found her lips, and we kissed. Together we tore off the remainder of my suit and fell into a fit of lust that seemed far beyond the capacity of our drained and weary selves. Flailing and groping, we somehow made it onto the bed, and she pulled me into her. For a minute or two, the creaks and moans of our mutual ecstasy filled the room. Then silence.

CHAPTER 35

When I awoke the next morning, the pillows were on the floor, the sheets were tangled, and we both lay flopped across the bed. The room was chilly, as it always was at dawn, and I thought I heard rain, although it might have been a passing airplane.

I got up and went into the bathroom to piss and brush my teeth. As I stumbled back towards the bedroom, I stopped in the doorway and stared at Ruth. With legs turned in opposite directions and her hair a ratty mess, she looked like a French prostitute after a rough night.

"What're you doing?" she whispered, stretching her arms.

"Watching you."

"I'm sure I look glorious."

"More than you know."

I left her alone and went to the kitchen, where I filled the teapot and lit the stove. I turned on the news, and Mayor White was giving a press conference at City Hall. At the first mention of St Kilda, my eyes popped open and I listened. The station cut to the abbey, where a mob was pouring through the front gates. What had been an orderly gathering a week before was now chaos as people shoved and thrashed to get in. The camera next went to a reporter on the street who was interviewing an elderly man and his granddaughter.

As I stared at the screen, the camera bounced around. Suddenly, I saw Sweeney's mother in the background. My chest got heavy, and I even felt afraid, although I didn't know why. For a moment, I thought our eyes met then realized it was absurd. The kettle was whistling, but I ignored it. Ruth ran out in a white bathrobe and turned off the burner.

"Are you okay?" she said.

The station flashed to the latest on the Tet Offensive and, sadly, I lost interest. Having lived through the Second World War and fought in Korea, Vietnam was like a hangover. And considering that I didn't drink, it wasn't my problem.

"Pardon?"

"Never mind."

She poured two cups of tea and sat beside me on the couch. Her eyes were sullen, her expression blank.

"Was that about the monk?"

"No. That hasn't gotten out yet," I said.

"What do you think happened?"

"I think it was murder."

"Ugh," she said. "What a world."

"How're you feeling?"

She looked at me.

"Sad. Sad and scared."

I leaned over, put my hand on her leg, and kissed her cheek.

"It'll be okay."

"You promise?"

"I promise."

I finished the tea and went to shower and get dressed. When I came out, she was lying on the sofa with her eyes half-shut. The Lucy Show was on, but the volume was down, and she wasn't watching it. I got a blanket from the closet and draped it over her.

Before I left, I leaned over to give her a kiss.

"Don't sleep all day," I said.

"I have to pick up my check."

"I'd stay away from the hospital for a few days."

I grabbed my coat off the rack and opened the door.

"Jody," she said, and I turned around. There was a faint despair in her voice, more of longing than of sorrow. "Are you mad?"

"I asked you to pull Jackson's record."

"That's not what I'm talking about."

The Ivory Snow commercial that was on the TV couldn't have been more poignant—a woman holding a newborn in her arms. If Ruth noticed, she didn't let on, but she waited for my response. I looked at her with a vague but heartfelt smile.

"What's not today, will be tomorrow."

I PULLED into The Armory just before 8 a.m.—a record time for me. The sun was bright, and the days were getting longer. Even in the darkest pit of winter, the indications of a weather salvation were never far off.

When I parked and got out, Harrigan was crossing the lot towards me.

"It's two hours before your start time," he said as he approached.

Considering how upset he was the day before, it was a relief to hear him joke.

"I'll put in for OT."

Together we walked up the front steps and into the building. As we went by the front desk, the brunette secretary was at the counter in a black polka dot dress, her hair in a bun. She was assisting an officer from another town or county, and I didn't recognize the badge. In the corridor, we passed two captains, and I overheard them talking about the abbey. The situation was reaching a crescendo and, with only five days until the eviction, everyone was anxious about what would happen.

We walked over to Jackson's door, and I knocked once. When after a minute there was no response, I opened it and peered in. The room seemed empty at first, then I heard a feeble voice call out, "Ah, Detectives." He was standing by a file cabinet in the corner, his hands buried in the top drawer. His trademark tweed coat hung over his frail body like an oversized robe; his hair was brittle and uncombed.

"Brae," he said.

He almost never used my last name. It was *lieutenant* for business and, on the rare occasion, *Jody* when it was personal.

"Good morning, Capt."

"Morning it is," he said, looking at the wall clock. "Good? We'll see."

He waved us in, and we sat down. With a folder under his arm, he closed the file cabinet and returned to his desk. He had a hunched back; his arms were thin. There were stains on his white shirt, either from a spill or the persistent coughing. He looked almost helpless.

"Now," he said, clearing his throat. "What's the story with Vigliotti?"

"We went to his aunt's house, and he walked into us in the foyer—"

"And he immediately ran," Harrigan said.

"Down a hill, into an intersection."

Using my hand and fist, I motioned an automobile running into somebody, and Jackson winced at the impression.

"His condition?"

"Don't know. Grave yesterday."

He clasped his hands, looked beyond us, and wondered aloud.

"Is such behavior an indication of guilt?"

"Probably," I said.

"Probably not."

He opened the case folder on his desk and took out some documents. He adjusted his glasses, something he did more frequently now.

"The prints on the railing in the tower were a match for Vigliotti," he said.

I looked over to Harrigan, who raised an eyebrow but was otherwise unmoved. With the reluctance of someone forced to defend a scoundrel, I said, "It puts him in the tower but doesn't implicate him. He had access. He goes up to the belfry to clear off ice, etc. He was the first person to see the image."

Jackson acknowledged my reasoning with a slow nod then flipped to the next page.

"Speaking of divine intervention," he said. "It would seem someone's been playing God. Tell me. How old was Brenda Mardini?"

I blinked and said, "Twenty-six, I believe."

"And what year would that put her birth?"

"1942."

"Well," he said, and he slid a document across the desk towards me. "How about 1912?"

Still confused, I reached for the paper and read it. It was a Xerox copy of an old birth certificate, handwritten and stamped with the Department of Live Births seal. The words were heavily faded, as much from the copy as from age. Harrigan leaned over and examined it too.

I looked up and said, "I don't get it."

"Look closer at the birthdate."

The longer I stared at the line, the more I detected something funny about the text. I studied the tiny swirls, following where they started and ended. It took a moment, but eventually, I realized the number "4" was superimposed. More significant than that, however, was the word "stillborn" at the bottom, just above the signatures. I handed it back to Jackson.

"A fraud?" I said.

"A damn fraud."

I shook my head and mumbled, "Ansell was right."

"Pardon?"

"Doctor Ansell," I said, speaking up. "When Mardini came in to claim the body, Ansell didn't believe it was his niece."

"Not a niece," he said. "Perhaps his grandniece. Her father Frank was Sid Mardini's uncle."

"Mardini said his brother's name was Frank."

"Must be an Italian tradition."

"They're Armenian."

The captain paused with a curious look. Being a Yankee from Maine, as generic as Johnny Appleseed, he struggled with the cultural distinctions of Boston's ethnic stew.

"Nevertheless," he continued, "he's covering up for someone."

"Then we have him dead to rights."

"Hardly. We have him on perjury, nothing more. We can't even prove he altered the document. He's got someone in the vital records office, that's obvious."

"We could question him, get him nervous," Harrigan suggested.

"A man like Mardini doesn't get nervous."

The captain looked at us with a long, simmering glare, the kind he used to give when he was well. For a fleeting second, I imagined that he was.

"Who's he covering up for?" he said. "And why?"

It would have been too easy to pin Anthony Vigliotti as a killer. There was no doubt he had a mean streak and my own experience that Halloween night was proof enough. But an old resentment was no basis for a murder charge, and it was hard to find a motive in someone who hadn't even had a parking ticket in a decade. Growing up in Roxbury, we all inherited an inner rage that had no reason or origin—it was just there. Maybe Vigliotti had, in fact, changed.

"Something...was...said," I said shakily. "Yesterday, after the accident—"

I didn't have to look up because I could feel Jackson's gaze.

"Go on, Lieutenant," he said.

"Vigliotti mumbled something. It was hard to tell, he was fading..." I shifted in the chair like a nervous witness. Withholding small but crucial details would make any detective feel inept. "...he might have said 'Mardini'...or maybe 'Martina,' his aunt's name."

"Or maybe *Martini*," the captain joked, and we all laughed, "Maybe he was crying out for a drink."

I shrugged my shoulders.

"I don't know. It probably wasn't 'Mardini.'"

"Or maybe it was."

There was silence. Jackson leaned over the desk thinking. His mind worked like a machine, considering all the possibilities and outcomes. But despite his reasoning skills, he operated more on instinct than on fact. He was a man who believed that, in the grand scheme of life, a compass was more important than a map.

Finally, he looked up.

"The priest was certain he saw Vigliotti leave the abbey?"

"Father Vogt?" I said, surprised. "If he wasn't sure, he was determined to be."

With a subtle squint, he acknowledged the implication and said, "He was also determined to have the abbey evacuated. The chief told me so."

"Vogt said it was the Archdiocese."

"At the abbot's behest." He coughed into his hand and said, "Why is a man who is so committed to the poor and vulnerable so determined to dash their hopes?"

"Who says he's committed?"

"He's been there twenty-five years."

"Twenty-three," Harrigan corrected. "He arrived after the war."

The captain's thinning white eyebrows furrowed.

"*Arrived*? From where?"

"Berlin?"

"A German?"

"Yeah, but you'd never know by his accent."

Jackson looked over to Harrigan.

"Get me everything you can on Vogt. His background, education, previous assignments."

Harrigan stood up and snapped to like a soldier.

"Should I consult with immigration?" he asked.

"Call Interpol, call the CIA. Call his mother for heaven's sake. I wanna know what this guy had for breakfast."

His enthusiasm made me smile because it was like the old days. Harrigan took his things and flew out the door.

"I don't trust Vogt," Jackson said to me. "I haven't met him, but I don't trust him."

"That makes two of us."

He leaned forward with a penetrating look that demanded I elaborate.

"There may be more to it," I said.

CHAPTER 36

RUSSO AND I NEVER FORGOT CHESTER SWEENEY OUTRIGHT, BUT WITH the whirlwind pace of young adulthood, we began to think of him less. Then two weeks after graduation, the incident at the abbey came raging back into our lives like a curse. It was a sunny Saturday morning, and Russo picked me up in his father's '36 Plymouth P-6. Because he was still *waiting to sprout,* as his mother would say, he could barely touch the pedals, and I was amazed he had passed the license exam. The trees were all in bloom; the scent of summer was in the air. There was stubble on our chins and sex on our minds.

"You sure about this place?" I said.

"Sure as shit."

He reached to the backseat and handed me a can of Pabst Blue Ribbon.

"It's warm."

"Take it or leave it. It's free."

For the whole day, we drove around Roxbury, stopping by all the familiar hangouts: basketball courts, city parks, drug stores, pool halls. There were gangs on every street corner, and each group—Irish, Italian, black, Jewish, etc.—guarded its territory like a contested national border. Having a car meant status in a neighborhood where probably one in ten families owned one, and we felt like princes of the world. But we weren't on parade, and once we had finished a few beers, we headed eagerly to our destination.

"How much?"

"Eight bucks," Russo said, reaching back for another beer. I dug in my pocket and pulled out a handful of nickels, dimes, and quarters. "Don't worry. They'll take whatever you got."

I couldn't decide which was stranger—that a whorehouse accepted change, or that they charged such a random amount. Either way, it was a lot of money at a time when most people made forty cents an hour. I had emptied my entire savings for the occasion.

"You got rubbers?"

"No," he said, shaking his head. "They put them on."

In the year and a half since Sweeney's death, Russo had gone from a boy to a man. Although still thin, he was growing, and his high-pitched voice had settled to a passable baritone. He had always been like a little brother, but he was fast catching up.

We passed through Dudley Square and went down a narrow lane of commercial buildings and empty lots. Wedged between a machine shop and glass company was a three-story row house, left over from a time when the area was still residential. He turned at the next corner and parked on the curb.

"Where is it?" I asked.

He pointed his thumb.

"Back there. That house back there."

"Looks empty."

"Oh man," he said with a mischievous smirk. "If that's empty, then we're in empty heaven."

Like most of his quips, it didn't make sense but was funny. We guzzled two more beers, then he took out a pint of Bacardi rum and handed it to me.

"Go on," he said. "Get nice and sauced."

The first swig burned, the second wasn't as harsh, and by the third round, my body began to tingle. We passed the bottle back and forth until it was gone, washing away the jittery anticipation of what was to come.

We got out of the car and stumbled up the sidewalk, so drunk we bumped into each other—twice. As we turned the corner and went towards the building, I saw a dirt parking lot across the street.

"Why didn't you park there?"

"You crazy?" he said. "All I need is for one of my pop's friends to drive by and see his car."

"Who are you kidding? They're probably all inside."

We both chuckled and walked up to the door. The wood shingles were splintered; the window shades were all drawn. It looked like a haunted house. Russo knocked more times than necessary, and we waited.

Moments later, the door opened, and a black lady peered out. She was the first woman I ever saw in blue jeans, and because she didn't look like a hooker, I was worried we had the wrong address.

"What's doin' boys?" she said with a flair.

"We're here for the card game."

She looked up and down the street.

"Come on in."

She brought us into a shabby foyer and turned around.

"Phew," she said, waving her hand. "Now ain't you drunker than Cooter Brown!"

We looked at her with guilty grins.

"How old is you boys?"

"Old enough," Russo said, trying to suppress a hiccup.

When she laughed, every joint in her body seemed to swivel.

"Okay, you got some money?"

Russo and I immediately reached in our pockets. While he pulled out a neat stack of bills, I took out a few crumpled singles and a mound of coins. The woman cupped her hands, and we dumped everything into them. She stuffed the cash into her jeans then reached for a cigar box on the radiator. She took out some playing cards and handed us each one.

"Now get on up there, find yo rooms, sweet thangs."

She strutted into the next room, and we stood gazing at the staircase. If Russo was apprehensive, I was outright terrified, but I couldn't let him know. So I started up first, and he followed. As we slowly ascended, the steps creaked, and I couldn't tell if our swaying was from the booze or because the stairs were uneven.

We came to a second floor with a long hallway and many rooms. I heard muted voices, and somewhere a radio was playing. We crept forward, side by side like soldiers on reconnaissance, facing in opposite directions. When we reached the third door and saw a Queen of Hearts taped to it, I glanced down at my card and it was a match.

"This is me."

Russo looked at me, bug-eyed and red in the face.

"See you in a bit," I whispered. "Any problems...shout. You hear?"

He nodded and continued down the corridor. I took a deep breath, grabbed the knob, and opened the door. Inside a woman was standing by the far wall in a white negligee. She was close to thirty, with curly blonde hair and freckles. She may have been average-looking, but she was voluptuous, and that meant more than beauty for a horny teen.

"How old are you?"

"I...I'm seventeen," I said.

"You ever been with a woman?"

"Tons," I said, and she smirked.

I held up my card, and she told me to come over. When I looked around, there was a mattress in one corner and a table lamp on the floor. Otherwise, the room was barren.

Before I got close, she pushed off her straps, and the gown floated to the floor. Her bare white body, with its endless curves and crevices, made me gasp.

"Take your clothes off, Romeo," she said, and I grinned nervously.

While I undid my belt and unbuttoned my shirt, she laid down and watched me with a seductive glare. I was so excited that I tried to walk before my pants were off and tripped. I stumbled forward across the room and somehow landed beside her on the mattress. She giggled and pulled me towards her.

"Had a little too much to drink?"

Before I could answer, she started kissing my face and neck. She reached down to my crotch, and when I felt her hand, I froze up.

"Do you have a rubber?" I asked.

She swung her leg over and mounted me like a steed. She put both hands on my chest and said, "A rubber? Why? You have syphilis?"

"W...what's that?"

"Never mind. I don't use them. I'm allergic to latex."

She lowered herself onto me, and the moment I went inside her, a wet tingle rippled through my body.

"Now take your eight bucks out of me, you little stud," she said.

She started to rock up and down. She was heavier than me, and the floor creaked under us. I frantically grabbed her hips, ass, breasts—anything I could reach. The room began to spin, and soon I got dizzy. She went faster, harder. It should have been the most exciting three minutes of my life, but I was too drunk to enjoy it. All I could think was *please make it stop*. Then in one surge of unbearable pleasure, it all came to an end.

Instantly, she rolled over and curled up at the edge of the mattress. With her back to me, I stared at the ceiling and listened to her breathe. My heart pounded; my legs were trembling. I was overcome by a warm sentiment that I mistook for love, and it gave me the urge to caress her.

"Take your things," she said. "Go."

I gazed tenderly at her, wondering who she was and where she was from. I was just ready to touch her shoulder when she barked, "Go, kid! Will ya? And shut the door."

Still, she wouldn't look at me. I rose from the mattress and staggered across the room to my clothes. Somehow, I pulled on my pants, shirt, and shoes, and got back to my feet. As I headed for the door, I looked across to her with a vacant longing. I recalled Russo's earlier remark about *empty heaven,* and he couldn't have been more right.

I quietly closed the door as I entered the hallway. I was so drunk I had to cling to one of the banisters for balance. I heard somebody downstairs, and in one of the rooms, people were talking. An older man who looked like a doctor or a lawyer came up the stairs and walked by. I averted my eyes, and neither one of us acknowledged the other.

I waited and waited, but there was no sign of Russo. So I decided to look for him. I stumbled down the hallway, putting my ear against each door. I must have passed four or five rooms and was nearing the end when I heard giddy laughter and was sure it was him. I stopped at the last room and saw the King of Diamonds. In a feat of drunken chance, I turned the knob and opened the door.

What I saw next, I couldn't have imagined in my worst nightmare.

"Vat are you doing, you little monster!"

Terror did strange things to the mind because when I saw the priest from the abbey lean up in a bed, my first thought was, *why did my room only have a mattress*? I froze in the doorway, unable to speak or move. Except for black socks with garters, he was completely naked. The sight of his grotesque body between the two young whores was repulsive in so many ways.

When our eyes met, his expression went from rage to wonder.

"Do I knowz you?" he said, squinting.

I shook my head, and he started to get up.

"Yez," he said, climbing out of the bed, his penis dangling. "I know you, boy." With his hunched back and hairy chest, he looked like an ogre. As he came towards me, I yelled, "I'm a man!" and slammed the door.

I ran to the end of the hall and tumbled down the stairs, landing flat in the foyer. I got up and scrambled out the door. I sprinted around the corner and panicked when I saw that Russo's car was gone. Then someone beeped, and I turned to see him waiting across the street, revving the engine.

"Get in!" he shouted.

I jumped in the passenger side, and we sped off.

"Where the hell'd you go?"

Still out of breath, I struggled to speak.

"The priest," I said. "I saw him...in one of the rooms—"

"Are you okay, Brae? You don't look right."

And I didn't because I wasn't. My head spun, my entire body shuddered, and I had to piss so bad it hurt. I sat still and stared ahead, waiting for the rum to wear off.

"Priest? What are you talking about?

"Never mind," I said. "Just drive."

CHAPTER 37

TELLING THE CAPTAIN ABOUT CHESTER SWEENEY WAS LIKE REMOVING A weight from one shoulder and putting it on the other. Any relief it brought was replaced by a new burden. For years, I ignored what happened that Halloween night, but now I could no longer pretend that Vogt wasn't involved in Sweeney's death. And if one thing was certain, it was that any man who could murder a child twenty years earlier was capable of much worse now.

"You didn't realize it was him?"

Still shaking from the admission, I looked at Jackson.

"I wasn't sure. When I was a kid, I was drunk both times I saw him. The night with Chester and then at the brothel. The memories are fuzzy."

Considering the captain's irritable state, I expected an admonishment. He could understand my reluctance as a boy, but as a lieutenant, there was no excuse for not disclosing it. I sat nervously while he chewed his lip thinking.

"And he had on black garters?" he said, finally.

The fact that he found some humor in the encounter told me I was off the hook. I made a sheepish grin and said, "He looked like Burt Ives in drag."

We both laughed.

"And the Sweeney case was never solved?"

"I don't believe so."

He coughed once and said, "Get the autopsy, if there was one. I'll try to pull the file."

As he reached for the phone, I stood up and almost felt like saluting.

"Yes, Sir."

THE MOMENT I exited The Armory, I saw a news truck parked at the end of the lot. A pretty blonde reporter dressed in a beige coat and scarf was waiting in the cold for a scoop. I hurried down the front steps and headed towards the Valiant, walking between the rows of cars to avoid her. But once she saw me, she scurried over with her cameraman and cut me off.

"Pardon me," she said. "Are you with BPD?"

"You saw me walk out of headquarters, right?"

When she frowned, she had the impeccable teeth of a newscaster.

"Mind if we ask some questions about the St Kilda Abbey in Roxbury?"

I looked at the cameraman.

"We have a public relations department."

She held out her arm, and the man put the camera down. When I realized her good faith, I nodded with a halfhearted assent that meant ask but don't expect much. She took out a small notepad and came close enough that I could smell her perfume.

"Are you familiar with the alleged miracle?"

"Who isn't?"

"Is it true the department is planning to remove people by force next Monday?"

"I don't know if it's true," I said. "But it would be a damn shame if they did."

Across the lot, I saw three men in suits come out the front doors. I couldn't tell who they were, but they looked like brass, and I didn't want to be seen talking to the media. When the woman and her colleague looked over too, I darted between the cars and was gone. As a matter of professional pride, she tried to follow me but soon gave up. I jumped in the car, started the engine, and drove away.

I got to City Hospital in no time and parked out back. Officially, I was in no rush, but for some reason I found myself walking faster and faster. By the time I reached The Crypt, I was out of breath. I knocked once, and Mayonnaise opened the door.

"I'm sorry, we're not open yet," he said.

I almost thanked him for the laugh, then I pushed through and into the office. Dr. Ansell was at his desk, a coffee mug in one hand, a newspaper in the other. He swiveled in his chair and greeted me.

"Lieutenant, bright and early."

"Morning, Doc."

His expression changed to concern.

"What's wrong? You look rattled, kid."

Feeling lightheaded, I unbuttoned my coat collar.

"I'm fine, thanks."

He glanced down at the paper and shook his head in disgust.

"Wish we could say the same for our boys in Nam. We're getting slaughtered." He looked at me and said, "And for what?"

"For freedom," I blurted, almost as a reflex.

"Freedom? A pretty word. Wish I knew what it meant."

When he noticed the intern dawdling in the distance, he called out, "Mayonnaise, get those scalpels sterilized."

The young man jumped at the order and went into the next room. Ansell took a sip of coffee and said, "So what is it, kid? What brings you here?"

"I have a favor to ask."

"Shoot."

"Could you pull an autopsy report from twenty-three years ago?"

He looked at me curiously.

"Whaddya wanna find out? How your dog died?"

"It's a friend…from childhood. He was found dead."

"What year?"

"'45…October."

He looked up at the ceiling lamps thinking. The intern came out from the back room and tried to get his attention but was quickly shooed away.

"Maybe, kid," he said. "We go back about 10 years here. Older records are in the Archives on Harrison Ave. What's the name?"

"Chester Sweeney."

He scribbled on the back of an envelope. When he was done, he gazed at me with tender concern. Maybe I looked more distressed than I felt because he said, "You've got the world on your shoulders."

"How do you mean?"

"Well, for one…"

He turned over the newspaper and there on the front page, was a large photograph of the entrance gate at St Kilda. The story dominated the news more than Vietnam, and the headline read: *Abbey Situation Grows Dire*. In the picture, the crowd looked like Revere Beach in August.

"That's not my problem," I said.

"But Ruth is."

"Pardon?"

With a soft, sympathetic voice, he said, "I heard what happened."

"You did?"

"I've got friends up there," he said, pointing upwards.

"In heaven or in administration?"

"I didn't know there was a difference."

"She'll be alright. It's not the first time someone's pulled a record unauthorized."

He was so startled he instantly got up and came over. I knew something was wrong when he put his hand on my arm.

"A record? No, kid. That may be true. I was told a nurse got canned this week for stealing drugs."

My face dropped, I stepped back.
"Ruth?"
"He didn't have a name, but said she stole barbiturates."
"Barbiturates?"

CHAPTER 38

THE GAS TANK WAS CLOSE TO EMPTY AS I RACED THROUGH THE afternoon streets towards Roslindale. With everything that was happening, I was more terrified now than I had been in all the weeks prior. Despite the cold, I drove with the window down and chain-smoked the whole way. My mind raced with thoughts of Ruth suffering under a depression that she could no longer bear. It was the illness I knew the least about but had the most experience with. I couldn't understand why she didn't tell me about the drugs.

I sped up the hill and slid to a stop in front of our house. I ran up the two flights, reached the landing, and searched frantically for the key. Seconds later, I turned the lock and threw open the door.

Inside, the living room was empty, and Ruth's coat was on the coat rack. I dashed into the bedroom and saw a tiny figure folded up under the blanket. Thoughts of the worst—fears of the unthinkable—raged through my head like a horror film, and I was sure I was losing my mind. I knelt down beside the bed, put my hand over her, and crumbled.

"Ruth," I said. "I'm so sorry. I want to help you. But I can't. I don't know what to do. Please, let me help you...oh God, don't. I can't—"

"Jody?"

When I heard a voice behind me, I froze. I stood up and turned around to see her in the doorway, fully dressed and made up. At that moment, my eyes must have gone from her to the bed fifty times. I was confused to the point of delirium.

"Sir?"

I glanced down and Teddy was staring back. He pushed the covers off and sat up, rubbing his eyes like someone who had been asleep a long time. I straightened out my jacket, regained my composure, and said, "Can someone tell me what the hell is going on?"

Ruth came over and took my arm.

"Go back to sleep, Teddy," she said. "It's alright. I'll explain."

Without a word, he fell back to the mattress and was out before we left the room. We came into the living room, and she said, "He's exhausted. He's been on the run for a week."

"How do you know that?"

She came towards me, but I backed away coldly.

"Because he told me."

"Where are the drugs?" I said, and she winced in confusion.

"Drug? What drugs?"

"Don't lie to me!"

She raised her voice to match mine and said, "I don't know what you're talking about, Jody!"

"I was told you stole barbiturates—"

"Barbiturates?" she said. "That's fucking absurd! They said *I* stole?—"

"They said *a nurse*."

She stopped, and her expression completely changed. She looked away and put one hand to her mouth, "Oh my gosh."

She was the only woman I knew that could go from indignant to sticky sweet in a single exchange. I would have laughed if I wasn't so worked up.

"I went to the hospital this morning," she said, "to get my check. A nurse said Ms. Stuart was called into administration yesterday. She was in trouble, no one knew why. She wasn't at work today."

"You think she was taking barbiturates?"

"I don't know," she said, frustrated.

I took her hand and led her to the couch, where we both sat.

"It wasn't me for God's sake," she continued. "I could barely tolerate that damn Clomi...whatever the hell it's called."

When she saw my face, I could tell she realized what my suspicions had been.

"Oh no, Jody," she said, shaking her head. "No, no, no. I would never."

I looked down in embarrassment.

"I've been so worried."

She took my hand in hers, and I kissed her forehead. As the late afternoon sun came through the windows, we leaned against each other and gazed off. Several minutes passed before the daydream faded and I said, "Where'd you find him?"

"Chinatown," she answered softly. "I saw him in Chinatown. He came up to me. I didn't recognize him at first. He had on a fur hood, sunglasses. He was scared."

"What were you doing in Chinatown?"

When she turned, her hair fell to one side, and she faced me like a penitent daughter.

"It's silly, really," she said. "I'm such a fool."

"No, tell me."

"I knew you were disappointed about—"

"Please don't say that."

"A woman at work, an Oriental nurse, told me about herbs."

"What about herbs?"

"That they can help."

"Chinese herbs?"

Her eyes started to water; her voice cracked. When I rubbed her back, she looked at me with a mournful smile. She had been depressed so long I almost forgot the girlish cheer she once had.

"Have you eaten?"

"Not in weeks," I said.

It may have been an exaggeration, but it felt true.

"You look so thin."

I walked into the kitchen and turned on the kettle. While I waited for the water to boil, I nibbled on some Ritz Crackers.

"What did he tell you?"

"A lot," she said, calling over from the living room.

I stuck my head around the corner.

"How much is a lot?"

"Maybe more than I should know."

CHAPTER 39

It was close to 8 p.m. when Teddy finally woke up. He sat in the rocker but didn't rock, gazing ahead, groggy from his long nap. With his soiled pants, torn sweater, and stubble, he looked like someone who had been living in the woods. When Ruth offered him one of my outfits and he declined, I assumed it was less out of pride than from some Korean superstition about wearing another man's clothes. Either way, I felt bad for him.

"Three men came by the restaurant," Teddy explained. "I wasn't there."

As we spoke, the aroma of dinner filled the apartment, and I was so hungry I didn't care what Ruth was making.

"Were they Orientals? I said, and I could tell he didn't like the term.

"Chinese. One of the workers told me."

"What day was that?"

He squinted in thought.

"Thursday, the 8th. I had a physical exam at the recruitment office. I couldn't go to work."

"Thursday?" I said to myself. "That's when Mardini came to identify the body—"

"Sidney Mardini?'

"You know him?"

"He comes in the Lantern House with his wife."

"Blonde curly hair," I said, and he nodded. "That's his girlfriend."

"He is friends with Mr. Lee, the owner."

"You mean Johnny?"

Teddy grinned and said, "No one would call him that."

The flow of our conversation was interrupted when Ruth hollered, "Dinner."

"Why not?"

"It's a sign of disrespect. He's respected...and feared."

"I met him," I said, as we got up. "And he wasn't too fearsome."

"It's different where we're from. He's a gentleman, polite, good manners. But he has money, and money is power."

"Some things are universal."

"He can be vicious."

I recalled the day Harrigan and I watched him browbeat the employee in the alleyway.

"I bet he can," I said.

We walked into the dining room, where the table was beautifully set with a burgundy tablecloth and the white china we got for our wedding. In the center were the roses I had given Ruth the week before, neatly cut and resting in a vase. There was fresh bread, glasses of water, and two red candles. Teddy waited timidly by the radiator and wouldn't move until I ordered him to sit.

Ruth came in with spaghetti and meatballs, and she filled our bowls, one by one. She lit the candles and opened a bottle of wine, and for the next ten minutes, we ate with the solemnity of the Last Supper.

"So," she said, wiping her mouth. "I understand you've been called for the draft?"

Teddy nodded.

"I got a letter two weeks ago."

"Are you scared?"

I gave her a sharp look, but she ignored me. I was never comfortable talking about war, especially in my own house, and the thought of him going to Vietnam weighed heavily on my conscience, although I had no say in the matter.

"I guess I should be," he said, stirring his food. "But I don't feel it, yet."

"Have you ever thought about getting a deferment…for family hardship? You take care of your elderly uncle, right?"

I cringed.

"Can we talk about something else?"

"It's alright," he said. He put down his fork and looked across to her. "I want to serve. I love this country. I'll go…and I'll come home."

"Amen," I said. "To your safe return."

I raised my arm, and we clinked our glasses together. Ruth took a sip and glanced over to me with a sad smile. For the first time in months, it was a sadness that was not her own, but for someone else. And there was nothing like sympathy to cure the isolation of despair.

IT WAS close to 2 a.m., and Ruth had gone to bed hours before. Teddy had slept so sporadically while on the run that he suffered emotional jetlag and was wide awake. While he sat in the recliner reading Life Magazine, I lay half-asleep on the couch in my undershirt and pants. On the table, my .38 Smith & Wesson lay in a dozen pieces after teaching him how to field strip a handgun. If he was going to learn about weaponry, I thought, he might as well have a head start.

"Where'd you hide?" I mumbled.

"Sorry, Sir?"

"Where were you staying all last week?"

He put down the magazine.

"Mostly in Chinatown, with Korean friends."

"I went there looking for you. I asked around everywhere."

"They won't talk to *gwai lo*."

I tilted my head back, closed my eyes.

"White devil, eh?"

"Not to me. You saved my life. That night, in front of my flat, when you fired at those men, I ran. I ran and ran until I couldn't run anymore." Drifting in and out of sleep, I raised one eyelid and listened. "When I was a child," he continued, "during the war, our village was attacked by the NKA one night. They burned everything. My mother woke me up, we fled our house. She carried me as far as she could then I had to run on my own. It was cold. We ran all night, slept in the woods by a stream. I was probably three years old. It's one of the only things I remember—"

With images and sounds of Korea swirling through my mind, his voice slowly faded out and everything went black.

"Sir, sir!"

I awoke to the sensation of an earthquake. When I jumped up on the couch, I realized Teddy was shaking me. The doorbell was buzzing, and Ruth rushed out of the bedroom in a robe.

"What?!" I yelled, my heart pounding. "What is it?"

"Someone's at the door."

"Jody," Ruth said, undoing the deadbolt. "Maybe you should get it."

Dressed in my shirtsleeves, I stepped out into the stairwell and walked barefoot down two flights. I peered through the peephole and saw Harrigan, his coat collar upturned, a scarf around his neck. He never came by unannounced—something must have been wrong. I took a deep breath and opened the door.

"What are you doing here?" I said.

He swallowed once then spoke.

"It's the captain."

CHAPTER 40

I RACED DOWN COLUMBUS AVE., TRYING TO GET AROUND MORNING commuters and school buses. For anyone in the throes of a crisis, the world always seemed remarkably indifferent. By the time I blew the second red light, I knew Harrigan regretted taking my car and not his. But I loved the Valiant, and as much as I scorned superstition, I was sure it brought good luck.

At Massachusetts Ave., I cut the wheel, and we swerved in a large arc. He grabbed the door handle and said, "Whoa…" like he was on a runaway horse. After two blocks, I went up the driveway to City Hospital and screeched to a stop at the entrance.

"You coming?" I said breathlessly.

"I'll mind the car, Lieutenant."

"I won't be long."

I jumped out and ran through the front doors and into the lobby, where the morning staff was preparing for a new day. Orderlies walked by pushing carts of orange juice, toast, and tea. An old black janitor was emptying ashtrays and picking up trash. I went straight up to the reception desk and saw the same grumpy woman from two days before.

"I'm here for Captain Jackson," I said, and she looked puzzled. "Ernest Jackson. I was told he's here."

"Let me check, Sir."

She reached for the phone and looked up, her eyes blinking.

"And who are you?"

"His son."

What caused me to say it, I didn't know. A family member had more authority than a colleague or friend, but the claim might have meant something more profound. Regardless, there was nothing that could stop me from seeing him.

Seconds later, the woman hung up.

"3rd floor, room 323."

She proceeded to give me directions, but I was already halfway across the lobby. When I came around the corner to the elevator bank, the first person I saw was Sergeant Duggan. He was in his full winter uniform, with a long navy coat, boots, and gloves.

"Jody," he said, opening his arms as if to hug me.

"What the hell's going on?"

"Don't know exactly. They found him in the hallway. He collapsed outside his office. He was unconscious."

We were both red in the face and panting. The doors opened and we got in, sharing the ride with a group of young nurses. We didn't stop at any other floors, but it seemed to take forever, and by the time we arrived, I was ready to sprint.

Nevertheless, I kept my cool and followed Duggan.

At the far end of the floor, I saw blue uniforms and knew it was the captain's room. We rushed down the hallway, past a lavatory, an x-ray lab, and a kitchenette. When we went by the nurses' station, there were several women, but I didn't see Ms. Stuart. We came to room 323, and two officers were on guard outside. They looked familiar, although I didn't know their names, and they stood to attention the moment we walked up.

"How is he?"

"Sir," one of them said. "He's stable...we believe."

The first officer looked past me, and when I turned around a doctor was coming towards us. He was a middle-aged man, medium height and with brown hair, and from a distance probably looked much like me.

"I'm sure you're all concerned," he said.

"More than you know."

With a tense smile, he held out his hand.

"Doctor Quinlan. I'm with the trauma unit."

"Detective Brae, Jody Brae. This is Duggan."

As we shook, he asked, "Are you Mr. Jackson's partner?"

Had the circumstances not been so grave, we might have all teased him for the remark.

"No, no," I said. "Not partners. He's my boss...and friend."

Two nurses with a patient on a gurney came down the hall, and we moved out of the way. Dr. Quinlan waved Duggan and me aside, and we stood in a close circle. He lowered his voice, almost to a whisper, and said, "What do you know about his health?"

"I know he's not well."

He nodded.

"He has cancer, liver cancer—"

"Why'd he fall?" Duggan asked, and the doctor looked at him.

"Not sure. We're doing blood analysis now." He faced me and added, "It's not uncommon at this stage of the disease. We know it has spread—it's incurable. It may have gone to his brain; we don't know yet. That would cause seizures, which might explain why he collapsed."

When I looked at Duggan, the sarcastic smirk that was a permanent feature of his face was gone. He appeared more scared than worried, and the only reason I knew was because I felt the same fear within. He had known the captain as long as me, maybe longer, and the thought of the department without him was like imagining the solar system without a sun. For two battle-hardened city cops, there wasn't much that could shake us up. This was the exception.

Struggling to control my voice, I asked, "May I see him?"

Quinlan glanced over to the patrolmen, who kept their posts with a cool professionalism. A nurse walked by and went into the room.

"Okay," he said, "But only a few minutes. We haven't been able to contact next-of-kin."

"Don't bother. There aren't any."

There was a dramatic pause—Duggan and Quinlan both seemed saddened by the news. Then the doctor asked, "You're sure?"

"I'm sure."

And I was. The irony of Jackson's personal life was that it was more mysterious than any case we ever investigated. He had been on the force nearly forty years, yet no one had ever met any of his friends or relatives. The only thing certain was that he never married, calling himself *a bachelor's bachelor*. But I wasn't really convinced because, as with most people, a strong denunciation was often a sign of regret.

"I'll wait out here," Duggan said.

He walked away, and the doctor nodded for me to go in. As I reached for the doorknob, my fingers trembled. I knew at that moment that entering the room may have been the bravest thing I ever did.

When I stepped inside, the air was moist, and the smell of urine and commercial disinfectant was everywhere. I looked across to the only bed and saw a tiny body under the sheets. The nurse was taking his blood pressure, fixing the IV that penetrated his emaciated forearm. If someone had asked me to describe death with a picture, this would have been it.

The nurse skirted by and quietly said, "He's awake, but may be a bit disoriented."

I thanked her and walked towards the bed. When I leaned over the rail, Jackson opened his eyes and looked right at me. His skin was sallow, his pupils dilated. He tried to move his lips, but no sound came out. I knelt down, as if in prayer.

"How are you, Capt.?"

He raised one eyebrow, the most he could communicate, and I nodded with a loving smile.

"We're gonna get you home," I said, patting his arm.

It may have been a lie or a promise I couldn't keep, but when he smiled back it was well worth it. His eyelids began to sag, his breathing slowed. I didn't think he was dying, but he was too weak to remain awake. I squeezed his hand then let go.

The windows of the room faced south towards Roxbury from an angle I had never seen before. It was a cloudless February day, with a sky so blue it seemed almost pastel. I looked beyond the brick buildings, housing projects, and triple-deckers and thought I saw the tower of St Kilda in the distance. Or maybe it was just an illusion.

"Lieutenant?"

When I spun around and saw Harrigan in the doorway, I was startled but not at all surprised. He had opted to wait in the car out of propriety and not because he wanted to. In the end, his heart overcame his etiquette, and he had to come.

I motioned for him to enter and he did. He glanced down with a reluctant dread, and I could tell he was relieved the captain was asleep.

"How is he?" he asked.

"Dying."

"I know. When?"

I shrugged my shoulders, curled my lips.

"Not today. Maybe this week, maybe next month."

"How are you?"

Until that point, I had been calm, perhaps even cold. But the question hit me like a pinprick to an overfilled water balloon, and I could no longer contain what I felt inside. Instead of answering, I swallowed my tears and stormed out of the room.

As I walked down the hallway, I heard Harrigan's footsteps behind me, and he was closing in. By the time I reached the elevators, I was finally composed enough to talk.

"Lieutenant?"

"Teddy's at my apartment," I said, the first thing that came to mind.

"Pardon?"

"Teddy...I've got him. He's at my house."

"How—?"

"Ruth found him...or he found her. In Chinatown." I lowered my voice and leaned in. "He's been hiding. Someone's out to kill him."

He rubbed his chin, shook his head. Too much was happening at once, and we were all suffering psychological overload.

"What did you find out about Vogt?" I asked.

He looked up, still perplexed.

"A whole lot of nothing."

The remark was enough to make me chuckle, some humor I desperately needed.

"He was a foreign national," Harrigan went on, "until '52. Then became a naturalized citizen."

"There's nothing natural about him. Any dirt?"

"Not even a parking ticket."

Just as the elevator arrived, Dr. Quinlan came out of a nearby room. I looked at Harrigan and said quickly, "I'll meet you downstairs."

Without a word, he got on, and the doors closed. I followed Quinlan down the corridor and caught up to him at a waiting area.

"Doctor," I said, and he turned around.

"Can I have a word?"

He glanced down at his watch.

"Certainly," he said with a smile. "I have a couple minutes."

We stepped over to a quiet corner, beyond the view of the nurses' station, and I asked, "Do you know a Ms. Stuart?"

He looked side to side, then said flatly, "I do."

"Was she caught stealing medication?"

He began to fret—he shifted his weight from one foot to the other and back again.

"I…I'm afraid. I can't—"

"I was told she was taking barbiturates."

He scratched his head.

"Sergeant—"

"Lieutenant."

"I'm sorry. Lieutenant."

When a nurse passed by, we both waited until she was gone. I stepped closer and said, "Can you at least tell me if the police were involved? If so, I can get the file myself."

"No," he said, holding out his hands, unable to look me in the eye. "It was internal. That's all I can say."

"Thank you."

Downstairs, the lobby was bustling—a big change from thirty minutes before. As Harrigan and I went towards the exit, Duggan came in yelling to clear the way. People stopped what they were doing, and everyone turned to look. Paramedics rushed in carrying three stretchers, and a triage team ran over to escort the injured to a trauma room. The scene went from routine busyness to complete chaos in a split second.

Nervous and sweating, Duggan got out of the way and let the professionals get to work. When he saw me, he came right over.

"What's going on?"

"Oh, Jody," he said, taking off his cap, wiping his forehead, "I heard the call on the two-way. I met the ambulances out front."

He reached to his belt and turned the squelch down on his radio.

"What happened?" I asked.

"A fire...at the abbey. One of the tents...from a candle...I think...I don't know..."

His face strained as he tried to catch his breath. I had never seen him so overwhelmed, and just the sight of it made me anxious.

As soon as he was able to form a complete sentence, he looked at me and Harrigan.

"They've gotta get things under control. It may be a shrine, but it's gonna be a graveyard."

"How will they clear five thousand people?"

He shook his head, and beads of sweat fell off.

"I don't know. Fire hoses and German Shepherds?"

When he saw me snicker, he looked over his shoulder and said, "But serious. People are nervous, jittery. Everyone's heard the rumors about Monday. They're ready to resist. I'm telling you, some will go easy, many won't."

A patrolman called over and Duggan said, "Gotta go..."

As he hurried off, I said, "Sarge," and he spun around.

"Watch out for the captain."

"You know I will."

Harrigan and I went out the front doors, and Doctor Ansell was standing on the curb trying to get a cab. I usually only saw him in The Crypt or at a crime scene, and he looked less distinguished in daylight. I could have mistaken him for just any old person.

"Doc," I yelled as he opened the rear door of a taxi.

When he turned, I waved him over.

"Don't waste your money. I'll give you a lift."

The cabbie looked over his shoulder with a frown, and Ansell shut the door. He walked up and said, "How do you know I'm not going to Providence?"

"You're dressed too nice for Providence."

We both chuckled, but Harrigan did not. Seeing Captain Jackson lying in the hospital bed had sent him into a quiet despondency that only I could detect. If concealing emotion was a strength, then he was Atlas.

He handed me the keys, and we all walked over to the Valiant. On the windshield was a blue parking ticket, the kind issued by hospital security. When I noticed an officer watching from under the portico, I folded it up like a paper airplane and flung it in his direction. Ansell laughed aloud, and Harrigan couldn't help but smile. In a city as territorial as Boston, even cops couldn't get along, and there was a historic tension between the public and private police forces.

"Funny we should bump into each other, kid," the doctor said. "But let's talk on the road."

As we got to the car, Harrigan offered him the front seat, but he declined. I started the engine and asked, "Where to?"

"Home."

"Where's home?"

"Charles River Park."

I rolled down the end of the driveway and into the city streets. Harrigan sat still, staring out the window, almost catatonic. His response to Jackson's condition was worse than mine, something I attributed to the fact that he was five years younger. It didn't help his mood when the doctor lit a cigar, and I had a cigarette.

I looked in the rear-view.

"Whaddya got for me?" I said.

"For one, I found the record of your friend Sweeney..."

Luckily, we were slowing to a red light because I would have hit the brakes.

"...the autopsy was slim," he went on, "...looked like a rush job. But his neck was snapped like a chicken bone...that was clear."

Never delicate with his imagery, Ansell was more concerned with making his point than being polite.

"He wasn't hit by a train?"

"Train?" he scoffed. "No way, kid. Trains make mincemeat outta bodies. This guy was intact. Just some bruising, alcohol in his blood."

I turned onto Storrow Drive, and we followed the Charles River towards downtown. The walking paths along the shoreline were empty; high winds whipped up flags and litter. On the opposite bank, the stately buildings of Harvard University faced Boston like a dare.

We exited at Cambridge Street, and I drove into Charles River Park, a complex of posh apartments that had replaced the slums of the West End.

"What's it like living among the mucky-mucks?" I said.

Harrigan gave me a nervous smile, unsure whether I was taunting or just teasing the doctor.

"They have a laundry service and they shovel. At my age, that's most of what matters in life." He pointed, then said, "Take a right here."

I came up to an entrance with wide glass doors and fake plants in the foyer. Sleek and impersonal, the high-rise had a modern design that was somewhere between chic and tacky. I leaned forward and looked up.

"Pretty swank," I said. "Is this what we get for kicking three thousand people out of their homes?"

With one foot out the door, the doctor stopped. Like anyone raised in poverty, he had an ambivalent pride about his own success.

"Don't preach to me, kid. My mother grew up in a cold-water flat on Blossom Street. I was born here. We moved to Roxbury when I was six."

"Then you were neighbors with Sid Mardini?"

He sat back down and shut the car door.

"Mardini?" he said, crouching forward. "I know two things about Sid Mardini: that broad from the dumpster ain't his niece, and he was no friend of the West End."

"Jackson said the same thing."

"About the girl or the neighborhood?"

When I turned to look at him, our faces were so close I could see his nose hairs.

"He said Mardini's company made millions off the project."

"I don't agree with Mr. Jackson about much, but he's dead on."

A Cadillac pulled up, and an older woman got out carrying a small dog. With her long white coat and oversized sunglasses, she smacked of new money.

"Turned against his own people," I mused, shaking my head.

"If Mardini didn't, someone else would've."

"You sound like you're defending him."

Ansell scoffed.

"My ass. I'm as much of a Democrat as you, kid. But look at this place..."

I glanced around at the shiny buildings and neatly cut pathways. If it was elegant in the snow, it must have been like Versailles in summer.

"...Imagine what this land was worth?" he went on. "Every developer in Boston wanted a piece. And they'd do anything to get it."

A chill went up my back, and Harrigan and I instinctively looked at each other. The silence that followed was just an afterthought.

CHAPTER 41

THE MEDIA PRESENCE AT THE ARMORY WAS SO HEAVY FRIDAY THAT SOME employees were parking on the street and using the side entrance. Always sensitive to the politics of public perception, Chief McNamara wasn't about to order the news trucks off the property.

To avoid the lobby, I walked to the top floor and down the rear stairwell, approaching my office from the other end of the building. When I got there, the door was wide open. I looked in to see a man from the maintenance crew crouched by the wall with a toolbox.

"What the hell's going on?" I snapped.

"Somebody called about the radiator knocking."

"That was two weeks ago."

I may not have kept my office tidy, but it was as personal as a bedroom, and I resented the intrusion.

"Lieutenant," I heard, and I turned to see Harrigan coming down the hall. "We can meet in the captain's office," he said, holding up a key. I nodded coldly to the janitor and walked off.

When we got to Jackson's office, Harrigan unlocked the door.

"Where'd you get a key?" I asked.

He gave me a curious look.

"You have one too."

It could have been true—I really didn't know. Even though his office contained all the open case files, going in when he wasn't there seemed a sacrilege, and I never would have done it.

I walked in after Harrigan, but it didn't feel right. The room had the somber stillness of a museum at night. The only thing that moved was the second hand on the wall clock. When we got to the chairs facing the desk, we both realized the awkwardness of sitting so close together.

"Wouldn't you be more comfortable there?" he said, nodding to the captain's seat.

"As a matter of fact, I wouldn't."

Still standing, Harrigan said, "You might want to start."

Coming from anybody else, the insinuation would have sent me into a rage. But he wasn't being sarcastic—he was simply being honest. If and when the captain passed away, I was next in line for his position, something that terrified me more than his death.

I went around the desk, past the watching eyes of General Eisenhower, and sat down. Even in a building where everything was ancient, the swivel chair seemed old. It was made of hand-carved oak, with slats on the back and casters on the feet. Considering that Jackson was from the backwoods of Maine, I wouldn't have been surprised if he made it himself.

On top of the desk were piles of folders so high I worried they would fall over if I sneezed. I looked across to Harrigan from a position of authority I always had but never asserted.

"We have to get the chief to stop the eviction…" I stated.

With his legs crossed and hands resting on his lap, he responded with a gentle nod that indicated neither agreement nor dissent.

"…It's a backroom deal. We both know it. Vogt pushed for the abbey closure. None of the monks knew about it. They thought he was advocating for them."

"Is that true?" he said.

"Emmanuel said it when I met him…said Vogt was fighting with the Archdiocese to keep St Kilda open."

I shook my head in frustration and leaned forward over the desk.

In all my years as a cop, I had operated mainly on instinct and left the analysis to my superiors. I knew now that that would have to change.

While Harrigan listened patiently, I continued, "Brother Emmanuel, the woman, Chester Sweeney...they all died of asphyxiation...from neck breaks. Very deliberate, very skilled."

"Might be circumstantial."

I acknowledged the remark, but said, "A guy the size of Vogt could do it."

"He could. But what motive, Lieutenant?"

His cool skepticism was beginning to annoy me. But I realized he was only playing the role that the captain always played.

"Emmanuel must've found out about Vogt and Mardini. Maybe he caught Vogt trying to destroy the image."

"What about the woman in the dumpster?"

"I don't know. Vogt was screwing her?" I guessed. "Maybe she found out about the plot too—wanted a cut or threatened to tell authorities. Remember what Doctor Ansell said about the West End... *Every developer in Boston wanted a piece. And they'd do anything to get it.*"

"We have nothing to tie them to the dead woman."

"Teddy's uncle saw one of Mardini's trucks dump the body."

"And Teddy's uncle is missing."

When someone knocked, I jumped up like a child caught playing where he shouldn't. The door opened, and it was the brunette secretary from the front desk. Her once feminine glow was now more of an anxious pallor. With the situation at the abbey growing dire, the chief was under tremendous pressure, and everyone was on edge.

"There's a woman here. She wants to speak with a detective."

I looked first at Harrigan then said, "A woman? What's she want?"

"I don't know. She's upset."

"Where?"

"The lobby."

Harrigan must have sensed my reluctance because he said, "I'll get her."

"Yeah, okay. Thanks."

He got up and left with the secretary. The room went silent. While

I sat alone, I looked around and observed the things both personal and professional that seemed to be the summation of Jackson's life. The walls had framed citations, honors, and news articles. There was a photo on the desk of him and a former police chief, fishing rods in hand, smiling. On the far wall, there were two large file cabinets, the heart of homicide, which contained dossiers on almost every case we had ever handled. The captain may not have been present, but his spirit was.

"Lieutenant."

Startled, I looked up, and Harrigan was in the door. Beside him stood a black woman, her skin tone so similar to his that my first thought was that she was an aunt or cousin.

"This is Mrs. Bynoe," he said.

She was probably sixty, but with her orange turtleneck and tall leather boots, she was dressed like a woman twenty years younger.

"My pleasure," I said, straining to get up. "I understand you want to talk with a detective?"

"Yessir."

Like a lot of blacks who came to Boston after the war, she retained the faded twang of her Southern roots. I gestured for her to sit, and Harrigan took the chair next to her.

"I...I didn't want to come," she said.

"If you have something to tell us, we're glad you did."

"One...one of my girls...she been gone. I know it ain't right neither..."

She stopped.

"Tell us, Ma'am," I said warmly, and she smiled like she was unused to such courtesies.

"I have some girls, they work for me..." I gave her a reassuring nod, letting her know I understood what she meant. "...One of them, Martha, she had some trouble with one of her men. She got pregnant..."

When I glanced over to Harrigan, he was already looking back.

"...I knew he was bad news, I said so. But she wouldn't listen—"

"Madam," I said, realizing the irony of the term. "Who is this man?"

"You know, I'm a Christian woman at heart..." Her face trembled, she wrung her hands. "...I sure ain't free o' sin, but I'm God-fearing." Finally, she worked up to the crescendo of her confession. "...He's a priest, Mister. A holy man doin' unholy things."

The way she pronounced *things* like *thangs* unleashed a memory. Suddenly, I recognized her from the whorehouse that Russo and I had visited many years before.

"When did you last see her?" I asked.

She put her hand to her chin and thought.

"It'd be three weeks, I'd say. She was close to due, I know that."

I stood up and she flinched. I came around the desk and leaned down to shake her hand. "You've done a good thing, dear," I said, and she turned away bashfully. When she looked back, our eyes met, and she stared at me curiously. I let go of her hand, a moment of private embarrassment, thinking that maybe she, too, remembered me.

"Would you be kind enough to give a statement?" I asked.

"That's why I came."

CHAPTER 42

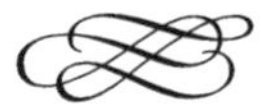

I STOOD BY THE OFFICE WINDOW AND LOOKED OUT AT THE SAME VIEW the captain saw each day. Buildings old and new were stacked against one another, city streets wending between them like the trails at the foot of a gorge. On all the various floors, I could see the office lights of people who were still working—lawyers, clerks, admen, and traders. Out front, the equipment from a news truck illuminated the half-empty parking lot, reminding people that something big was going on.

The scene was hardly a vista, but Jackson loved it. Many were the mornings I arrived to find him staring out the glass, hands clasped behind his back, humming a tune.

I reached over to the desk for my coffee, the only thing I had had to eat since breakfast. My suit coat was on the back of the seat, my tie was on the desk, and the file from the investigation was open. With nothing more to do until Harrigan returned, I leaned back in the chair and tried to relax.

"Lieutenant?"

When I opened my eyes, my head was slumped forward and there was drool on my chin. I shook myself awake and looked up to see Harrigan.

"What time is it?"

"Almost eight."

I yawned and said, "Did you get the affidavit?"

"Yes. I just came back from giving her a lift."

"Where to?"

"An old house behind Dudley Square."

Just as he sat down, the wall clock struck 8 p.m.

"It's quite warm in here," he said.

"Which reminds me. It's time to make Vogt sweat a little."

I picked up the phone and dialed the operator. The woman put me through to the abbey, and it rang several times. Finally, a man answered.

"Hello?"

"Is this St Kilda?"

He paused and said, "You've reached St Kilda."

"I'd like to speak with Father Vogt."

"I'm afraid he's not here at the moment."

"Where is he?" I asked, and I knew the question was brash.

"I'm sorry, to whom am I speaking?"

"Lieutenant Brae, Boston Police."

There was a muffled silence, and I could tell he was covering the receiver. I winked at Harrigan, and he raised an eyebrow, acknowledging but not approving of my mischief. With the captain incapacitated and the deadline for the abbey eviction looming, I was beginning not to care who I pissed off.

I heard some shuffling on the other end of the phone.

"I'm sorry," the voice said. "He had a meeting with the Archdiocese at five. He may be on his way back. Is there a message?"

I thought for a moment.

"Yeah. Tell Vogt he looks good in black garters."

CHAPTER 43

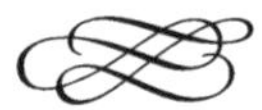

THE HEADQUARTERS OF THE ARCHDIOCESE OF BOSTON WAS AT SAINT John's Seminary in Brighton, five miles from downtown but worlds away from the desolation of Roxbury. Much like the abbey, it was a vast complex of classic stone structures set against acres of open ground. The buildings were four stories high, with pitched roofs and arched windows, and had the ivy-covered elegance of a college campus.

Harrigan and I turned onto Lake Street. In the distance, I could see the conical towers that capped the corners of the main building. In terms of audacity, visiting the Archdiocese was the Catholic equivalent of walking into the White House and expecting to meet with President Johnson.

We continued ahead and were almost at the gate when Harrigan said, "Keep going!"

"What?"

"Keep going."

I drove by the entrance and pulled over.

"The truck. The Dodge truck," he said.

"Where?"

"Out front. I'm sure of it."

"Well," I said, putting the Valiant in gear, "let's go find out."

We drove another block and turned into a secondary entrance that was probably for delivery trucks and maintenance personnel. After we passed a baseball field, the road curved, and we came to a rear lot with a few cars. I turned off the headlights and rolled in quietly, stopping in the shadow of an administrative building. I turned off the engine and looked at him.

"You ready to do this?" I said.

"I don't know what we're doing. But I'm ready."

I gestured with my chin.

"Let's go."

We got out and walked towards the main building. As we came around the corner, I heard voices and stopped. With Harrigan close behind, I peered out and saw three men in the front lot, standing in a circle under a streetlamp. I gave Harrigan a suspicious glance and looked again. Even with the distance and bad lighting, I could tell it was Mardini and Father Vogt. The third man had his back to us, but he was dressed in a cassock and purple mozzetta, the vestments of senior clergy.

I watched as the three men shook hands and dispersed. Father Vogt walked over to a black Delta 88, and the driver started the engine. Mardini lit a cigarette, crossed the parking lot, and got into the Dodge WC54. Moments later, the vehicles pulled out and disappeared down the driveway.

"C'mon," I said.

We hurried towards the front of the building. As we neared the entrance, the priest was at the top of the stairs and almost to the door. He must have heard our footsteps because he spun around.

"Who's there?"

As if on cue, we stepped out of the darkness.

"Beautiful night," I said.

"I'm sorry. And who are you?"

While Harrigan waited, I walked towards the man and stopped at the bottom of the stairs. He was somewhere between middle-aged and elderly, with thin lips and a thin nose. He had the stern expression of an academic—the kind of person who only smiled when challenged or threatened.

"Detective Jody Brae, BPD. Mind if we ask some questions?"

Even with the loose vestments, it was clear that his body was tense. He hesitated, looked around, and then said, "Perhaps. Would you be kind enough to come inside?"

I called to Harrigan, and we followed him through the doors and into a long hallway. Inside was even more lavish than the exterior. There were large, gilded mirrors and beaded lamps. The wallpaper was dark and ornate, and an Oriental runner ran the length of the floor. We turned at the first doorway into a sitting room.

"Please," the priest said. "Have a seat."

Harrigan and I sat down and looked around in wonder. Bookshelves covered every wall from floor to ceiling, and a large hearth crackled with pine logs. A smokey warmth filled the room and, as awkward as I felt among such luxuriance, it was an easy place to be uncomfortable.

The man stoked the fire then came over and took a chair facing us.

"I'm Bishop Severin. Can I get you gentlemen anything?"

I appreciated his tact, but we weren't there for an aperitif.

"We could use some answers," I said.

He averted his eyes with a polite modesty.

"I'm afraid I don't know what the question is."

"Who were those men you were just talking with?"

With a slight hesitation, he said, "Business associates."

"Father Vogt?"

"You know him?"

"We've met. You know there's a humanitarian crisis at St Kilda?"

The bishop smiled.

"All will be well after Monday."

"You're aware there was a murder there last week?" Harrigan asked.

"I'm aware of the tragedy. Yes."

"And that there was another murder, three weeks ago, a young woman, downtown," I added.

We had only been there a couple of minutes, and already I could tell the bishop's civility was waning.

"I don't quite see what you're getting at," he said.

"We believe Sid Mardini is involved with both murders."

The statement was so blunt it even caught Harrigan off guard. The bishop sighed and said, "I don't know what evidence you have, but I assure you the Archdiocese's relationship with Mr. Mardini is purely professional."

"And what is that relationship?"

He paused thinking.

"Well, seeing it will be official Monday, I don't think it inappropriate to say: Mr. Mardini is in the process of purchasing the abbey."

"A murderer?"

"What evidence do you have?" he said curtly. "He's not under investigation, as far as I know."

"We have a witness who saw one of his trucks dump a body. Mardini's people have been looking for the man—to silence him." When I got up from the chair, the bishop flinched. "They tried to kill his nephew—" I almost said *for chrissakes*, but quickly changed to *for crying out loud*.

"This is all quite absurd."

"The young man is scared for his life," I continued, raising my voice. "And he's a draftee. He'll be in Nam in ten weeks. He's at my house right now, terrified he's gonna lose his life BEFORE he goes to war!"

Finally, the man stood up.

"Mr. Brae, calm down or I'll have to ask you to leave!"

When I glanced over, Harrigan was standing too.

"I don't know who your 'witness' is," the bishop went on, "but Mr. Mardini did not murder his niece. He's a well-respected member of the community and a great benefactor to the Church. We will cooperate in any way we can but not like this." He softened his tone and said, "Listen, when Cardinal Cushing returns—"

"Returns from where?"

"Rome. He's in Rome until next Friday. When he's back, I'm sure he'd be happy to meet and discuss any concerns related to the Archdiocese." He gave a sideways, probing look and said, "And who is your superior?"

"Captain Ernest Jackson."

"Very well, please ask him to—"

"If I could," I said, and he blinked in surprise.

"Pardon?"

"He's dying."

IT WAS pitch dark when we left the Seminary. We walked through the complex along brick walkways that were iced over from the drop in temperature. We reached the rear lot, and the same cars were still there. I started the Valiant and waited a couple of minutes for it to warm up.

"Are you satisfied?" Harrigan said, taking off his gloves.

"I'm never satisfied."

"Do you still think Mardini and Vogt are complicit?"

I turned to him and said, "And the bishop too."

He had the expression of someone who is told something so preposterous they question their own hearing.

"He said *Mardini did not murder his niece*," I said. I put the car in gear then looked dead at him. "I didn't mention his niece. And I didn't say he had anything to do with the death of that woman."

Harrigan swallowed and looked straight ahead. I lifted my foot off the brake, and we started down the driveway. As we drove, I couldn't tell what he was thinking, but I was damn sure he knew what I was.

A side of law enforcement that no one spoke about but which many accepted was the reality of civilian power and influence. The law was for everyone, but prosecution was for the ordinary. Presenting evidence that might implicate a bishop, an abbot, and one of the wealthiest builders in Boston was like asking the DA to indict the Lord himself.

When I pulled up to my house, we sat idling for a few minutes.

"Where do we go from here?" Harrigan said.

"You go home."

He made a tired smile, tried to keep from yawning.

"That's not what I meant."

"Get some rest," I said. "We'll talk about it tomorrow."

I turned off the engine, and we both got out. As he walked over to his car, he said, "You know, Lieutenant, your instincts are almost as good as the captain's."

I was just ready to thank him when he added, "*Almost*."

CHAPTER 44

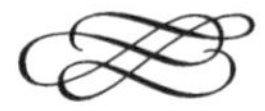

I AWOKE TO THE GLARE OF THE MORNING SUN THROUGH THE SHADES. When I turned over, Ruth was on her side, her arms tucked into her chest. The hum of her soft breath reminded me of a cat purring. I rubbed her back, kissed her shoulder, and then headed to the bathroom.

When I walked into the living room, Teddy was eating a bowl of cereal and watching Captain Kangaroo. He wore the same dirty pants, but the undershirt must have been mine because it was sparkling white and three sizes too big. The moment he saw me he stopped everything and stood up.

"Morning, Sir."

"Carry on," I said, waving for him to sit. "You're a guest."

I looked at the TV then at him, raising one eye sarcastically.

"I used to love this program," he said, like he had to justify his reason for watching it. "It's how I learned English."

I just shook my head and walked into the kitchen, where I filled the kettle and lit the stove. I made tea and grabbed a banana from the counter. When I came back out, Teddy had changed the station, and the news was on.

The headline story was the crisis at St Kilda, which was now competing with the Vietnam War for coverage. There were more officers than I could count, and people filled the street from end to end like a Macy's Day Parade. A group of protesters stood by the wall with placards that read *OUR LADY IS OUR RIGHT* and *GOD REVEALS, THE MAYOR STEALS*. Much of it was orderly, but even through the camera, I could sense a collective tension that was only one scuffle away from becoming a riot.

"Wouldn't want to be there right now," Teddy remarked.

I was going to reply but stopped. As he stared at the TV, I watched him with a warm pity, knowing that where he was going would make the abbey situation look like a traffic spat.

I was about to go get dressed when something caught my eye. The camera was getting knocked around from all the activity, but when it steadied, I saw Sweeney's mother in the background. It was only for a couple of seconds, but long enough for me to read the sign she was holding:

FOR JUDGMENT IS WITHOUT MERCY
TO ONE WHO HAS SHOWN NO MERCY.
– JAMES 2:13.

IN AN INSTANT, she was gone. I stood stunned. The station flashed to Mayor White, who was giving a press conference. Behind him were members of the community—city councilors, local business owners, clergy—an ambitious assemblage for a Saturday morning. And there, towering over them all, was Father Vogt, his brown cloak concealed under a long coat like he was trying to blend in.

What came over me, I didn't know. But without a word, I ran to get ready, and minutes later I was out the door. My stomach gurgled and my head throbbed as I raced through the streets to the abbey. The clock was ticking; time felt like it was accelerating. I knew that if I didn't do something to stop the eviction, a world of blood would be on my conscience.

As I neared St Kilda, I felt the presence of the multitudes like a thick humidity. Even five blocks away, automobiles lined the streets, took up every possible spot. Pilgrims trudged along the sidewalks through slush and cold in a long procession of the faithful. Notice of the Monday expulsion had created a new urgency, and everyone everywhere wanted to visit. It seemed like the eyes of the country were on Roxbury.

Even using my sirens, I was only able to get within a few streets of the abbey. The roads were jammed, and traffic was at a standstill. Some cars had run out of gas, and a few broke down. I watched one family push a rusted Ford van into a driveway; another towed their things in a toy wagon. The steady determination reminded me of refugee columns in Korea, those miles-long convoys of trucks, mule carts, and foot-travelers.

I was lucky enough to find a spot, and I got out, joining the procession in the long march to the miracle. Some people joked, others conversed, but for the most part, everyone was silent. Walking among them made me realize how distant I had grown from ordinary residents. When an old drunk asked for a cigarette, I handed him two and gave him a light.

I soon reached the street that descended to the front gates. Ambulance lights were flashing; patrolmen shouted through bullhorns. There were media vans everywhere, and a helicopter hovered above. The exhilaration of the scene was something I hadn't felt since the war.

I was thirty yards from the entrance when someone shouted my name, and I looked over to see Duggan. Had it been anyone else, I might have overlooked them in the chaos, but he towered over the crowd, his lanky body pushing through the swarm. When he finally got to me, he was almost distraught.

"This is nuts."

"This is more than nuts, Giraffe," I said, looking around in astonishment.

"Have you seen Sergeant Yelmokas or Houlihan?" When I shook my head, he went on, "Manning? Piero?—"

"No!" I said. "Nobody. I haven't seen anyone. I just got here."

"I'm waiting to get relieved—been here all night. I gotta get home, Jody—"

When I glanced up to him, his face was red, and it wasn't from the cold. His voice shook from both fear and fatigue, a dangerous combination for any cop.

"You know the mayor asked for National Guard troops Monday?" he said.

"I heard the rumor."

"It's no rumor, it's gonna happen. And this place is gonna turn into a battlefield."

"Then I'll feel right at home."

I felt someone watching and swung around to see two hippies behind us. When they flashed the peace sign, Duggan waved for me to follow, and we walked to the sidewalk, where the Red Cross had a table with water, snacks, and first-aid supplies. He reached for a paper cup and a young female volunteer smiled.

"I guess we're not the bad guys," I said.

In one continuous gulp, he drank the water and stared at me.

"Not yet."

He tossed the cup in a barrel, and someone called over the two-way. He responded, then struggled to hear with all the noise. His expression changed from worry to surprise, and my pulse rose at the thought that something was about to happen. He ended the chat with 'over' and looked down at me.

"Just when things can't get any stranger."

"What's wrong?"

"Not sure, come on," he said, and we began to walk.

We went against the tide, up the street to a paddy wagon parked on the curb. Four patrolmen stood beside it, and I noticed a civilian among them. I wasn't sure if they had someone in custody, but I could tell it was serious. The moment we approached, the officers nodded to Duggan and acknowledged me.

"Detective," one of them said.

When he turned aside, I saw an old man in the middle. He was small and wiry, with a plaid overcoat and a white beard. He moved his hands around as he spoke, and the men looked spellbound.

"What's the problem?" I said.

"Sir, you won't believe this," one of the officers said.

"Try me."

He came closer and lowered his voice, making sure no passersby could hear. Duggan stood at my side and leaned in.

"This guy's a survivor…of the death camps."

"Where?"

"Germany. You know? Auschwitz."

"Auschwitz was in Poland."

He ignored the correction and continued.

"He was over by the wall, blabbering away, shouting, haranguing people. I was told to shut him up." The cop took out a napkin and wiped his nose. Whether it was from the cold or the excitement, I couldn't tell, but he was teary-eyed. "This place is a tinderbox anyway. The precinct captain doesn't want any instigators. I get to talkin' with the guy. He says he knows the abbot. And the abbot's no abbot. He says the abbot was a guard. A guard at Auschwitz."

All the uproar faded into the backdrop, and the three of us stood stunned. I glanced over to the abbey, where the bell tower hovered atop the hill, and a sinister tingle came over me. In that instant, everything that had occurred in the previous weeks took on a new clarity. I stood for a moment thinking, then I held out my hand.

"What's your name officer?" I asked.

"Katz, Sir. Paul Katz."

I thanked him and walked over to the man. He was visibly upset, but not with the police, and his hollow eyes revealed a deeper indignation than I could ever have hoped to understand. He was one of those people who looked old but was even older. When I stepped up to him, the other cops moved away.

"I'm told you have some information on Abbot Vogt."

"Vogt?" he said, opening his arms, looking up at the sky, "A victional name for a victional man. Heez no Vogt, I tell you." He had a heavy accent; he spat when he spoke. "Heez Hans Volkmann. I know that man like I know my own son. A bastard! A scoundrel." He pointed his gnarled finger at me. "A filthy murderer!"

As he worked himself into a frenzy, I put out my hands to calm him.

"And if so, he'll be arrested. But I need a statement from you. Can you come to the station?"

One of his eyebrows lifted, "Eh?"

"The police station. Can you come down?"

His expression softened, and he seemed almost honored by the request.

"Ye," he said in Yiddish. "I shall be of service in any way to get that devil."

I smiled and said thanks. Then I looked at Duggan and said, "Take him down to headquarters immediately. Get a statement." I lowered my voice so the other officers couldn't hear. "If this doesn't buy us some time, nothing will."

"What time is that, Jody?"

I looked over to the abbey.

"Time to let this whole thing die a natural death."

CHAPTER 45

WHEN I GOT TO THE ARMORY THERE WERE MORE CARS THAN I HAD ever seen on a weekend. A CBS van was out front, and a female reporter, different from the one before, lingered by the stairs with her cameraman. She was young and pretty and wore a Jackie Kennedy pillbox hat that was a few years outdated. As I crossed the lot, I knew it wouldn't be easy to avoid her.

"Excuse me," she said, holding up a microphone. "CBS. May we ask?—"

"Sorry, I'm with the Red Cross."

I didn't look back to see her reaction, but I knew she wasn't amused. I pushed through the main doors and went up the stairs. The reception area was complete mayhem. There were photographers, public officials, freelance reporters, concerned citizens, and insiders from the mayor's office. The phones were ringing off the hook, and three secretaries, understaffed and overwhelmed, worked feverishly behind the counter. The place had the frenzied rush of a passport office on the eve of an invasion.

I kept my head low and walked quickly towards my office.

"Lieutenant!" someone yelled.

I looked back, and Harrigan was coming towards me, almost in a sprint. He never shouted, and his voice sounded different when he did.

"Anthony Vigliotti is dead," he said.

The news was unfortunate, but it wasn't a shock, and I even felt a twinge of sorrow. With people rushing up and down the corridor, we stepped over to the wall.

"Too bad—"

"The hospital called twenty minutes ago."

The interruption wasn't like him, but I knew he was close to panic.

"Have someone notify his aunt."

As I started to move away, he held out his arm to stop me.

"They think it was not unintentional."

Even under stress, he practiced an understatement that was not easy to understand. I had to repeat the sentence in my mind twice to be sure I knew what he meant.

"He was killed?" I said.

He looked me dead in the eye.

"It appears to be so."

Without another word, we headed to the nearest stairwell, scrambled down three flights, and reached the alley on the side of the building. To get to the front lot, we had to run through a foot of snow, but avoiding the lobby was worth the discomfort.

We hopped in the Valiant and pulled out, and Harrigan hit the sirens.

"I saw Duggan bring the witness in," he said. "Is it true?"

"I hope so and I hope not."

He acknowledged the contradiction with a slow nod.

"Whether he was a Nazi or not, he's still a bastard," I added.

"To me, they are one and the same."

"Amen, brother."

Because it was the weekend, traffic was light, and we got to City Hospital in five minutes. I sped up the driveway and there were three cruisers out front. Hospital staff and visitors gathered in small groups, chatting about the incident, exchanging gossip and hearsay. We parked at the curb and hurried into the lobby, where I went up to the counter and flashed my badge.

"BPD," I said, interrupting a secretary on the phone. "Where's the incident?"

She whispered something to the caller and hung up.

"Yes, Sir, um, it's, go—"

While she continued to stutter, a colleague came over.

"Gentlemen, it's room 223," the woman said. "The whole ward is on lock-down."

I called over to Harrigan, and we ran to the elevator bank. When the door opened to the second floor, the first thing I heard was Doctor Ansell's voice. We started down the corridor, and there was more blue than white. I saw patrolmen, detectives, BCI officials, and even a guy I knew from the canine unit. We hurried down to the end, and Ansell was standing with his intern, Dr. Quinlan, and two officers.

"Brae," he said, and his face beamed. "Fancy seeing you here."

"Where's Vigliotti?"

"Dead."

"Where's the body?"

"In there on the bed. All ready to roll."

When I leaned in to get a view of the room, I realized that 223 was directly below the captain's—323. A man from BCI came out with dusting equipment and measuring tape.

"Shouldn't be much longer," he said.

I looked at Ansell.

"You could've had him delivered."

"Don't even need a stretcher. Easiest call I've ever had, kid."

Dr. Quinlan stood with his arms crossed, lips pressed together, annoyed by our sarcasm but trying not to show it. I turned to him and said, "Who had access to him?"

"He wasn't under any special protection. We weren't informed that he was a suspect."

"He wasn't a suspect," I said, loud enough for everyone around to hear. "Maybe a witness. What the hell happened?"

"One of the nurses found him unconscious. When she checked his vitals, he barely had a pulse."

"But he had severe internal injuries, am I right?"

Quinlan looked at Harrigan then to me.

"Can you follow me, please?" he said.

While Ansell and the intern stayed behind, the three of us walked down the hallway and turned the corner. Outside an office, two officers were standing guard, and they seemed relieved when we approached. Quinlan lowered his voice and said to me, "I didn't want to alarm anyone, and I certainly don't want to prejudice an employee."

I nodded to the officers, and they moved aside. When Quinlan opened the door, a woman was sitting in a chair with a nurse comforting her. She looked up as we entered, and her eyes were red from sobbing. I immediately recognized her as the Irish nurse Harrigan and I met when we first came to investigate the dumpster homicide.

"Detectives," Quinlan said, "this is Miss O'Toole, one of our floor nurses."

She went to stand, but I held out my hand.

"Please, stay."

"Would you tell these gentlemen what you saw?" the doctor said.

The other nurse stepped back. Miss O'Toole wiped her eyes and looked up. "I'd just come back from lunch," she said nervously. "I...I...I seen, um, Ms. Stuart come out of the loo. I knew she had been in some sort of, um, trouble, but I didn't know how. So I says, 'Ms. Stuart, how're ye?' She said she'd come to get her pay and that we mightn't be seeing one another for some time..."

Maybe it was the woman's melodic brogue, but it sounded more like she was telling a story than recounting an event.

"...About, um, thirty minutes later," she went on, "I was behind the station counter, and I noticed her come out of a patient's room. My lady goes to the end of the hallway and out the utility stairwell—"

"Vigliotti's room?"

The other nurse handed her a tissue and Miss O'Toole continued, "I couldn't tell, you know? It was a bit of a distance. I only recognized her because of, um, the blue coat. I thought nothing of it. 'Bout ten minutes later, I was making me rounds. That's when I realized—"

Harrigan stepped forward and asked, "But you're not positive it was his room?"

She looked over to Dr. Quinlan, and we turned to him. He reached into his jacket and took out an eyeglass case. As we watched, he opened it, and there was a small implement inside. Using a napkin from his pocket, he took it out and said, "This was at the foot of the bed."

When he held it under the light, we saw that it was a syringe. I looked at Miss O'Toole.

"You found that?" I asked.

She nodded but didn't speak.

Quinlan looked at the other nurse and said, "Would you please take Miss O'Toole to get some water."

The two women left the room, and when he shut the door, I gave him a cold look.

"Why didn't you show this to BCI?"

"I wanted to talk with you first," he said, and he was either clever or I was gullible because the flattery softened me. "You're the only one outside of hospital administration that knows about Ms. Stuart's... ah...situation."

"You mean stealing drugs?"

"Yes," he said, a hint of professional humiliation in his voice.

"Toxicology will know if it's barbiturates or not."

When I held out my hand, he put the syringe back in the case and handed it over. I nodded to him and turned to leave.

"Officer," he said, and Harrigan and I stopped. "Does Ms. Stuart's misconduct need to be made known? I prefer the hospital's reputation not be put in jeopardy."

I turned around and looked him straight in the eye.

"My wife, Ruth Brae, was reprimanded by Stuart for something she didn't do. She's terribly upset. You fix it and I'll see what I can do."

His forehead strained; his eyes twitched. In the high culture of medical ethics, no doctor was comfortable making a backroom deal.

"Agreed," he said, looking down.

Harrigan and I walked out of the room and saw the Irish woman and her colleague sitting in the hallway. We smiled as we passed and turned down the main corridor. The floor was desolate—the only staff I saw were some nurses pushing carts, attending to their patients.

As we waited for the elevator, Harrigan said, "You have a way of getting your way."

"I just try harder."

The bell rang, the doors opened, and we got in. When I pressed the button for the third floor, Harrigan didn't have to ask because he knew where we were going. Moments later, we arrived and headed for the nurses' station. In the intimate corridors of the hospital, news spread fast, and there was a subdued busyness as staff went about their daily tasks knowing that someone might have killed a patient.

As we walked by the charge nurse, she said, "May I help you?"

I pointed ahead.

"Going to see Ernest Jackson."

"He's been released."

Harrigan and I stopped immediately, and I walked over to the desk.

"Released?!" I said angrily. "What do you mean released?

She recoiled, more out of fear than indignation.

"I'm sorry, Sir. He was transported home this morning."

From the moment I turned to leave until we came out the hospital doors, I was in a controlled rage. Harrigan waited by the entrance while I walked over to an empty bench to smoke. He always seemed to know when to intervene and when to leave me alone.

As I sat thinking, a plane took off from Logan Airport, and I watched it bank east, probably heading to Europe. I thought of our honeymoon in Ireland, and it made me want to go back there with Ruth.

After a few minutes, Harrigan strolled over, his coat buttoned up and hands in his pockets. It had been cold for so long that I didn't even notice anymore.

"Are you okay?" he asked.

I stood up, flicked my cigarette, and walked away without answering. He followed me to the Valiant, and there was a parking ticket on the windshield. I was glad the security officer who issued it wasn't around because he would have become the target of all my fury.

"We'll need a warrant for Stuart...immediately," I said.

"You haven't answered my question."

I looked at him across the roof of the car.

"I really don't know."

BY THE TIME I got home, it was midnight. I opened the front door, and Teddy was lying on the couch with a blanket and pillow. The only light was the television; the volume was down all the way. On the screen, I saw the fluttering flag of the nightly sign-off. Soon there would be only static.

I hung up my coat, loosened my tie, and sat in the rocker.

"Hi, Sir," he said in a drowsy voice.

"Don't let me disturb you."

"I can't sleep."

"I don't blame you."

I rubbed my temples, trying to soothe a bad headache, but it didn't work. I looked at him and said, "You're thinking about your uncle."

He nodded.

"Will we find him?"

"I believe he's safe. I don't know why, but I do. Any man who's lived through Kim Il-Sung can dodge a few American thugs."

I kicked off my shoes and leaned back in the chair, struggling to keep my eyes open. I had every intention of getting up and going into the bedroom, but my body felt like a suit of armor, and it was so much easier not to move.

"How was Ruth tonight?" I mumbled, my eyes slowly closing.

"We had dinner then she went to bed."

"She cooked?"

He said something that I thought was 'yes' and I added, "She's an awful cook, huh?"

Although I said it for a laugh, it was also true, and she would have admitted it. But Teddy wouldn't comment out of respect. Instead, he said, "When I came to this country, I had rickets. I don't remember much from childhood, just that I was hungry all the time."

"You should've told the draft board. They would have given you an exemption."

My eyes were almost shut; I saw only a sliver of the world. The second before I sank into sleep, I heard his voice.

"I don't want an exemption."

CHAPTER 46

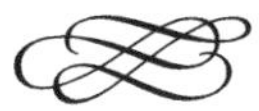

I AWOKE TO THE SOUND OF CHURCH BELLS. IT WAS SUNDAY. TOMORROW, the city would evict the pilgrims from St Kilda. Tomorrow, the Archdiocese would clear the frost from the windows. Tomorrow, the hope and faith of countless people would be shattered.

I sat forward in the rocker and looked around dizzily. Sleeping on the couch with the covers over his head, Teddy looked like a mummy. I got up quietly and peeked in the bedroom to find that Ruth was also out cold. Not wanting to wake them, I tiptoed into the bathroom, where I brushed my teeth and splashed water on my face. Then I grabbed my coat and headed out the door.

Outside the temperature had risen twenty degrees since yesterday, and it was almost mild. It was so early the streets were deserted, and even churches weren't open yet. When I reached The Armory, the lot was empty, but I took a spot near the street anyway. With less than 24-hours until the abbey eviction, city officials, auxiliary staff, and the media would soon be on-site, and I didn't want anyone to box me in.

I must have been paranoid because I went down the side alley to avoid the lobby. When I opened the door to my office, I looked at the minefield of boxes, crates, books, and other things, and just shook my head. The captain had asked me several times to organize it, and, in a way, I felt like I had let him down.

As I stepped over the clutter to my desk, I noticed that the frost on the windows was starting to melt. In a few weeks, the apparition at St Kilda would also fade due to the rising temperatures. If the Archdiocese could hold off from erasing it, I thought, the miracle would die a natural death and prevent the disillusionment of the many believers.

"Lieutenant."

The soft voice made me jump, and when I looked, Harrigan was in the doorway.

"Do you ever knock?" I grumbled.

"It was open."

"No. I closed it."

"I just walked up. It was open."

"No," I said sternly. "It was closed."

When he held up his hands in surrender, we both grinned, and he entered. He climbed over the mess and got to the leather chair beside my desk. Showered, sharply dressed, and wide awake, he reminded me just how disheveled I was.

"You look tired."

I leaned forward in the seat and said, "I'm beyond tired."

"I have the warrant for Ms. Stuart."

"How about the address?"

"11 Tennyson Street, West Roxbury," he rattled off.

"You're good."

"Should we go?"

"Naw, let her sleep in," I said, and he smiled. "Can I buy breakfast?"

"Are you paying?"

"I said I'd *buy*."

"With you, that's not always implied, Lieutenant."

WE WALKED DOWN to the cafeteria and took a table near the coffee urns. The night shift just got off, and throngs of weary patrolmen came in for a snack before going home. We each got a donut and coffee then sat down under an unspoken tension that was ready to burst.

When Harrigan reached to the next table for the newspaper, there was a large front headline: *COMMUNITY WEIGHS IN ON ABBEY EVACUATION.*

"Now they're calling it an evacuation?"

"A gentler term," he said, skimming the story. "The chief is giving a press conference at 2:00 p.m."

"We have to get him to call off tomorrow."

"And how do you propose we do it?"

I sipped from my cup and stared ahead helplessly. Without Jackson, the confidence that for years I carried like a medal seemed to collapse. I felt like a rookie again. It was a hard thing to be scared but even harder to be uncertain. I thought of the captain and imagined myself asking for his advice. Then like a prayer answered, a surge of inspiration came over me, and I knew what to do.

"Give the warrant to some junior detectives," I said, turning to him. "Explain the situation. Then to go to my house and get Teddy. He's the only witness we—"

"He's not a witness."

"Until we find his uncle, he's the closest thing to it."

When two sergeants walked by, I stopped talking. It was strange being secretive among my own, but the abbey was a political and humanitarian disaster, and, at this point, no one wanted the clearance postponed for fear that it would only get worse.

"I'll get the birth certificate of 'Brenda Mardini,'" I said, "It's gonna take more than a theory to convince the chief."

He shoved the rest of his donut in his mouth, guzzled his coffee.

"What will you do, Lieutenant?" he asked.

"I'll call Bishop Severin, tell him we know about Vogt. If McNamara doesn't call off the eviction, the Archdiocese might."

We got up from the table and faced each other like two soldiers before a mission. It was a sentimental moment I didn't expect, and for some reason, we shook hands.

"Be back here at noon."

"Yes, Sir."

We parted at the stairwell, and Harrigan headed towards the lobby. I went into my office and made sure the door was shut. I called the operator for the number then dialed the Archdiocese. It rang a dozen times before someone finally picked up.

"Archdiocese of Boston."

"I'm trying to reach Bishop Severin."

There was a short pause.

"He may be getting ready for Mass, but I can check. May I ask who is calling?"

"Lieutenant Jody Brae. Boston Police."

Again, there was a pause.

"Hold please."

I waited anxiously and listened to the static. Bishops weren't accustomed to getting unsolicited calls, and I doubted they would put me through. I never had strong feelings about religion, but the Roman Catholic Church had a control and command that, as a former soldier, I had to respect.

"Hello," a timid voice said, and I immediately sat up. It was him.

"Bishop, this is—"

"Yes, officer," he said, "I know. How may I be of service?"

"You need to call off the eviction of the pilgrims tomorrow," I blurted, the words tripping off my tongue. It was a bold demand, but with the deadline fast approaching, there was no more time for diplomacy.

"I'm afraid that's not possible."

"We have some information that might change that."

"Excuse me?"

"Your abbot, Father Vogt, is no priest. He's a former Nazi. He was identified by an Auschwitz survivor. I spoke with the man yesterday. He's given a statement, and he'll testify."

"Mr. Brae, this is—"

"You need to call Chief McNamara. Tell him the Archdiocese no longer supports this."

"I can do no such thing. I haven't the authority."

Unable to contain my anger, I stood up in the chair and squeezed the receiver.

"You have to! The sale of the abbey is a sham. You know it, I know it. Mardini's firm is involved in the murder of a young woman. We have a witness. Vogt is a Nazi...and he probably killed Brother Emmanuel—"

"Enough!" he said. "Please!"

I lowered my voice and spoke with a slow and threatening intensity. "Oh, and there's more. Much more." It was a bluff he could have easily called, but one I had to make, and when he didn't scoff, I knew that he was part of the plot. "We can let this whole ugly episode die a natural death. Mardini's going to jail. Vogt too. But if you call off the eviction, the investigation will end with them."

"I...I...I...," he stuttered, "don't think—"

"I'll go to the press right now. They're parked out front. I'll tell them the Archdiocese is conspiring with criminals to sell the abbey... at the expense of all those helpless people. There'll be hearings in the legislature."

There was dead silence at the other end. For a moment, I thought he had hung up. But as I listened, I heard faint, rapid breathing. When he eventually spoke, it was with the angst-ridden voice of a remorseful man.

"I...I'm afraid...it's not that simple."

"I never said it was."

"Please, Mr. Brae. Let me talk with some of my colleagues."

"McNamara is holding a press conference at 2 p.m. If the eviction isn't canceled, I'm going public with ALL the evidence!"

I slammed the phone, swiped some papers off my desk, and sat furiously. I reached in my coat for a cigarette to calm down, but I couldn't find my lighter. When I opened the top drawer to look for matches, I saw a key marked 'Capt.'s Office'—Harrigan had been right. I grabbed the keyring and left, going down the corridor until I reached Jackson's door. I unlocked it and peered in to see only darkness. I groped along the wall for the switch and when I hit it, the captain's world suddenly appeared.

I went over and raised the window shades, and the mystique of the place vanished in the morning light. I got straight to work, rummaging first through the cabinet then the drawers of his desk. It wasn't until I looked on the desk itself that I found the case file, a thin manila folder marked with only the date of the first homicide.

I took out the documents and sat in his chair, flipping through pages of autopsies, police reports, witness accounts, etc. I found the birth certificate of Brenda Mardini, the doctored date more obvious each time I saw it. On top of everything and folded in half was a Xerox copy of an old news article whose text was light but still readable. My hand trembled as I read it.

The Boston Evening Globe - June 14th, 1960.

DEVELOPER INDICTED IN CORRUPTION SCHEME.

BOSTON – *Authorities have announced a federal indictment against a local man whose company secured millions in government contracts to demolish the West End. The indictment alleges that Sidney "Sid" Mardini, 64, of Weston, Mass. engaged in an elaborate scheme to charge the government for equipment and services not rendered. Named also in the indictment is a business associate of Mardini, Wei "Johnny" Lee, 53, of Boston. A spokesman for Attorney General Elliot Richardson's office said, "While the investigation is ongoing, we can only confirm that the defendants acted together to defraud the Federal Government...*

. . .

I PUT down the dossier and looked across the room, stunned and yet strangely relieved. The only thing I knew about Jackson's organizational system was that he filed documents in the order he obtained them. And considering that the article was at the front of the folder, he must have only recently discovered it.

Learning that Mardini and Lee were crooks was no great revelation but seeing their names together in print somehow completed the circle of treachery and deceit that had been dogging me for weeks. They must have beaten the indictment because both men were free, and I would find out how another day. For now, I was satisfied in knowing they were collaborators.

Someone knocked at the door, and I froze. They waited a few seconds then knocked again, this time quicker, harder, with much greater urgency. When I shifted in the chair, it made a loud creak, and I could no longer hide if I wanted to. So I got up and went to the door. I turned the knob and opened it a few inches to see the petite brunette secretary. There was alarm in her face.

"Lieutenant," she said nervously. "There's an incident. Dispatch told me to look for you."

"An incident?"

"Roslindale Avenue. Your house."

CHAPTER 47

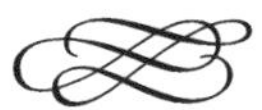

I RACED THROUGH THE CITY STREETS IN A COLD SWEAT, TREMORS rippling through my body like a seizure. I kept the gas floored and turned only when I had to. Knowing what I knew, it mattered little whether I lived or died.

By the time I got to Roslindale, I had blown at least one tire, and the engine was overheating. I approached my street and saw a police car turn onto it with its lights flashing. I skidded around the corner and followed it up the hill. At the top, there were three more cruisers in front of my house, all parked chaotically. Officers were hiding behind open car doors with their pistols drawn and aimed.

A wave of nausea came over me. When I sped up and screeched to a stop, some heads turned. The moment I got out, I realized I didn't have my .38. I crouched down and made my way to the trunk, where I fumbled with my keys and opened it. Inside I unlocked the shotgun case that I kept hidden under a gray blanket. I took out the shiny Browning 12-gauge and cocked it once to load the chamber.

As I moved towards the scene, I couldn't believe how quiet it was. Squirrels scuttled between the bare trees; the gutters dripped with melting snow. I crept to the nearest cop car, feeling neither fear nor dread. My brain, as well as my body, had slipped into an automated trance and, just like in combat, I returned to a state of primal instincts—readiness, survival, revenge. Inside that apartment lay my entire world, and I was either going to protect it or die trying.

"What the fuck's going on?"

The officer looked over as I came near.

"Shots fired, Sir..."

Anything beyond that I didn't hear. I continued on, leaping to the next closest vehicle, exposed for a few perilous seconds. I came up to a rookie, who was holding out his gun with one hand and talking on the two-way with the other. He turned and looked at me with complete terror.

"Who's in there?" I said.

"D...d...don't know," he answered, his trigger hand shaking. "A... a...a call came in, a...a...a suspicious car..."

I went around the back of the vehicle and peered across to see Sergeant Duggan kneeling in the passenger door of his cruiser. With a hiss, I got his attention, and he glanced over, squinting in the sun. The moment I darted towards him, he put out his hands, but it was too late. As I dashed between the cars, I heard a whoosh above my head followed by the crack of gunfire. Gripping the shotgun, I hit the ground and rolled once like they had taught me in boot camp.

"Stay the fuck down," Duggan snapped.

"What the hell's going on?"

Hugging the side of his cruiser, he looked back and said, "Don't know. We got a call. I was in the area. Showed up. They opened up on me. Harrigan was already here—"

"Harrigan?"

He nodded ahead, and I peered around the car door. Because I had been searching for any sound or movement, I almost overlooked the presence of Harrigan's vehicle. I got flat down and looked under the cars to see a large hulk on the sidewalk by the front steps. Then I heard the moaning.

"I gotta get him!" I said frantically, and I started to get up.

Duggan turned back and put his big hand on my shoulder.

"Brae," he said. "Stay down, brother, or you'll get your head blown off."

"Ruth's in there. Are they in the house?"

When he shook his head, a bead of sweat fell from the tip of his nose.

"Don't know. I don't think so. One guy is on the lawn. I got him good, real good. There's another in the foyer." He looked at me, his face twitching in discomfort. "There were three, I think. I don't know where the third is."

He made a grim smile and struggled to breathe. It was then that I noticed blood under his arm, just below the ribcage.

"You're hit."

"A scratch, just a scratch."

With his dark wool coat, it was hard to know whether it was or wasn't so I had to take his word for it. As I started to back away, he mouthed, "Don't be a hero—"

I put up my thumb then circled the trunk to the other side of the cruiser. From that angle, I could see the walkway, and a body was lying in the snow. I got on my stomach and shimmied to the front tire, where I looked out and saw a figure in the vestibule of the house. He was jumpy, nervous, darting wildly in every direction. For a split second, he peeked out of the doorway with his gun raised. When one of the officers fired, the man shot back and a windshield shattered.

I gripped the shotgun firmly and took some deep breaths. I watched the man's movement in the shadows and tried to guess when he was facing away from me. And once he was, I sprung up and ran across to the neighbor's driveway. I slid on the ice and landed on my hip, fast enough that the assailant didn't see me. My heart pounded; I was dizzy with adrenaline. I stood up and went to the corner of the house, where I looked over and signaled to Duggan and the others.

With my back to the wall, I tiptoed along it and approached the doorway. The shotgun was upright to my chest, my finger was on the trigger. Suddenly, there was another exchange of gunfire—a bullet hit the grille of one of the cruisers. As I stepped closer to the entrance, I heard panicked voices, the scuffle of feet. The third man was inside.

I looked over to Duggan, whose face was half-concealed by the car door, his eyes visible behind the barrel of his .38. I motioned to all the officers that I was going in, and I waited for each to respond with a nod. Everyone was edgy, and I didn't want to die from friendly fire.

Finally, I gazed up to the sky and thought of Ruth and Jackson. I looked over to Harrigan and prayed for him also. Then I moved closer to the doorway, so close I could hear the man inside breathing. In a single motion, I jumped onto the front steps, spun around, and aimed the shotgun. A second after I fired, I saw the man's eyes. I pulled the trigger again and again. Blood splattered. The hall filled with smoke. I heard a thud. I got him.

I yelled to the officers, and everyone came running. At that moment, I was torn between helping Harrigan or going in for Ruth. But when he glanced up from the sidewalk and raised his thumb, I knew it was not fatal.

I went into the dark vestibule and stepped over the body. The hallway door was slightly open, its wood splintered by bullets. As I ascended the stairs, I heard another gunshot from the third floor. The bang knocked me back—my ears rang. I held the shotgun tight and charged up screaming. What I saw when I reached the top was beyond joy.

"Sir!"

There stood Teddy, dressed in the white undershirt, my .38 in his hand. Lying on the landing with a bullet hole in his cheek was one of the Chinese men I had encountered in front of his house two weeks before.

"Where's Ruth?" I yelled, and I ran into the apartment.

"Jody," I heard, and she came out of the bedroom in a bathrobe, her hair wet. She dashed over and we embraced.

"What the hell happened?!"

"The doorbell rang," Teddy said. "She was in the shower. I called down but no one answered. So I tiptoed to the door, looked through the peephole. I saw Mr. Lee's men—"

"Johnny Lee?"

He nodded and continued, "I know them from the Lantern House.

They come in late...with other men. They sit in the back. Mr. Lee sits with them. They drink, talk business."

Still holding me, Ruth looked up into my eyes and said, "They tried to break in."

"I heard them doing something with the lock, so I ran up and called the police."

She looked at him and then to me.

"Teddy yelled for me to get under the bed."

"I heard the foyer door open," he said. "I leaned over the railing and saw the big man coming up. When he saw me, he fired. I shot back."

"He held them off until the police came," she said, her voice cracking.

She let go of me and looked at Teddy with warm and grateful admiration. I reached out to shake his hand, but he gave me the pistol instead. When he grinned at the misunderstanding, I leaned forward and hugged him like a son. His body was tense; the back of the t-shirt was sweaty. Then he stood with a bashful silence, proud but in a humble way.

"I guess I'm a soldier now."

"You always were," I said, checking the gun and locking the safety. "You always were."

I turned to Ruth and saw a glimmer in her eyes that hadn't been there for months. The horror of being present at a near-assassination would have traumatized most people. But she wasn't most people, and although she was far from calm, the experience seemed to enliven her spirit.

Two officers came in and looked around, knowing they should do something, not sure what.

"Um," one of them said, "everything secure in here?"

I pushed the door a little to shield Ruth from the body on the landing. I leaned into one of them and whispered, "Check with the guy out there?"

The cop made a wry smile and looked at his partner. Only a fellow officer would know that, in such a situation, sarcasm was not only appropriate but necessary. Teddy didn't hear me, and Ruth was busy picking things up in the living room, ever concerned about tidiness. More police cars arrived, and I looked out the window to see patrolmen scouring the street and sidewalk for shells. When Duggan came in, he was visibly distressed.

"You okay?" I said.

"Told you. Just a scratch."

"And Harrigan?"

"Head wound," he said, and everyone was silent. My face dropped and I went for the door, but he got in front of me. "No, no, no…I'm sorry. I'm not thinkin' right. He got grazed in the knee, fell back, banged his head. He's fine."

Nevertheless, I looked at Ruth before bolting out the door. Outside on the front lawn, someone had already thrown a sheet over the assailant—he was dead. Two paramedics were attending to Harrigan, who was lying on a stretcher in the middle of the road. His left knee was a bowling ball of white gauze, swelling and wet with blood. I ran over and was glad to see he was conscious.

"Hello, Lieutenant."

He spoke like he was greeting me at a dinner party.

"You alright?"

"I believe so. My knee hurts."

"How about your head?"

He rolled his eyes back as if trying to observe his own crown.

"Too thick to feel pain."

I grinned.

"I gotta go see the captain. I need your car."

He groped for his coat pocket but couldn't find it, so I reached in and got the keys myself. The paramedics looked at me for permission then they lifted the stretcher. As they slid him inside, Harrigan stopped them halfway and glanced at me.

"Make it count, Lieutenant."

I patted his arm, and he responded with a soft, contented smile. The two men loaded him the rest of the way and closed the doors. As the ambulance sirens faded behind me, I walked over to Harrigan's car. Duggan, Ruth, and Teddy came out of the doorway and into the sunlight, stunned but unhurt. Ruth met me at the bottom of the steps, and I said quietly, "I'm going to see the captain. It's urgent."

She looked up to me, her eyelashes fluttering.

"You go then."

I took both her shoulders and looked at her tenderly.

"Are you alright?" I said, then added, "for now?"

She nodded.

"For now."

An unmarked car pulled up and parked in the street. Two men from the Bureau of Criminal Investigations, overweight and bald, got out leisurely and looked around. One of them stretched—the other yawned. It was too early for them to be drunk, but they were probably hung-over.

I looked over to Duggan.

"Take her and Teddy. Get something to eat. This place is gonna be under the microscope for a while."

When he nodded, I took Ruth in my arms and hugged her one more time. The warmth of her body in the cold air was as soothing as a campfire, and I didn't want to let go. I gazed into her eyes and said, "Go with him. I'll see you in a bit."

She kissed her fingers and put them to my lips.

"Be safe."

When I got in Harrigan's car, the position of the seat and mirror reminded me how much larger he was. One of the cruisers started to reverse to let me by, but the street was so clogged two other vehicles had to move in the process. Once there was enough room, I squeezed through and sped off down the street, watching in the rear-view the mayhem I was leaving behind.

CHAPTER 48

As I headed to Jackson's place, I turned on the radio but couldn't find any news about the abbey. I lit a cigarette and rolled down the window, smoking obsessively, my eyes fixated on the road. My mouth was dry and my hair itched with splinters and plaster from the blast. It was the first time I had ever shot a man without seeing him first, and I felt fortunate to have won the draw.

I drove fast but not dangerously. With Ruth and Teddy safe, and Mardini's henchmen eliminated, I no longer had good reason to be reckless. I may have sympathized with the pilgrims, but their plight wasn't worth my life. My attitude now was something they could surely have understood—the outcome was in God's hands.

When I got to Back Bay, I slowed down on Commonwealth Avenue and searched for the address. The captain always walked to and from work. But two years earlier, he had asked for a lift when a freak summer squall hit the city. I remembered the day well, and the awkward conversation of two men not used to discussing things outside of work. It might have been then that I realized his devotion to the department, a commitment so strong that he had sacrificed a home, a wife, children. He may not have been religious, but he pursued the job like a divine calling.

I didn't have the number, but I knew it was a few doors down from an old Baptist Church that, according to him, he sometimes attended on Christmas or Easter. Just before I reached the intersection at Clarendon Street, I saw it and stopped. There were no spots anywhere, so I parked in a no-parking zone and got out. Sweaty and shaking, I couldn't tell whether my nerves were the result of where I had just come from or where I was going.

He lived in a garden-level apartment, which was a fancy way of saying the basement. The only thing I recalled from that ride two years prior was that his were the only ground-floor windows without bars. He must have been either claustrophobic or exceptionally trusting because he made it a provision of his lease. And no landlord in the City of Boston would refuse to accommodate a police captain.

I walked along the sidewalk, looking at the stately brownstones with their granite front stairs and black double doors. I had only gone a few steps when I spotted the windows. I went into the foyer and reached for the button beside his name: *E. JACKSON*. A few seconds later, the door buzzed open, and I went down a stairwell to the basement floor. At the end of a short hallway, there was a door. When I approached, it opened, and a middle-aged black woman greeted me.

"Allo."

"I'm here to see Ernest Jackson."

"Do come in," she said with a smile. Inside it was dark, and the first thing I saw was a refrigerator and a basket of laundry. As with most efficiency apartments, the layout was odd. There were walls where there should have been rooms and rooms where there should have been walls.

"I'm Beatrice," the woman said, "Mr. Jackson's caretaker. Please come."

She led me into a room that was both a kitchen and a den. The only light was from candles that were strategically placed at regular intervals, emitting an almost sickly glow. There was an old couch, a coffee table, two chairs, and a console radio. On the far wall was a row of oak cabinets and above that, the basement windows that looked out to the street. The ceiling was so low I crouched just to be safe.

Another entranceway led to the bedroom, but with the door closed, I couldn't see in.

"How is he?" I whispered.

"Tired."

"Any pain?"

She shook her head.

"No. He's taking Darvon."

"I'm sorry," I said suddenly. "I'm Lieutenant Jody Brae—"

"I know."

"You do?"

"He talks about you."

I swallowed my emotion and proceeded towards the door. I pushed it gently open and peered in. After his criticism about the condition of my office, I was surprised that his own bedroom was a mess. In the corner was a bureau with three of its four drawers open and clothes hanging out. Piled on top were jars of change, a leather belt, a coffee mug, magazines, a keychain, pencils, etc. When I looked at the wall, the first thing I saw was a large painting of mountains and a stream. It could have been real or imagined, but I was sure it reminded him of the Maine landscape of his youth.

I heard a cough and looked over to the bed. On the side table, two candles were burning. Beatrice poked her head in and said, "I'll be going to the market for some things."

When I nodded, the captain said, "Don't forget bath salts," and I couldn't tell if he was joking.

She left and I heard the front door shut. I stood speechless, allowing the moments to pass like a temporary reprieve, unwilling to face what I knew would devastate me.

"Don't just stand there, Brae. Say something."

His voice was strained, raspy. It sounded like it had dropped a whole octave since the last time I saw him. I stepped to the edge of the bed but could barely see him. Never before had I been so thankful for the darkness.

"What's with the candles?"

He hacked and said, "She insists it's soothing. I think it's Voodoo. She's from Haiti."

"How are you?"

"Terrible."

"How terrible?"

He sighed.

"I guess if there's a scale of terribleness, I'm somewhere in the middle."

"Mardini's men came to my house looking for Teddy."

"Mardini's men or that Lee fellow?"

"I saw the article," I said, moving a few steps nearer, "about the indictment of Mardini."

"I think that's what made me collapse," he said with a chuckle. "It's the last thing I remember."

"I never would've imagined an Armenian teaming up with a Chinese."

"Crime has a tendency to bring people together. A beautiful irony, isn't it?" He cleared his throat then said, "Well, at least I know it turned out alright, otherwise you wouldn't be here."

"We got 'em."

"And how's Ruth?"

The candle flickered, and I saw him for the first time. His eyes were distant, and his face was like a skeleton with a gray sheet over it. I looked away and took a deep breath.

"She…she's well," I said uneasily. "Not well, really, shaken but—"

"Not stirred..."

I smiled and said, "You could say that."

"You love her Brae, don't you?"

All at once, my lips began to tremble; my eyes welled up.

"Of course."

"Don't let go of that. It's the most precious thing on earth."

"I won't."

I spoke in short gasps, fighting the sensation to breakdown.

"Come closer," he said, and it sounded like an order. "I can't see you."

I moved forward into the candlelight and watched as his yellow, sagging eyes tried to find me. I knew when they did because he made a wistful smile.

"Why are you here?"

"To see how you are—"

"Don't bullshit me, Lieutenant. You never could lie well. But it was never a weakness, always a strength."

"I need your help."

"That's better."

"The chief needs to call off the eviction of the abbey. The Archdiocese is selling the property to Forbes & Peabody—Mardini's company. I think it's an inside job. I think Father Vogt convinced the Archdiocese to sell. I think he murdered the woman too. I think Lee and Mardini helped him cover it up—"

"That's a lot of thinking. But *why* do you think this?"

When he looked up, his eyelids were quivering. I paused for a moment and said, "For one, he's a murderer."

"Because you believe he murdered your friend?"

"Sweeney?" I said, shaking my head in wonder. "We'll never know for sure."

"Nothing is certain, Jody."

"A local resident, an old Jewish man, recognized Vogt this morning, remembers him from the death camps in Europe."

"A Nazi?"

"A devil."

His head fell back to the pillow and he grunted. There was a short silence as we each reflected on both the absurdity and the gravity of the situation.

"This certainly is news," he muttered to himself. "And a tragedy."

"Which is why we have to halt the operation tomorrow."

"Go on," he said with a cough. I could see the strain in his eyes—hear phlegm deep in his chest. I took one step forward and knelt beside the bed, speaking into his ear.

"Capt., if those people are forced to leave, they'll be devastated. It's their solace—they believe in it."

With a sideways glance, he asked, "And do you?"

I shook my head.

"No. I think Brother Emmanuel fabricated it. I think he found out Vogt was trying to have St Kilda closed. Thought the attention would change things."

He lifted his head slightly and looked at me.

"And will it?"

Our eyes met.

"It's up to us."

"What do you suggest?"

"Let the pilgrims stay. Let them have their miracle." I felt the increasing eagerness of someone who was gaining the edge in an argument. "Spring is a few weeks away. The ice will melt. Let it die a natural death."

The room went quiet. The only sounds were the knock of the heating pipes and traffic outside on Commonwealth Avenue. It was strange that the candles flickered because there was no draft.

"You know, Lieutenant," he said, "I never liked when you were right. It always meant I was losing my grip on you."

"I guess that's a compliment."

He coughed again and pulled the blanket up.

"Okay, I'll call the chief."

"You will?"

"If what you say is true, it's the right thing to do." He winced, as if from a jolt of pain, but his voice remained unaffected. "Clearing the abbey should be postponed, at least until all this corruption is sorted out."

"Can you convince McNamara?"

Jackson put his head back, looked at the ceiling.

"He'll do it. He has to. He owes me."

"Owes you?"

He nodded and said, "Something from years ago, not a scandal but certainly unbefitting. I kept it quiet." He turned to me and added, "We all cover for one another, Brae, whether intentionally or not."

"No wonder you got all those promotions."

He looked at me with a mischievous smile.

"Knowledge is a useful ransom."

I got up because my knees were sore from stooping. Every twist, turn, or bend seemed to indicate that my body, too, was aging, that life wasn't forever. As I stood over him, I had the ghastly sensation that he was in a coffin, and I was at his wake.

In the distance, a church bell rang. More than anything I wanted to stay with him, but with the press conference an hour away, time was running out, and I had to get back to The Armory.

"I'll make the call. Consider it done."

"Is there anything I can get for you, Capt.?"

His eyes opened a little.

"No, but there's something you can do."

"Name it."

"I have some old friends coming down from Maine. If it's not too much trouble..." He started to hack but quickly calmed himself. "...Can you give me a shave?"

"Well...I...sure."

"I could always ask Beatrice."

"No," I said. "No problem. Where's the kit?"

"Through there on the right."

When I left, I was shaking beyond control and couldn't understand why. I walked into a tiny bathroom with a bath, a toilet, and not much more. I turned on the hot water and found a clean towel. Then I grabbed a razor and shaving cream off the sink and returned to the bedroom.

Like a newborn, Jackson was drifting in and out of sleep. But aside from a few twitches of pain or discomfort, he looked at peace. I crouched down beside him.

"Have to look good for these things," he said.

I chuckled at the remark, although I didn't know exactly what he was referring to. I rolled up my sleeves and noticed goosebumps on my arms. As I spread the cream over his cheeks and neck, he kept his head firm and didn't move. A tear fell off my nose and landed on the blanket.

Once his face was covered, I took the razor and started under his chin. I wiped the stubble on the moist towel and continued with the next run. My struggle was not in giving a final shave to a man I loved and admired, but in trying not to move while doing so. By some miracle of human physiology, my entire body trembled, but my arm and hand were perfectly still.

When he began to cough, I quickly pulled away.

"Gotta warn me," I said.

"Now's not the time to worry about nicks."

I finished with his neck and started on his cheeks in long, steady strokes. By the time I got to his upper lip, the towel was full of stubble. I heard Beatrice come in the front door.

"I gotta clean this off," I said.

I hurried into the bathroom and shut the door. As I soaked the towel, I looked in the mirror and saw a face wrenched by sadness. Tears rolled down my cheeks; my chest heaved. I breathed deep and tried to gain control.

When Beatrice knocked, I snapped, "Be right out!" but I didn't mean to be rude. I cleaned off the shaved hair and went back in the bedroom to finish.

"Brae," Jackson said as I came over to the bed, "Is that you?"

"Yeah. Me and Beatrice. She's back."

"Ah, good."

Any composure I got in the bathroom was lost the moment I put the razor to his skin. I turned away every few strokes to wipe away tears. I thought he was unaware until he patted my arm.

"All is well, Lieutenant."

I couldn't answer.

"We've been through worse…"

I ignored him and continued to work.

"…These things are not for us to decide."

With a final swoosh of the blade, I finished his shave. I dropped the razor and collapsed to the floor. In the shadow of the wall, between the bed and side table, I curled into a ball and cried into my fist.

Sometime later, I awoke as if from a dream, staring blankly into the darkness, listening to Jackson's labored breathing.

"Brae," he called, "Are you still here?"

I wiped off tears with my tie.

"Yeah, yeah. I'm still here."

"Get me to the phone."

Beatrice knocked once and peeked in the room. I got to my feet before she could see me and said, "He needs the phone."

"Ah, yes," she said with her warm Caribbean accent. "It's in here."

The captain tried to get up but couldn't. Beatrice rushed over, and together we helped him out of the bed. He put his arms over our shoulders, and we took him into the other room. We lowered him onto a sofa chair, and she handed him the phone. He dialed the numbers and waited.

"This is Captain Jackson," he said. "Put me through to the chief, immediately."

He looked up to us, and his bushy white eyebrows flickered. The wait was an eternity, and by the time the call went through, Beatrice was at the kitchenette preparing something to eat.

Finally, Jackson said, "Ed. This is Ernie." There was a pause. "I'm comfortable, the medicine does wonders. Thank you. Listen, this is about the abbey in Roxbury—"

He winced in confusion, and I could hear the nasally voice of the chief.

"I'm sorry? Right now? Who?"

The captain's expression went from surprised to severe, and I could tell something was wrong. He asked the chief to hold then put the receiver under his arm.

"There's an incident at the abbey...shots fired."

"I—"

"I'll tell him. Get over there. Now!"

CHAPTER 49

I SPED BY THE PUBLIC GARDEN AND DOWN ARLINGTON STREET. AS I approached Park Square, I saw four cruisers and an ambulance parked in front of the Statler Building. I should have gone straight, but I turned towards the scene and stopped short. I rolled down the window and yelled to an officer on the sidewalk.

"What the hell's going on?"

He walked over and squinted in the window.

"Oh, hey, Detective," he said casually. He stood with a patrolman's nonchalance, his hat tipped back, his coat unbuttoned. "Looks like a double suicide—a man and a woman. BCI is up there now."

With my foot on the brake, I tapped the gas impatiently, and the car bucked.

"Where?"

"Top floor."

I craned my neck and looked up the granite façade. I wasn't sure which windows were Peabody & Forbes, but it didn't matter because I knew.

"They think it was an overdose," he added. "Prescription drugs —barbiturates."

I stared ahead through the windshield and mumbled to myself, "This day's never gonna end."

"Did you hear about the shootout in Roslindale?"

"No," I said, revving the engine. "Tell me—"

The moment he spoke, I let go of the brake and peeled away.

I raced south down Tremont Street, blowing red lights and swerving through intersections. I got to Roxbury in five minutes and spent another ten trying to get to the abbey. Finally, I dumped the car in a snowbank and continued on foot. As I looked down towards the entrance, there were cruisers everywhere, and it seemed like half the department was on-scene. Officers screamed through bullhorns while crowds of protesters stood beside the gates chanting. With news of shots fired, I would have expected a stampede, but there was no panic.

Instead of going straight, I turned and followed the course of the wall, circling the entire property. Soon I reached the street where, years before, Vigliotti and his gang had chased me, Sweeney, and Russo. I continued down the sidewalk, staring into the overgrowth until I found the old gate. I ran over, pushed away the weeds, and started to climb like a reenactment of that terrible night.

I got to the top, took one look back at the neighborhood, and then jumped. I landed in some snowy shrubs and fell over. Dusting myself off, I focused on the bell tower and hurried towards the abbey.

As I came up the shallow hill to the courtyard, there was smoke coming from the main building. I broke into a full sprint, along the gravel paths, passing by the statue of Jesus ministering to the three boys. Somewhere beyond I heard the sound of two-way radios, the urgent voices of men. I ducked under the arcade and followed the walkway to the rear maintenance door. It was locked. I stepped back and kicked it in.

I went through the annex and into the hallway, where I began to smell the smoke. I came to an abrupt stop at the intersection of two corridors. Looking right, I saw the entrance to the bell tower; left would have led me to the atrium and offices.

Suddenly, I heard voices and footsteps. Two officers came flying around the corner with their guns out. Reaching into my jacket, I took out my own .38 and ran towards them.

"What's going on?"

"The abbot," one man said, so winded he could hardly speak. "He's armed..."

"Forensics came by," the other explained, "to do more analysis. The chief ordered it."

The first officer said, "When they came in, the abbot unloaded on them—"

"How are they?"

They shook their heads with grim expressions, and I gritted my teeth.

"Where is the bastard?"

"Don't know. We had to wait for a battering ram. Front door was like a brick wall. We just got in."

"Okay," I said, pointing to the end of the hallway. "You guard the tower door."

The cops nodded.

"Fire department on the way?"

They nodded again.

"Get to it. Don't mistake him for a monk."

"How will we know?"

"He's a giant."

They dashed to their post, and I went in the other direction. The smell of fire was getting stronger, and I began to see a thin haze of smoke. I reached in my coat for a handkerchief and covered my mouth.

I came around the bend in the hall and saw flames in the distance. When I entered the atrium, the benches and wood paneling were smoldering. The smoke was thick, the heat intense. Fire was creeping up the side of the wall, where it would soon reach the once-rescued statue of Christ.

My eyes stung, and I began to cough. I was just about to turn around and head for the front door when I heard a faint noise. I held my breath and listened. Somewhere beyond the crackle of burning wood was the unmistakable sound of a baby. I leaped through the flames and down the hallway, following it through an open door that led to an office.

The moment I stepped in, I stopped and froze. Hunched forward over a desk, blood seeping from the top of his head, was Abbot Vogt. I ran over and felt his neck for a pulse, but there was none. The cries of the infant were getting louder. At the back of the room was a small door that looked like a closet. I turned the knob, but it wouldn't open. In a single thrust, I booted the door, and the lock crumbled.

What I then discovered was beyond my worst nightmares or my greatest dreams.

I stepped into a small alcove with the numb astonishment of someone first entering the tomb of Tutankhamun. Much like the pilgrims on the hill outside, Vogt kept his own shrine.

The walls had portraits of Adolph Hitler, swastikas, flags, and tapestries with Nazi symbols. There were framed pictures of SS Leadership and news clippings of their early triumphs. Against the backdrop of all that horror, however, sat a crib, shoved into the corner, obscured by the clutter of the obscene memorabilia. In that split second, the events of the past and present converged. Father Vogt, the man I had always suspected of killing Chester Sweeney, was, in fact, a monster.

I ran over and peered in. A tiny baby girl peeped back, her arms flailing, shrieking, hysterical. The room was fast filling up with smoke. When I picked her up, she was as light as a loaf of bread. I curled her in my arms and ran—out of the room, out of the office, down the hallway. I reached the atrium, and it was engulfed in flames. And there, looming over the room, was the statue of Jesus Christ, saved from a church fire only to burn again.

At the end of the opposite corridor, I saw black uniforms and helmets rushing towards me—the fire department had arrived. But the atrium was impassable. So I turned around and went down the hallway until I reached the exit door Brother Emmanuel had taken me through weeks before. I pushed it open and immediately began coughing as the fresh air filled my lungs.

Outside, I stumbled to the middle of the cloister, the spot where Sweeney, Russo, and I had pummeled Vogt many years before. I looked over to the main building, and smoke was coming from the roofline and through the closed shutters of the small windows. Holding the child tight, I walked around to the side of the abbey. I kept close to the wall, following the steep embankment, and made my way to the front of the building.

When I came around the corner, two fire trucks were by the main door, their diesel engines rumbling. Hoses crisscrossed the pavement, going off in different directions; men with equipment scurried to and fro. A fire captain noticed me and quickly came over.

"Detective, you okay?" he asked, then he noticed the baby. "Was that child in there?"

"Yeah," I nodded. "She was."

I stood in a daze and watched the scene with a detached wonder. My face and coat were black with soot, and my eyelashes were singed. The warmth of the little girl seemed my single source of life, and I wasn't sure who was clinging to whom. I turned away from the captain, as if in a trance, and continued down the long driveway. The ground was melted from the sun so I didn't worry about slipping.

I looked right, over to the hillside, and watched the thousands of people. The sight of smoke and fire trucks did nothing to stir the crowd and maybe, I thought, the pilgrims had more restraint than anyone had given them credit for. For the first time, I admired their faith and perseverance. Their beliefs may have been different than mine, but at least they believed. I walked steadily on.

When I approached the front gate, everyone parted to let me by. There was awestruck silence as I staggered forward with the child in my arms. I heard 'ohs' and 'ahs' and other expressions of astonishment. An old woman put her hands together, looked up to the sky, and started to pray. I breathed shallowly; my eyes welled up.

At that moment I understood that, despite my years of cynicism, every act of love was a mini-revolution, a strike against the apathy and hatred of an unforgiving world. When I pushed the blanket from the child's face and held her up, there was a great applause. I smiled as if for the first time.

I walked out the front gates like a savior, something I never intended to be. For as far as I could see, there were cheerful faces. A police cruiser stopped in front of me, and Ruth, Teddy, and Sergeant Duggan got out.

"Lieutenant!" Duggan said. "I knew you'd be here."

Ruth came up, and I handed her the child. She was so elated that I worried she would faint. But she didn't. She held the little girl in her arms and gazed at her with a mother's love. When I saw the joy in her eyes, it was as if she, too, had just been born. Teddy looked on too, as well as some bystanders, and a photographer snapped pictures.

"Vogt," I said to Duggan then started to cough. "...Vogt is dead."

A Red Cross volunteer handed me a cup of water, and I drank it in one gulp.

"Sid Mardini, too," Duggan said. "He was found at the Statler with his—"

"Mistress," I said. "I know."

"But why?"

"Why? Because he wouldn't get out of this one. And he wasn't going alone."

Cradling the baby, Ruth looked up and said, "The eviction has been canceled. They announced it at the press conference thirty minutes ago."

I crushed the paper cup in my hand and tossed it.

"I was wondering why everyone was so happy," I said.

"Is that a child?"

I spun around startled, and it was Mrs. Sweeney. For some reason, her eerie mystique was gone, and she looked like nothing more than an eccentric old bag lady.

"It's a girl," Ruth said, dipping down to show her.

As she looked, a crooked half-smile broke across her face.

"I had a child once," she said, chewing her gums.

I wanted to say I was sorry, but sometimes apologizing for the past did more harm than good. She mumbled words I couldn't hear then turned away and blended back into the crowd. I knew I would never see her again.

"You're a hero, Jody," Duggan said.

"You told me not to be."

"Never listen to me."

He patted me on the back, and we both laughed. Two paramedics came rushing over with first aid equipment and went straight to Ruth. I could tell they wanted to attend to the baby, but she wouldn't let go, and the best they could do was convince her to come over to the ambulance.

I reached in my coat for my cigarettes, but they were gone. When Duggan held out his pack, I looked inside, and there was only one left.

"I guess we'll have to split it," he said.

We stood in the middle of the swarm, people going every which way, and looked through the gates to the top of the hill. Thin plumes of smoke rose from various parts of the roof, but otherwise, the fire appeared under control. The pilgrims were remarkably calm—there was no panic. While a small group had gathered near the front to watch, the majority remained at the shrine and in the scattered encampments along the slope.

"It's peaceful," I said.

"The people or the abbey?"

I blew smoke out my nose and handed him the cigarette.

"The people are the abbey."

CHAPTER 50

In the end, the bell tower survived the inferno, much like a chimney remains after a house burns down. The main building was totally gutted, as was the annex, and every window was black from smoke and ash. The Archdiocese relocated the monks to St. John's Seminary, ironically, but they wouldn't have to worry about Bishop Severin. He was in Charles Street Jail awaiting formal charges once the investigation into the scandal was complete.

It was a mild March day, and there wasn't a cloud in the sky as Harrigan and I drove to the North End to see Mrs. Vigliotti. In the backseat was Teddy, his face pressed against the window and staring out at the city. I would have said he was quiet, but none of us spoke much during the ride. After all that we had been through, silence wasn't something we took for granted.

When we turned onto Hanover Street, awnings were down, and some shop doors were even open. People walked cheerily up and down the sidewalks like a summer day. Maybe it was the sun, I thought, or the fact that spring was just a few weeks away.

We drove down Prince Street, and the snowdrifts were half the size they were before. Old men sat on stoops smoking cigars, waving to friends, chatting with neighbors.

We turned right onto Margaret Street, and I parked along the curb.

"Wanna wait or come in?" I asked Harrigan.

"I'd prefer to wait, Lieutenant. I'm in no condition to climb stairs."

I looked down at his knee, the thick padding obvious under his loose trousers. I had never seen him incapacitated, and his pride was probably hurt as much as his body. But he had done well these past few days, walking when he could, resting when he needed to.

Teddy and I got out and went up to the front door. There weren't many people on the narrow lane, but I knew eyes were watching from every window and alleyway. And I could only imagine the head-scratching wonder of the Italian locals when they saw a white guy, a black guy, and an Asian. If they didn't think we were cops then a vaudeville act was a good second guess.

We stepped into the foyer, and I pressed the buzzer. Almost immediately Mrs. Vigliotti opened the door at the top of the stairwell and called for us to come up. When we reached the landing, she stood in the doorway with a somber smile. She was dressed all in black, but I didn't think it was an expression of her mourning.

"Please, come in," she said.

We followed her into the small apartment where seated by the window was Teddy's uncle.

"Baekbu!" Teddy exclaimed, rushing over.

The old man greeted his nephew with an emotionless nod. Then, without warning, he grasped the arms of the chair and stood straight up. Teddy stepped back, as stunned as I was, and we looked on amazed.

"Has he walked the whole time?" I asked.

Mrs. Vigliotti winced in confusion.

"Walked? Yes. Why? Shouldn't he?"

I glanced over to the old man.

"Of course he should."

"Will you have some tea?"

"I can't."

"Please," she said. "Don't leave just yet."

I paused and looked over to Teddy, who shrugged his shoulders. Then I turned to her and said, "Any more of those Italian cookies?"

IF MY PARTNER was anyone else, I would have worried about leaving him out front. But Harrigan was the most self-sufficient person I knew, and he always found some way to stay busy. As I sipped my tea, Teddy and his uncle sat in the corner and conversed quietly in Korean. The language brought back memories of the war, but not of the enemy because we were never close enough to hear them. Instead, it reminded me of the kind civilians who worked at division rear or the peasants who poured in from the countryside looking for help.

"When I walked in the garage, he scared the dickens out of me," Mrs. Vigliotti said.

I smiled at the old-fashioned phrase.

"It would've scared me, too."

She sat forward on the couch, elbows on her knees. She held the cup with both hands, and her eyes flitted nervously. There was suffering in her face, but there was also the strength that came from it. In the respectable slums of the North End, life was a succession of woes interrupted by moments of joy. I only knew the intensity of the experience because I had lived it too. For those in Boston's poorer parts, winter was always the longest season.

"He just stood there," she went on, nodding at Teddy's uncle. "Wouldn't say a thing. Thank God Anthony's friend walked in. He told me the man's life was in danger, that he was from the abbey, that Anthony was hiding him." She turned to me and said, "We watch out for our own, you know? Even if they're not ...our own."

We both smiled at the contradiction. With much to lose and nothing to gain, protecting a stranger was somehow nobler than protecting a friend.

"Anthony was a good man," she said.

"I know he was."

"He wasn't always, but he changed."

"I know he did."

For the first time in many minutes, she looked at me and said, "He must have known about that priest...knew they were going to kill Jong-soo." When she said the name, Teddy and his uncle glimpsed over.

I drank the last of my tea and put the cup down with a contented sigh. Harrigan was patient, but he wouldn't wait all day.

"What made you go to the garage?" I asked.

"I wanted to get his things. He used to make pictures. He's an artist," she said, switching between tenses, still not used to her nephew's absence. She got up and went into the other room, returning with a thin panel of wood about the size of a college diploma. When she held it up, I saw an engraving of a horse grazing in a pasture with mountains in the background, clouds above. The image was lifelike, the detail remarkable.

"Anthony could draw anything," she said. "He loved to carve scenes of the country."

Recalling our childhood in the congested streets of Roxbury, I said, "I'm not surprised."

I glanced over to Teddy and indicated that we had to leave. When he rose, his uncle got up too and stood with his arms at his side, staring blankly. He was a strange old geezer, I thought, but considering the horrors he had lived through, I understood why. The fact that he acknowledged only Teddy was a sign of his love and his loyalty, and those things meant far more than charm.

As we walked to the door, Mrs. Vigliotti stopped me.

"Please, take this," she said.

I looked down at the engraving.

"Sure, thank you."

Before we left, Teddy's uncle turned to her, took a deep bow, and let out a flurry of harsh sounds that neither of us could comprehend. We knew it was an expression of thanks, but it seemed more like a tirade.

We walked out to the landing, waved goodbye, and started down.

"Oh," she said, leaning over the railing. "Come visit sometime, will you?"

"Of course I will," I said with a smile.

Outside someone was blaring the Rolling Stones from a tenement window. I looked down the sidewalk and saw Harrigan talking to a gang of boys. They circled him like a pack of dogs, firing off questions, making jokes, moving with that spastic energy all ten-year-olds had. They were a ragtag bunch, with rolled-up denim jeans and hand-me-down coats. They had dark hair and olive skin, and only one looked like he might have been something other than Italian.

"Looks like you made new friends?" I observed.

When Harrigan saw Teddy's uncle walking, his face dropped. One of the boys ripped a ball out of his friend's hand and taunted him with it. Then he turned around and ran off, and the others followed.

"My word, Lieutenant," Harrigan said as Teddy helped his uncle get in the backseat.

"Ever seen anything like it?"

"Never."

I opened the trunk and laid the picture down next to the shotgun case and the crutches. Harrigan peered in and said, "I wondered what took so long. Was there a yard sale?"

"What would you say if I told you Tony Vigliotti made that?"

He hesitated and gave me a long and telling stare. We both wanted to say what he was thinking, but the time for theories and speculation had passed. With Vigliotti and Brother Emmanuel dead, it was just as easy to accept that what happened at St Kilda was, in fact, a miracle.

"I'd say he was quite an artist."

CHAPTER 51

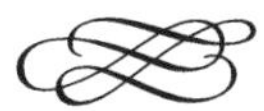

JACKSON ROLLED DOWN THE CAR WINDOW FOR SOME AIR. HE HAD BEEN feeling *nauseated* since we got in the Valiant, but he was determined to hang on. As we drove through Dudley Square and down Warren Street, he sat quietly and observed the endless blocks of brick buildings and triple-deckers. He was born in the wilderness of Maine and would die at the center of a major metropolis. But this was his home and had been for fifty years. Even if he wasn't a Bostonian by birth, he had been naturalized through and through.

We turned at a liquor store and drove into the thick of the residential jungle. In an abandoned lot, little black and white children were playing together, hurling wet snowballs at a fence. Roxbury was changing fast, but on the fault lines of that racial shift, there was a glorious unity that somehow signaled hope for mankind.

"Any update on the woman in the dumpster?"

"Nothing," I said, shaking my head. "I'm sure some relative will eventually file a missing person's report—"

"Or not," he said, and he coughed into his hand. "Don't expect it. Maybe she has no family. She could be from out of state. The world is filled with drifters, Brae, nameless and unaccounted for. It's tragic but true. These are the times we live in, unfortunately."

We soon came to the crossroads near the abbey. Already I could tell the crowds had diminished; the surrounding blocks were no longer crammed with cars, vans, and busses. Residents were out shoveling, clearing away the soft snow from driveways and porches. The only sign that anything big had occurred was that there was more litter than usual. Otherwise, the neighborhood had been restored to peaceful neglect.

I cut left and went slowly towards St Kilda. There was no rush—no urgency. Across from the entrance was a single cruiser, the lone remnant of a force that, at one point, consumed a quarter of the department. There were still scattered groups of people lingering by the front gate and along the wall. I saw hippies and beatniks, a few tourists, and some curious locals. A young man in a black turtleneck and sunglasses was taking photographs. But compared to the throngs from a week before, it was desolate.

As I turned onto the property, I beeped to the patrol car and waved. Jackson and I looked up the hill and saw the devastating aftermath of the occupation: trash, filthy blankets, ripped tents, overturned shopping carts, abandoned grills, and children's toys. The thousands of footsteps had melted the snow and destroyed the grass, and what remained was a mud pit. Curls of smoke here and there told me some pilgrims still remained, but for the most part, it looked like a vacated refugee camp.

We went up the driveway and parked at the turnaround by the main building. The front door was covered in plywood, as were all the windows. When I got out, all I could smell was ash, and it reminded me of campfires as a boy. I got Teddy's uncle's crutches from the trunk and went around to help the captain. He was too weak to get out himself, so I leaned in and he took my shoulder. As I hoisted him up, he was lighter than a child, and everywhere I touched I felt bones.

Once on the crutches, he was stable enough to walk. We saw the bell tower, twenty yards in the distance, and headed towards it. Every thirty seconds he stopped to rest, and I could see that the short stroll was a challenge. But the crisp air seemed to soothe his lungs, and he hadn't coughed once since leaving the car.

We walked across the grass and came to the paved area around the tower. When I looked ahead, I saw melted candles, photos of loved ones, handwritten notes with pleas and words of gratitude. More chilling, however, were the wheelchairs, crutches, and other prosthetic aids left behind by the pilgrims.

The top of the hill was perfectly quiet. Jackson and I stood side by side and observed the shrine with a mystical wonder. We were there for a few minutes when I heard a faint sound and thought someone was playing music in the distance. Then I realized it was the captain, humming to himself like he used to do. I didn't know if it was a sign of resignation or inspiration, but I was glad to have part of him back.

"You know, Brae," he said, breaking the silence, "I think we all reach a point in our lives where we ask, *what the hell happened?*"

"You mean the abbey?"

"No," he said with a chuckle. "I speak figuratively."

He looked down, kicked aside some snow. His shoe hit an object, and we both saw that it was a cross in the mud, similar to the one Mrs. Sweeney had. Much like the former battlefields of Europe, the abbey grounds would yield paraphernalia for generations to come.

"There're worse places to be," I said.

"I'm sure you know, Jody. You've stared death in the eye once already."

"When you're twenty-two, you don't know it."

"Well," he said, turning to me. "Let me tell you...when you're sixty-six, you damn sure do."

He stepped away and hobbled to the base of the tower. With his last bit of strength, he laid down the crutches and knelt before the open-air altar. He clasped his hands and bowed his head. Although his back was to me, I could hear whispering and knew he was praying.

All at once, I began to tremble. My eyes got teary, but I told myself it was from the wind. I gazed up to the highest window and gasped when I didn't see the Madonna and Child. With the rise in temperatures, the frost had finally melted—the image was gone. Just as I had hoped, the miracle at St Kilda had died a natural death.

"Brae," I heard, and I jumped. I must have daydreamed because Jackson was beside me again.

"Where was it?" he asked.

I pointed above.

"There...the highest pane."

He looked up and squinted.

"And it was quite real?"

When I stared at the clear window, I saw the reflection of the sky and clouds.

"Yeah," I said, nodding. "Real enough."

BRINGING Captain Jackson back to City Hospital was the second hardest thing I had ever done in my life. Leaving him there was the first. But with a urinary tract infection, high fever, and constant pain, it was the best place for him. For someone with no family, just being around other people was enough to make those last weeks and days easier.

"I need to check someone into the hospice."

The lady looked up from the front desk.

"Name please."

"Jackson."

"First name."

"Ernest."

As we headed to the elevator bank, he went so slow that an orderly asked if he wanted a wheelchair. But he declined, more out of determination than pride, and we eventually made it. We signed in at the hospice reception and met a kind older nurse. She was pretty for her age, and when Jackson made a remark about her knee-highs, she raised an eye flirtatiously.

Before she took him to his room, he spent a few minutes discussing our caseload, giving me orders, telling me what to follow up with and when. Deep down he knew I had things covered, but it was his way of saying that, whatever happens, he was still in charge. I patted his shoulder and said I would see him tomorrow, although I really didn't know.

I left the hospital and drove through the wet streets in a hypnotic daze. I felt neither sorrow nor joy, but more of a numb indifference that I could only attribute to my utter exhaustion. It may have made the pain more bearable, but it didn't make it go away. By the time I got to my apartment, the ride home seemed like a dream I could only partially recall.

When I entered the foyer, I heard the baby cry. I rushed to the top of the stairs and the door swung inward. Ruth stepped out to the landing and gave me a long, passionate hug. "You'd never believe it," she whispered. "The president of the hospital called me—personally. He asked me to come back to work, said the incident was a mistake."

"Why the secrecy?"

"She's here," she said, nodding inside.

We walked in and went to the kitchen, where a woman was sitting at the table.

"Jody," Ruth said. "This is Mrs. Ellis from the Department of Child Services."

"My pleasure," I said, bowing slightly.

With a beige suit and hat, she had the feminine but conservative style of a government official. A briefcase was on the floor, her coat was on the chair, and several documents were spread across the table.

"I was explaining to your wife," she said, "that as long as there is no paternity claim, the adoption should be finalized within a few months."

"I don't believe the father is alive."

She smiled curtly.

"In any case, you have sole custody *for now*."

From the bedroom, the child whimpered then was quiet—I knew she was napping. Ruth and I took each other's hands, excited beyond words, and the joy in her eyes made up for the many months of sadness. The woman watched with the awkward poise of someone not used to either seeing or showing affection. It was an odd trait, I thought, considering her role, but I had to remember she was a bureaucrat.

With our business concluded, Mrs. Ellis began to collect the papers and put them in order.

"I'll just need a signature," she said.

I stepped over to the table, and she pointed to a line. I scribbled my name and, as insignificant as the act was, I somehow felt my entire world change.

"Oh," she said, holding the pen, reading the fine print. "There's one more thing. Have you considered a name for the child?"

Ruth looked at me and shrugged her shoulders.

I thought for a moment and said, "Ernestine."

"Ernestine?"

"Ernestine," Ruth said in agreement. "That's a lovely name."

Mrs. Ellis wrote it down and placed the documents in the briefcase. She stood up, put on her coat, and we escorted her to the door. Once she was gone, Ruth and I gazed at each other with the contented silence that only comes from true happiness. Then the baby cried, she laughed, I sighed, and we both ran into the bedroom.

EPILOGUE

Boston Record American - Obituaries

February 28th, 1968 – Boston, Mass.

Jackson, Ernest C. – Born in 1902, Cornish Maine. Loving son of the late Rutherford and Carol (Cote) Jackson. Captain, Boston Police Department, Homicide Unit. Funeral to be held Monday, March 4th, 10:00-12:00 a.m. at the First Baptist Church, 110 Commonwealth Avenue, Boston, Mass. Burial to follow at Forest Hills Cemetery.

July 4th, 1968 - Quang Tri Province, S. Vietnam

Kwan, Theodore (Teddy), Pvt. USMC – Born September 1949, Seoul S. Korea, from wounds suffered in the Battle of Khe Sanh. Teddy came to the United States as a young boy and lived under the care of his uncle, Jong-soo Kwan. Graduate of Boston Latin School, class of '67. Worked several years at the Lantern House Restaurant in Boston. Special friend to Joseph H. Brae, Lieutenant, Boston Police Department. Memorial service Wednesday, July 24th, at St Kilda Abbey in Roxbury.

. . .

August 15TH, 1968 – Boston, Mass.

Kwan, Jong-soo – Born in 1896, Kujang, North Korea. No services scheduled.

End

The story continues in book 3,
***The Polish Triangle*. Continue reading for a sneak peak, or follow the link below to purchase.**
https://links.liquidmindpublishing.com/9QtV

Sign up for Jonathan's newsletter for updates on deals and new releases!
https://liquidmind.media/j-cullen-newsletter-sign-up-2-jody/

THE POLISH TRIANGLE

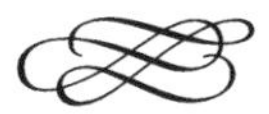

CHAPTER 1

September 1970

I HAD JUST ARRIVED at Harrigan's apartment when I heard the call. The two-way was faint and staticky, the reception bad from all the brick buildings. But it was clear enough. *Shots fired.* My hand shook as I turned the squelch, and it wasn't from the coffee. There was urgency in the dispatcher's voice.

Officer down.

Just then Harrigan came out the front door, his suit pressed and black skin gleaming from a fresh shave. He walked with a swagger that I sometimes took for slowness, a consequence of his childhood on St. Kitts in the Virgin Islands.

I hit the horn. Startled, he ran towards the car, moving clumsily with a briefcase in one hand, a mug in the other.

"Lieutenant?" he asked as he got in.

"Officer down!"

He was barely in the seat when I turned on the sirens and pulled into traffic. We raced to the location, swerving around cars and buses. Morning was the worst time to get anywhere in the city. Harrigan braced himself for the ride, clutching the side of the door, having already spilled coffee on his pleated pants.

"What happened?" he asked.

"A bank robbery, I think."

I reached for a cigarette, fumbling to light it.

"Any idea who?"

Not knowing if he meant the suspects or the victim, I shook my head. Anytime an officer was hurt on duty, the entire force held its breath.

We sped down Massachusetts Avenue, where the leaves on the trees were already starting to turn. Soon the Citgo Sign peered above the buildings, and we were almost there. Blowing through the last two lights, we went under an overpass and came into Kenmore Square.

In the distance, I saw a dozen emergency vehicles: police cruisers, ambulances, fire trucks. People were watching from the sidewalks; a helicopter hovered overhead. Several officers stood in the middle of the intersection, attempting to direct traffic through a square that was a chaotic juncture of two wide boulevards and several smaller roads.

With no place to park, I stopped in the street, and we jumped out. We ran towards the scene, but there was so much activity it was hard to know where the scene was. On the corner, I saw Edmund McNamara, the barrel-chested chief of police, standing beside a Delta 88 with some police officials. Easy to spot in a crowd, he wore a fedora, something that had been out of fashion since Eisenhower was president.

I ran towards him, Harrigan trailing behind, and by the time I got there, I was out of breath.

"Chief," I said.

"They hit the Shawmut Bank," he said, nodding to a small two-story building on Beacon Street with a stucco façade. "Sergeant Duggan has been shot—"

"Giraffe?"

McNamara frowned as he nodded, probably unaware of the nickname.

"How is he?" I asked.

Pausing, he looked at the men around him; a local precinct captain, two detectives from Area B, and a few others I didn't know.

"We don't have an update yet. They rushed him to City Hospital."

It was a diplomatic answer, but I understood why. Things changed quickly after an incident, and giving no information was better than giving the wrong information.

I looked around, stunned, dizzy from exertion. Jerry Duggan was a fellow officer, but he was also a friend, a 6' 6" half-Irish, half-Italian giant who was raised in public housing in Charlestown. We had joined the department the same year and even lived together as rookies. With five kids at home, he worked mostly nights, priding himself on never having missed a Little League game or a school recital.

"Brae," the chief said, startling me. "This is Paul Shine...FBI..."

I nodded to the agent, and we shook hands.

"...and Mark Marecki."

I turned to his partner, a short and stocky man with dark sunglasses. He was built more like a bricklayer than an FBI agent, and when we shook, his grip was firm.

"Jody?"

"Joseph," I said, thinking he had misheard the chief. "But everyone calls me Jody."

"It's Marcus."

Something in his voice, perhaps the way he said his name, was familiar, and we stood shaking far longer than necessary.

"Marecki?" I asked, confused.

"It used to be *Evans*."

My mouth dropped when I realized who he was.

"Marcus," I said, and my cool expression melted into a smile.

No one seemed surprised we knew each other—the FBI and Boston collaborated more than either organization wanted to. But my acquaintance with Marcus went beyond my job or even the war, back to my childhood over thirty years before. It was hard to reconcile that pug-nosed boy with the polished agent who stood before me, and in those few short seconds, I had a thousand questions. But I couldn't get out the first because the moment I went to speak, the chief interrupted.

"We got an ID on the car. Looks like the same group that hit the armory."

Marcus and his partner acknowledged the remark, but they were mostly just listening. Agents never said much around cops. Only three days before, the National Guard arsenal in Newburyport had been robbed, the culprits taking guns and ammunition and lighting the place on fire.

"How'd it go down?" I asked.

"They were parked in that alleyway," McNamara said, pointing to a narrow lane beside the bank. "When the officers showed up, Stapleton went in the front. Duggan went down the back to where the perps were parked. We don't have the logistics yet, but it looks like they fired on him as they were pulling out."

"They were leaving?"

"Already had the money," the precinct captain said, and one of the detectives added, "Almost sixty grand in cash. Biggest heist in years."

"Anyone else hurt?"

"No. The bank manager had just gotten there. He was opening the back door when someone with a mask came up from behind. Stuck a gun in his ribs."

"A lucky hit," I said.

"It wasn't luck," McNamara said. "This bank transfers cash every week. The days rotate and are confidential. The money was already sorted and packed, waiting for Brinks."

Someone called, and the chief looked over. Two plainclothes officers were at the corner with a group of reporters and news anchors, a pile of cameras mounted and ready. McNamara had to make a statement—he couldn't avoid it. He was good with the rank-and-file but awkward with the press, and public speaking wasn't his strength.

"If they had the money, why'd they shoot?" I asked.

"Because no one likes pigs."

It was harsh but true, and the past decade had been hard for law enforcement. With anti-war protests and student demonstrations, cops had gone from heroes to villains, the scapegoats for the problems of a society that was coming apart at the seams.

As the chief walked away, Marcus reached into his pocket and took out a card.

"Let's get lunch," he said, handing it to me. "We'll catch up."

I glanced down: *Marcus B. Marecki, U.S. Department of Justice, Federal Bureau of Investigation.* I didn't know what surprised me more, that I had run into him after all these years, or that the FBI issued business cards.

"I'd like that."

"Good to see you, Jody," he said.

He nodded goodbye to Harrigan and then hurried to catch up with the others. Squinting in the sun, I watched as he blended into the crowd of officials, reporters, and bystanders. Sometimes I envied the attention, although I never sought it, and it seemed some small validation for the stress of the job. But I was a lieutenant, too high in rank to avoid scrutiny and too low to deal with the public.

"An old friend?" Harrigan asked.

With my eyes still on the press conference, I said, "What?"

"Was that an old friend?"

"Just a guy I used to know—"

"Lieutenant!" someone shouted.

I looked across the street, and an officer was waving. When we walked over, his partner was leaning over a young woman sitting on the curb between two parked cars.

"She says she saw the suspects," the cop said.

"Why wasn't she interviewed?"

He looked at his partner, who just shrugged his shoulders.

"Don't know. We were looking for shell casings. She was just sitting here."

They moved away, and I knelt beside the girl. She was hysterical, her head in her arms and sobbing.

"Miss?" I said.

When she looked up, her eyes were swollen, her cheeks covered in streaks of mascara. Still, she was pretty, with full lips and a petite nose. Wearing a fur-collared coat, she looked more dressed for a night out dancing than a day of work or school.

"What did you see?"

Moving closer, I looked straight at her. Those precious minutes after an incident were critical, first impressions always being the most reliable.

"It shouldn't have happened," she said, stumbling. "I...I was walking up the alleyway. There was someone in the car. It was running."

"Can you describe him?"

"It was a woman," she said, wiping her face. "A student—"

"How did you know she was a student, Miss?" Harrigan asked.

Something about his voice put people at ease, compelled them to cooperate.

"She had a red sweatshirt on, Boston University."

"What happened next?" I asked, pressing her.

"A man came out the door of the bank."

"Did you see what he looked like?"

"Long hair. A mustache, I think. The way they all look."

The way they all look. I grinned because it was a phrase I would have used.

"He got in the passenger seat," she went on. "A police officer came down the alley. He yelled for them to stop. I heard a loud pop, like a firecracker, and they drove away. I didn't know what happened until people started screaming."

Standing up, I looked around. Over at the bank, some cops were running tape along the front, blocking it off until the area had been thoroughly vetted. Otherwise, things were returning to normal, people going into the subway station, students on their way to class. A couple of news trucks lingered at the intersection, but overall, the excitement was over. The quiet aftermath of a crime was as jarring as the crime itself.

"Miss," I said, turning back to her. "These officers are going to take you to the station to get a statement."

When she nodded, Harrigan held out his hand and helped her up.

"Thank you," I said.

She peered nervously at us, then the men escorted her over to the cruiser. In skintight jeans, she had a sexy figure, her hips swaying as she walked in high heels. Her short coat revealed the skin of her back, white and smooth, and I stared out of disapproval, not desire. I was no prude, but sometimes I couldn't believe how young women dressed.

"Rather unusual attire for a Thursday morning," Harrigan said.

"Who the hell would let their daughter go out like that?"

THE POLISH TRIANGLE

CHAPTER 2

THE DAYS WERE GETTING SHORTER, AND BY THE TIME I LEFT headquarters, it was already getting dark. I drove home along the Jamaica Way, a winding parkway that passed the mansions of Jamaica Plain and skirted some of the finer parts of Brookline. It was always a quiet ride home, and an opulence I wasn't used to because for most of my career I had lived in apartments. But three months earlier, Ruth and I had bought our first home in West Roxbury, the outermost section of Boston, a neighborhood of leafy side streets, baseball parks, and backyards. The houses ranged from grand old Victorians to tidy post-war ranches, but it was mainly middle-class and only considered upscale by those who had less. Nevertheless, it was the closest thing to the suburbs, and because cops and public officials had to reside in the city, it was where many of them chose to live.

Aside from my time in Korea, I had never been around so many trees and flowers, and I awoke some mornings to a silence that was almost unsettling. I had spent my entire life in the inner boroughs of the city, places so dense that heat still emanated from the buildings and sidewalks long after summer was over, places so crowded you could reach out a window and shake the hand of your neighbor, places where laundry hung from all the back porches, giving the impression of a fleet of sailing tenements cast adrift in a sea of brick and cement. There was no denying I missed the grittiness. Something about poverty and squalor seemed to reflect the deprivation in my soul. But with a wife and an infant, I chose quiet over the hustle-bustle, safety over the excitement. After years of living on the edge, I finally accepted there was honor in just being ordinary.

As I turned into the driveway, my headlights flashed across the small bungalow with white shutters that was our home. Someone next door peered through the curtain, but I couldn't see who it was—my eyesight was getting worse with age. It could have been Jim or his wife, Esther. He was a forty-something balding accountant who took the train each morning to his job in Copley Square; she was the stay-at-home mother of their two young daughters, a short brunette who wore day dresses and smoked Pall Malls. Like most of the neighbors, they were sensible and friendly, keeping their yards tidy and conversation light.

Turning off the car, I breathed deep and tried to relax, never wanting to walk in agitated after a tough day. As I gripped the steering wheel, my hands were steady, but my body trembled, which I attributed to hunger or fatigue or the fact that I had run out of cigarettes and hadn't had one in over an hour. The truth was, however, that after all these years, the job was finally getting to me. Maybe I was getting old, I thought, or something about having a child made me especially attuned to the fragility of life. A dear friend had been shot, his condition uncertain, and even if I didn't know who the killers were, I wanted to blame a whole generation.

I saw them every day, young people with long hair and tie-dyed shirts, unclean and unshaven. They congregated on downtown streets, playing bongos and other peasant instruments, waving signs or selling flowers, smug in their self-righteousness. There had been a massive protest on Boston Common the year before where the department was so short-staffed that even Harrigan and I got called in to help. It was a large but mostly peaceful event, one-hundred-thousand strong, with long speeches about demolishing the power structure and remaking society, the rantings of middle-class kids who probably had never made their own lunch or folded their laundry.

Suddenly, the front lights went on.

When I looked up, Ruth was in the doorway, her hair in a bun and her nurse's uniform showing under her coat. I reached for my briefcase, empty except for a yellow pad of paper and a few pens. I had never been organized like Harrigan, who took careful notes of interviews, evidence, thoughts, and theories. I operated on instinct alone. But my new captain said that if I wanted to continue working the streets, a lieutenant's role was also administrative, and I had to at least look like I was more than just a beat cop.

I got out and went up the walkway, the silhouette of Ruth looming.

"You're late again," she said.

"Sorry, there was—"

"This can't continue."

Sighing, I skirted by her, defiant but in no mood to argue. When I entered the foyer, I looked into the living room and saw Nessie, sitting on the couch in her pink sleeper, staring at the television and laughing at the slapstick antics of *I Love Lucy*. The moment she saw me, her eyes beamed, and she cried, "Daddy!" I ran over, picked her up, and she reached for my nose.

"She's already had some carrots and chicken..." Ruth said.

I raised Nessie over my head, and she giggled.

"...If she's hungry before bed, give her some crackers, but nothing sweet..."

As Ruth spoke, I spun Nessie around and around.

"...Her nose is runny. I think it's hay fever. There's some Teldrin above the sink..."

I was starting to get dizzy, but she was so excited I couldn't stop.

"Dammit, Jody! Are you even listening?"

Stopping, I turned to Ruth, who stood by the door with her arms tight to her side, containing her anger. Her shift started at 6 p.m. and she was going to be late—again. Although I always tried to get home on time, my schedule was unpredictable, and no one ever knew when and where a crime was going to happen. I had asked her to leave her job to be a full-time mother. Like a lot of women now, she preferred the independence of a career and an income. It made our life more complicated, but I didn't resent her for it, and I even felt a mild shame because, with the high cost of living, it was hard to live on a lieutenant's salary alone.

I put Nessie back down on the couch, and although she tried to resist, I reassured her with a smile. I walked over to the foyer and faced Ruth, looking her in the eye.

"It was a crazy day."

"You can't just show up when you want to!" she said, speaking in a forceful whisper. For all our arguments and petty spats, we never shouted in front of Nessie. "You've been late twice this week already!"

I lowered my head like a repentant child, and I was truly sorry. As she stood waiting for me to reply, I leaned forward and tried to kiss her, hoping some affection might ease the tension. But she frowned and walked over to Nessie instead, kissing her on the forehead and rubbing her back. I stood by the door with my arms crossed, tired and feeling rejected. But even in my moment of bitterness, I couldn't help being touched by a mother's love for her child.

When headlights flashed over the lawn, I knew a car was coming. It was another sign that we were living in suburbia because I never would have noticed before. A Volkswagen stopped in front of our house, and it was Ruth's coworker Janice. Ruth grabbed her purse from the table. As she whisked by me, she gave me a smirk that was more playful than scolding, and I knew her anger had subsided. She would forgive me for being late, but it probably wouldn't be until morning.

Once she left, I went into the kitchen and reheated some chicken stew, knowing that Nessie would soon start getting drowsy. Loosening my tie, I sat beside her, shoveling the food into my mouth like it was coal for a dying fire. What I felt wasn't hunger, however, but more the vacant longing of a body that hadn't had nourishment in several hours. I was uncomfortably anxious, and the first moments of calm after a hectic day were always the worst. In many ways, I envied Ruth's job because, even though she had to experience the horrors of illness and death, she also got to see people get better. In crime, there were no happy endings, only the bleak and uncertain satisfaction of justice, and even that was a rare thing.

When Nessie giggled, I looked up. The TV cut to a special bulletin. All at once, I felt my blood pressure rise.

We interrupt this program to report that the Boston Police officer shot today during a bank robbery in Kenmore Square has died.

I FELT a soothing warmth along my entire back, against my shoulders. Under the haze of slumber, the sensation blended easily with my dreams, and I could have continued sleeping. But when I smelled perfume, felt the delicate touch of fingers, I was startled awake.

"Shhh," I heard, and it was Ruth.

"Nessie..." I grumbled, my eyes still closed, my arms wrapped around the pillow.

"She's fine. Out cold, just like you."

Ruth ran her hands through my hair, her sweet breath tickling the side of my neck.

"I heard what happened," she said, a soft sadness in her voice. "Jody, I'm so sorry."

I responded with a nod, thinking about Jerry and the five broken-hearted kids who would be in the receiving line at the funeral. Of all the horrors I had seen, both in Korea and on the streets, I could think of nothing worse.

"Did you know him well?"

"Well enough," I said, staring out at the darkness, the vague form of the dresser, the outline of the closet.

"Were you two friends?"

Again, I just nodded. How could I explain the vast web of relationships I had made growing up? It was a city where everyone knew everyone, from the days of playing stickball to joining the military to eventually returning home and getting a government job. Boston was one giant, extended family, chaotic and fractured in its loyalties. Ruth had had two best friends her whole life, a girl from her childhood in California and her college roommate, who now gave skiing lessons in Vermont and raised alpacas.

"We were friends," I said.

"I'm so, so sorry."

"These things happen."

She paused for a moment, her mouth just inches from my ear.

"Do you have your appointment this week?" she whispered.

"Yeah."

With her lying behind me, I couldn't see her face, but somehow I knew she was smiling. She snuggled even closer, her breasts pressed into my back. Then I felt her hand slide around my stomach and down. In an instant, I was aroused. I craned my neck and our lips met, and only then did I realize she had on a negligée. It had all been planned. If it didn't make up for the argument earlier, it was a good move toward reconciliation.

I rolled over in the bed, and we embraced, her muffled moans sending me into quiet ecstasy. I had just started to slip her gown up over her head when we heard something and stopped. Our eyes met in the shadowy light, a look of mutual frustration. But it was a tender disappointment and one I could accept. The murmur in the distance soon turned to crying, and I watched with a smile as Ruth clumsily pulled herself together and went to tend to Nessie.

ALSO BY JONATHAN CULLEN

Shadows of Our Time

The Storm Beyond the Tides

Sunsets Never Wait

Bermuda Blue

Port of Boston Series

Whiskey Point

City of Small Kingdoms

The Polish Triangle

Sign up for Jonathan's newsletter for updates on deals and new releases!

https://liquidmind.media/j-cullen-newsletter-sign-up-2-jody/

BIOGRAPHY

Jonathan Cullen grew up in Boston and attended public schools. After a brief career as a bicycle messenger, he attended Boston College and graduated with a B.A. in English Literature (1995). During his twenties, he wrote two unpublished novels, taught high school in Ireland, lived in Mexico, worked as a prison librarian, and spent a month in Kenya, Africa before finally settling down three blocks from where he grew up.

He currently lives in Boston (West Roxbury) with his wife Heidi and daughter Maeve.

Made in the USA
Las Vegas, NV
20 October 2022